All Things Now Living

SEVENTH DAUGHTER BOOK ONE

BY

RONDI BAUER OLSON

An *Untapped* book by **Written World Communications**

All Things Now Living

Brought to you by the creative team at Written-World.com:
Kristine Hansen, Dale R. Hansen, Lynda K. Arndt

Cover design by the creative team at Damonza.com

Library of Congress Control Number: 2017907216
International Standard Book Number: 978-1-938679-10-0

Printed in the United States of America

For my dad and mom, Fran and Barb Bauer, for keeping my childhood shelves full of good books to read.

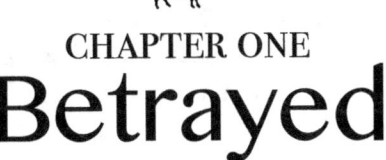

CHAPTER ONE
Betrayed

The wild boar lies on the far side of the river. I wriggle on my belly through the cattails and push aside the rigid stalks so I can see him on the screen of my controller. He's adorable, his snout half buried in mud, little brown tufts of fur on the tips of his ears, and tusks that curve toward the sky. He swishes his tail in the water. I zoom in with the recording eye. He wrinkles his nose and yawns. He has a seriously bad case of plaque build-up, but his eyelashes are long, dark, and curled. Beautiful.

"Amy!" Gilchrist calls from the trail.

The boar jumps. He spins. His beady black eyes focus on me. He charges toward the cattails.

I can't breathe. I'm going to be shish kebab.

Gilchrist shouts again. The boar turns and runs downstream. I exhale with relief. That is going to be some awesome footage.

I stand and slosh across the river. Gilchrist waits on shore, his arms folded across his chest and his lips pressed into a thin, straight line. If he were Mama I'd be trembling, but Gilchrist is about as intimidating as a puppy growling over a bone. He lacks follow-through.

"You don't have time to dawdle, young lady. We've got to make it across the valley before dark."

The spring sun sparkles on the river. The day is bright and warm, but behind us shadows creep from the mountain.

I adjust my backpack. "I can make it."

Gilchrist turns back to the road.

I replay the clip, name it *Sus Scofas* Male-11, and file it under *Suidae*. The recordings are my one consolation. Thanks to Gilchrist, I'm missing six weeks of school, but I've never been this far south. I've added tons of new specimens to my digital zoo. Suzanne will be impressed, or at least pretend to be, for my sake. Our on-going friendship has been a mutually agreed upon deception since puberty. We haven't had anything in common for years, but we're determined to hang onto the whole best-friends-forever thing.

"Hurry up." Gilchrist is already more than a hundred feet ahead of me.

"Coming." I hold tight to the straps on my backpack and jog. I near him and his steps quicken. I can never catch up. For a scrawny, old guy he can sure cover the miles.

Then I remember the Committee. I check the time and moan. I'm late, again. I drag my finger across the controller's screen. Icons pop up like rows of carrot and turnip. I scroll until I find the blue and green globe. I tap and the globe spins. At last a map fills the display. I capture our location, then hit send. This is the third time today. I'll do it once more before I go to bed. It's data collection, I tell myself, like the clips of the animals. Facts are neutral.

"How can you walk with your nose in that thing?" Gilchrist is at my side.

I jump. "I'm organizing files." I hurry to close the map and open the clip of the boar.

Gilchrist watches from over my shoulder. "What is it with you and pigs?"

"They're cute."

The edges of his mouth turn down ever so slightly. "They're unclean."

"It's not like I'm eating a ham sandwich."

"Put your controller away, Pumpkin, and pick up the pace."

Pumpkin. A squat, orange vegetable. He'd called me that the first time we'd met and somehow the nickname had stuck. I'd been six years old, at the annual gathering. Mama had taken me deep in the woods to a waterfall. I'd let the round drops of water roll off my fingers and stuck my tongue out to taste the mist. Then he'd stood there, a little taller than Mama, his dark hair slicked back.

Mama nudged me forward. "Amy, this is your father."

Gilchrist cupped my chin in his hand. "Aren't you the cutest little pumpkin?"

It would have made more sense if I had red hair.

I push a stray strand behind my ear. Mouse brown, Mama calls it, the same color as my eyes.

I settle into a comfortable pace. Broken fence lines the meandering road. The scent of apple blossoms floats on the breeze. We pass a rusted mailbox. A white farmhouse, its paint cracked and faded, stands at the end of a drive beside a red barn. My steps slow. Inside could be clothes that would fit a sixteen-year-old girl, gadgets like controllers and tablets, or food.

I am so sick of thirty-five-hundred-calorie bars. They taste like chewy lemon cake. You'd think they'd be good, and they were, for the first few days. When I get home I'm never eating lemon-flavored anything ever again. I fantasize about slurping fat little round spaghettis in tomato sauce. Most things in cans are fine ten, even fifteen years past their expiration date.

"Amy!" Gilchrist is so far ahead it takes me a second to spot him beneath a huge, lone poplar. The road dips, and he is out of sight again.

I run, my pack thudding against my back, until each breath aches. There's no use asking him to stop. We haven't scavenged once this whole trip, which is odd, considering we're supposed to be on a scavenging trip. We don't even stop to eat, hence the food bars, and we only sleep when it's too dark to move forward.

I keep up pretty well for more than an hour. Birds twitter overhead. Swallows, thousands of them, swoop across the valley. The western sky is red and purple. Dusk chases us. My feet feel their way over the broken pavement.

The road turns north on the far side of the valley. We continue east on a narrow trail that leads up the ridge. The crescent moon rises as the sun sets. The eastern horizon stays orange. I glance at it a few times as we walk. The light should fade, but it only grows brighter. Then it flickers.

My heart pounds against my chest. I've seen the sky like this once before, the night the pine barrens burned.

I run to Gilchrist. "Fire!" I fill my lungs, but there is no taste of smoke. He is steady on the path. "Not exactly."

"What is that supposed to mean?" I ask, but the moment the words leave my mouth I know. I can't believe he's brought us this close. "The lights are from New Lithisle, aren't they?"

"I'm sorry. I should have warned you. The trail parallels the border for ninety miles."

3

"Gilchrist." My fingers tighten into a fist. "You promised you'd stay away."

"Your mama was already upset you'd be gone so long. If we'd walked the other way it would have taken an extra week."

I pull on his arm. "But what about, you know. Boom. Crash. Burn." I don't want to be anywhere near New Lithisle when God sends his judgment on the pig people.

"Do you think I would have brought you this close if I thought the aegis was going to collapse tonight?"

"You tell me."

"Give me more credit than that." Gilchrist's boots scrape against the dirt and rocks as he continues on the path. "The aegis has its problems, but the solar storms won't peak until the summer solstice. We should be fine."

"Should?" The branches over the trail reach like spooks' arms across the glowing sky. I feel the cool, smooth edges of the controller in my pocket. I trudge after him.

The trail steepens. The sky grows brighter. The tree frogs are silent and even the mosquitoes stop buzzing in my ears.

Gilchrist stands on an outcropping of rocks at the top of the ridge. "There's a good view of the aegis from here."

"I don't want to see it."

"It's a little hard to avoid."

I step beside him. My skin prickles. A wall of fire stretches north and south, so tall I can't see the top of it; cities, fields, lakes, and streams, the entire east coast of what used to be the Lithisle Republic hidden inside a terrestrial sun.

"Beautiful, isn't it?" Gilchrist's voice is filled with pride.

Only he, once the lead engineer on the project, would think so.

"In a moth-to-the-flame kind of way," I say. Not that I'm a bug, drawn.

Gilchrist ignores me and moves to the edge of the rocks. I take his sleeve and hold him back. "I don't think this is a good idea."

He pulls from my grip and continues down the trail. "We'll be fine."

"Please, no. We can't go down there."

"It's not a big deal."

My feet won't move. "It is to me."

He doesn't look back.

"Fine!" I yell after him. "Go scavenging in Mason yourself. I'll be back at the farm in the valley eating a decent meal."

He disappears into the woods. I stand in the glare of the aegis.

"Gilchrist!" My voice echoes through the trees. The heat presses against my face. My breath grows short.

I tear through the woods after Gilchrist. Branches and trunks flash by. I bowl into him. We tumble to the ground. I spit dirt and rotten leaves from my mouth.

"People are calling you a sympathizer," I blurt. "The Committee thinks this whole trip is nothing but a front for you to fix the aegis and keep it from collapsing."

Gilchrist sits and groans. "Where did you hear that?"

"Suzanne's father was in his study with Committee Member Trumble the week before we left. They were arguing. You need to avoid the appearance of evil."

He brushes off his arm. "I don't care what anyone thinks. The other route is hundreds of miles longer. It's foolish."

He'd better just be taking a shortcut, but no matter his reason, being this close to the aegis isn't going to look good. And for 90 miles. How can I cover that up? I can't pretend to forget my transmissions or say I couldn't connect for two whole days.

I help Gilchrist to his feet.

He takes a step and stumbles. "Ouch."

Now he's got a sprain. "Sorry," I say, and I lift his arm over my shoulder.

Gilchrist grimaces and grunts as we walk. I raced down the first half of the trail in minutes. The second half takes more than an hour.

We come to the end of the trees. A few hundred feet away a wall of fire swirls orange, gold, and sienna, like molten glass being blown. Energy sparks from the base of the aegis. There is a loud crack. I shudder.

Gilchrist drops to the ground. "Don't worry. The aegis makes noise like that all the time." He props his foot on his sleeping bag. "Set my tent up for me."

I turn my back to the aegis, pull out the poles, and push them together.

Gilchrist unzips the front of his backpack and digs through rods, wires, and black boxes.

I run the poles through the sleeves, set the tent on the under pad, and stake it in place.

Gilchrist screws the rods together.

I clip the fly over the tent.

Gilchrist slides the bottom of his now six-foot tower through one of the boxes. He fastens it in place, takes a red wire and connects it to the inside of the box. He takes a blue wire and does it again.

"Your tent is ready."

"Thanks." He offers no explanation, but it's obvious. He's trying to communicate with someone in New Lithisle. Committee Member Trumble was right. Gilchrist is a traitor, or about to become one.

My stomach turns. I run from the trees across the dry, barren field. I'm at the aegis. I freeze. I see my reflection in the fire, transparent and light, shimmering like an angel, or a ghost. "What am I supposed to do?" My likeness offers no suggestions, but I know. I'll do what I've done every night. Data collection. Facts are neutral.

I tap the blue and green globe icon on my controller. The globe spins, then locks onto our coordinates. My finger lingers over the send button. I tap. A blue bar speeds across the screen. 5, 20, 100 percent. Delivered.

God have mercy on Gilchrist. And me.

My chest stings from the heat. I take a deep breath and let it burn. I reach for the fire. My image mirrors my movements, slow, poised, and graceful. My fingertips graze the edge of the flames. A spark leaps to my hand. I feel alive. I feel pain. I'm tossed in the air, then slammed to the dirt.

"Don't play with it," Gilchrist yells from across the field. I hear his lopsided gait pound toward me. He kneels at my side.

My hand throbs. Tears well.

"It's okay, Pumpkin. Let me see." Gilchrist pulls a small glass jar from his backpack, applies a cool, silver-white salve to my burn, and wraps it in gauze.

"How does it feel?" he asks.

"Better."

"I didn't think I had to warn you to stay away. You didn't even want to come down here."

"I wish we hadn't."

He slings his backpack over my shoulder. "Help me up."

6

We stand. I brace Gilchrist as he walks along the aegis.

"The antenna didn't work," he says.

I can't believe he admitted it. "I don't want to hear about what you were doing."

"Of course you do. You've been spying on me."

I press my lips together. I don't like that word, but I'm not going to argue.

"I don't blame you. They've had sixteen years to indoctrinate you. It's only natural you'd side with them."

"I haven't sided with anyone. The Committee asked me to send them our coordinates. I have. That's all."

Gilchrist rests his hands on my shoulders. "I know you did what you thought was right, but you must understand. So do I."

His grip tightens.

I duck, but can't pull loose. "Hey!"

His eyes narrow.

My stomach drops.

He shoves me into the flames.

Fire burns all around, bright as the sun. I gasp, but the heat steals my breath. Pain coils me like a snake, then screams from every cell in my body. I sway.

"Why?" I cry, but no sound comes from my lips.

"Keep going," Gilchrist shouts. "Don't stop!"

I try to walk, but my muscles tighten into knots. I only want the pain to end. I fall to my knees.

"Get up, Amy."

His words ring in my ears. My thoughts fade. I'm warm and cozy by the stove, snuggled in Mama's arms. Posey is curled on my lap. She purrs as I stroke her soft fur. Golden Star wags his tail at my feet. I smile. This is what eternity will be like, an endless winter night close to the ones I love.

Cold fingers encircle my arm. My eyes flash open. I can still feel. I look and realize my clothes aren't even singed. I see the hand that touches me, melted skin and charred muscle. Gilchrist holds me, but he has no strength.

"Hang in there," says Gilchrist. "I'll get you out."

He'll never be able to. I push at the dirt and rise to my knee.

I pull one foot beneath me, then the other. I waver. My head and hand throb.

"Walk forward. You can do it."

I take a step. My legs crumple.

"Don't give up!"

I fall into darkness.

CHAPTER TWO
Cursed

A loud crack shatters the quiet. I open my eyes. Sparks from the
aegis graze my cheek. I roll away. A dull *beep, beep, beep* sings from my
pocket. I lift on my elbow. My head fills with stars and my gut turns.

"Gilchrist?"

The aegis rumbles.

I push myself to my feet. My legs wobble, but I walk to the middle of
the field. Thin, wispy clouds float through an azure sky. The sun shines
bright, but I stare at it and my eyes don't water. The golden ball fades to
nothing then pops back in place. The sun is only a projection. I'm inside
the aegis.

Boom. Crash. Burn.

I'm going to die.

"Gilchrist!" I stumble to the wall. "Get me out!"

Not a bird sings. Not a squirrel chatters. The only thing I hear is my
controller, which hasn't stopped beeping since I woke. I take it from my
pocket and look at the screen. The word *Error* flashes with every note.
An upload bar is locked at 66 percent. I open the attached file. There
are lines of dots, dashes, and numbers, a program written in strophes,
Gilchrist's favorite coding language.

I look for his initials on my task bar and find them in a yellow circle.
He'd logged in remotely and tried to send the file, probably thought I'd
make a good mule when his pile of poles failed. At least his program
hadn't made it to...I open the details. The information is addressed to
greycat40@vlas.net.

I close the app and wipe tears from my cheeks. Crying won't
help. I need Gilchrist. I have no idea how I made it through the wall
without frying. The way he did. I gasp. The burns on his arm. They
were awful.

I stand as close as I dare to the aegis and wait for a break in the energy field. I don't see him through the swirls of light, but the tent I set up is still pitched near the trees. I call to him again. He doesn't answer.

I tap the blue and green globe icon on my controller. The screen reads *Please Wait, Searching,* but after five minutes it doesn't lock onto one satellite. The aegis must be blocking them. I won't be able to signal Gilchrist or the Committee, not that I want to tell the Committee anything, but without medical attention Gilchrist could die.

I check the time. I had thought it was morning and it is, two and a half days later. I've been out almost three days.

I can't breathe. Three days.

What if Gilchrist is already... dead?

I sink to the ground and think back to the day three years ago when Gilchrist had come to tell Mama and me about the Committee's decision to let me accompany him on some of his scavenging trips. He'd stood on Mama's porch, a broad smile on his face and a parchment in his hand. He'd said the Committee had finally given him permission to visit me, although not in Old Lithisle. I could come along with him on one of his scavenging trips.

My heart had leapt in my chest. I'd been so excited at the chance to spend more than a few clandestine minutes with this stranger who was my father and had been my biological mother's husband.

Mama had frowned and held out her hand. "Let me see." She unrolled the scroll and there, pressed in red wax, was the Committee seal on a writ of agreement. "Why now?"

"She's thirteen." He winked at me. "Old enough for an adventure." I guess he hadn't lied, but if Gilchrist had been completely honest he would have admitted he was doing more than collecting electronic doodads for the Committee. I was certainly too naïve to have figured out the Committee wanted me to spy on my own father. I should have known it wasn't going to end well.

I take a deep breath. *No.* Things haven't ended. Gilchrist is alive. He has to be and no matter what he tried to do, he didn't actually commit treason. His message didn't make it through. I just have to make sure he doesn't figure that out, get him home safely, and convince the Committee we didn't betray them. My heart shrinks. Scoring a triple save doesn't seem likely.

I look around the clearing. My head spins. My stomach growls. I reach for my backpack, but it's not mine, it's the one Gilchrist slung over my shoulder after he dressed my wound. I pull it open. There's a pair of men's pants and a couple of shirts but no meal bars and the water bottle is empty. I wipe the opening with my shirt and try not to think about Gilchrist spit as the last few drops fall to my tongue.

I turn the backpack upside down and shake. The first aid kit rolls out then one of his black boxes. The plastic case fits in my palm. A red circle glows on the front and its back is a solar cell. I glance to the fake sky. There is no sun. I lay it in a bright spot anyway.

I pull out my controller and play with the New Lithisle maps. There's a campsite with a stream six miles away, a twelve mile round trip.

I look down the path that disappears into the woods. I haven't seen anyone since I woke. Thank goodness. Committee Member Trumble says the people of New Lithisle have done even more disgusting things to themselves in the sixteen years since they sent Gilchrist, Mama, and the thousands of other pandemic survivors away for refusing the pig genes. The last thing I need is to run into one of Allarice's genetically altered abominations.

I'll wait here. Gilchrist could be napping or maybe he went to the house in the valley to find supplies. If he did, he'll be back.

I lie down and close my eyes, but I've slept too much already. I open them and watch the clouds. The sky repeats itself every half an hour. The sun is on a separate cycle. It's as accurate as my controller for telling time.

Hours go by. I go to the wall and call again. There is silence. I peer through the fire. The tent is still.

I roll my tongue, thick and wooly, dehydrated. I can't sit here and do nothing. I'll die of thirst before the aegis has a chance to kill me. I take the clothes from Gilchrist's backpack and form an S.O.S. on the ground. I write in the dirt with my finger, *Went to find food and water. I'll be back soon. Amy.*

I toss the backpack over my shoulder. The eastern path Gilchrist and I traveled continues inside the aegis. The trees at the edge of the forest are gnarled, but a few hundred yards in they grow tall and strong. I run my fingers along the bark, smooth beech, rough maple, and a tree that's shaggy.

A few miles from the wall the path leaves the hardwoods and enters a growth of pine. I reach a junction and kick through the dead grass for a trail sign. My foot hits a soft cedar post. I flip it and a cracked rectangular board turns. I wipe off bits of dirt and a fat white slug that leaves behind a pool of slime. Yuck. The paint is faded, but I trace the lines of the trail system. A florescent pink dot proclaims *You Are Here.* I examine the junction, then the map. The campsite lays a mile north but a welcome center is only four more miles east.

According to the map, the campsite doesn't even have an outhouse or shelter, but my thirst would be quenched and wild greens would quiet my stomach. The welcome center could have every offering of civilization, or nothing at all.

I count the miles in my head. Eighteen instead of twelve, twenty if I do the campsite and the welcome center. The hike wouldn't be bad. I'll go to the welcome center and be back to the aegis by midnight. If there's chocolate every step will be worth it.

I continue on the eastern trail. The miles hadn't intimidated me, Gilchrist and I go forty or more a day on our trips, but without food every step feels like the last in a marathon.

I rest for a minute and listen. There's no breeze to moan or rustle and I haven't seen so much as a chipmunk or sparrow since I woke. The air is too still and quiet for someplace so green and bright, like a museum filled with silk plants. I hurry on.

In the distance I see a brown, vine-covered building. The dirt becomes pavement beneath my feet. I run, then press my back to the brick wall. Shards of glass and a door ajar tell me the building has already been scavenged, but piles of untouched leaves and dirt show it hasn't been for a while.

I scoot alongside the building to the door and step inside. Maps are scattered across the floor. The plastic front of the snack machine in the lobby is shattered. The one for cold drinks is tipped on its side, but remains intact. I set the laser on my controller and slice through the thin metal back. The holding bins are empty. I reach down the chute and feel the rounded bottom of a can. I slip my fingers around it and pull. Orange. I pop the top and take a sip. The liquid is sweet and smooth on my lips and tongue. I gulp. My stomach bubbles. The lightness in my head fades.

Beyond the lobby are offices. Vines have grown in from the windows and cover the desks, bookcases, and chairs. There is a bathroom and a janitor's closet, but no place for extra supplies. I poke through the ceiling tiles. Pink insulation in the attic makes me sneeze. I go from room to room and peek out the windows. I don't see a shed or garage.

I wander through the building until I come to a back room with a counter, mini-fridge, and microwave. The fridge is empty, but in the cupboard I find forks with rust spots, plastic spoons, and packets of ketchup and mustard. I'll starve before I'll down the mustard, but the ketchup is worth a try. I empty it on a paper plate, sit at the table and lick it from my finger.

I lean against the wall. The table is jammed against an exterior door. Beneath it a rubber mat lays askew. The mat isn't where it belongs.

I drag the table to the center of the room and roll back the mat. A trapdoor lays flat in the floor. I pick the lock with my army knife, and lift the latch. Stairs lead to a basement. I pad down the damp concrete. In the dim light I see boxes of paper beside plastic utility cabinets.

I work my way around the basement. There are more maps as well as gift shop books, plush animals, and little spoons with different waterfalls painted on the handles. I scratch the neck of a fluffy wild boar. They're even adorable stuffed. I find pens, pencils, and staples. I swing open the last cabinet. Bottles of water in cardboard flats are wrapped in clear plastic. Cans of coffee fill an entire shelf. I pull a blue box of cocoa packets from the cabinet, sit on a box of paper, and spoon cocoa powder into my mouth. I wash it down with water. I chew a few red and white striped candies. The mint blends with the chocolate on my tongue. I don't think anything has ever tasted this good. I spot a box of ramen noodles. I munch them right from the package.

I want more, but I know I'll get sick if I eat too much. I shove as many bottles of water in the backpack as I can and carry the noodles and cocoa in my arms.

I dart up the stairs. Worn leather boots surround me like bars on a cage.

"What you got there, girlie?"

I scream and drop the boxes.

The men laugh.

I take a step back down the stairs, but there's nowhere to hide. I can't run. I can't fight. I pick up a packet of ramen and hurl it at one of the men. "Noodles, and you idiots made me drop them." I bend down to pick up the rest. My hands shake.

I'm dragged up the stairs by the backpack. My chest scrapes against the carpet.

"She's mine," a man says.

I roll over. An angular, bony ridge, like a fin, runs down the middle of his bald head. His eyes protrude from his skull and his teeth, the ones he has left, are as pointed as a pike's.

Fish people. *Sick.* Not even the most pessimistic Committee Member could have imagined this.

Fin-head grabs my foot and slaps a flat, cold piece of metal on my ankle. He drops me to the floor. "Stay."

The men push their way down the stairs like goats trying to get in the shed at grain time. I'm alone. I sit. No one reprimands me. I stand, then run to the door. Electric shocks jolt me. I twitch like a frog in biology. If I hadn't been through the aegis, it would be the worst pain I've ever felt. It's a close second. I fall back in the room. The shocks stop. I puke bits of cocoa, mint, water, ketchup, and orange.

"Never had a bracelet on before, have you? You wouldn't have tried to run if you had." Fin-head holds up his arm. On his wrist he wears a bracelet like the one he put on me. "Get more than twenty feet from this and you'll be in a world of pain."

"My people will be angry when I don't come back."

"Our scouts found you three miles away, alone, and followed you here. You've got no one." He walks to the lobby. I don't want to get zapped again. My legs shake, but I follow. He holds the door open even though the glass is gone and I could have walked through it closed.

A blue, rusted pick-up idles in the drive.

"Get in the back."

I take a hesitant step. I'd almost rather get shocked to death. "Where are you taking me?"

"Does it matter?"

Tears blur my vision. I can't get stuck in this place. I'll die with the cursed when the aegis collapses. *Boom. Crash. Burn.*

The skin beneath the bracelet tingles a warning. I climb over the tailgate. Patience is a virtue, Mama says. My chance will come. I'll get back to Gilchrist somehow. I sit with my back to the cab and pull my knees to my chest.

"Hurry up," Fin-head says to the men coming out of the building. "I want to make it to market tonight."

They move faster, but they laugh and smile as they carry boxes and pile them around me. I try not to gawk. They all have the pointed teeth, but I'm sure I see the glint of a scale or two. A few have deep creases in their necks. Gills.

When the bed is loaded, two men sit on the truck gate, their backs toward me, while the rest pile into the crew cab. A ball of smoke explodes from the general direction of the exhaust, the engine sputters, and we roll away. The brick building fades from sight. We enter woodlands. The truck slows, turns onto a forest road, then stops. The men on the gate hop off. The doors behind me open.

We've only traveled a few miles. I can't believe I'm not ready to run. I grab my controller and set the laser to its lowest setting. I aim the blue beam at the bracelet. The metal grows warm. I bump up the intensity. The bracelet burns. I lift it off my skin and bite my lip. The laser isn't going to work.

I hide the controller and wait for the men to empty the back of the truck. They don't.

"Tell Ruth we'll be back in the morning," says Fin-head. "Early afternoon at the latest."

"Sure thing, Leroy." The man by the side of the road holds the box of noodles under his arm.

Fin-head gets back in the truck. Three men climb in after him, the rest file into the woods.

I curl in a ball next to the cab. They won't be back until tomorrow. Only God knows where I'll be. The truck bumps along in a dull rhythm. I count. Each thump takes me further from Gilchrist. Will I ever see him, Mama, or Suzanne again? I fight the heaviness in my eyelids. I have to memorize every turn, remember the way back, but we pull onto an empty highway and drive for hours.

The truck gate falls with a shudder. I sit and shiver. I must have fallen asleep. The light in the sky has faded but electric lanterns strung on cables, light a worn, grassy stretch. Trucks and tents line a makeshift avenue. Merchants hawk their wares, and men, women, and children wander among the goods. I search for alterations. A woman with hair as yellow as the feathers of a goldfinch passes. A boy looks up at me with eyes as purple as the fins of a royal dottyback. No one here looks normal, but I don't see any others as bizarre as the fish people.

Fin-head and his men arrange the paper, pens, staplers, and paperclips on the tailgate. He announces the arrival of his merchandise. He doesn't mention the cocoa, mints, or water. They'd probably taken them to their camp with the noodles.

The paper sells first. Buyers exclaim how white and bright it is. The find would have been popular back home too. At school we write on slate. The paper we do have is recycled grey.

"What do you want for the girl?" A tall man dressed in a ruffled white blouse and black trousers speaks to Fin-head. He wears short bangs and a trim beard. His pale skin almost glows in the light. "Is she a virgin?"

I slide to the edge of the truck and take hold of the wall. If Fin-head names a price I don't care if I get shocked, I'm out of here.

"She's not for sale," says Fin-head.

"I'll give you ten thousand."

I stare in disbelief. I've watched the sale for an hour. At most they'd only made a few hundred credits selling the boxes of paper.

"I said she's not available."

"Looks like she is to me. I'll give you fifteen thousand credits." A second man, his face and neck bushy with hair, counters the first.

Fin-head waves to one of his men. "Get her in the backseat."

I do as I'm told. I should be grateful, but I wonder what they're saving me for.

The cushion feels better on my backside than the truck bed. The sun sets and the night projection rolls across the aegis. The moon is full, surrounded by constellations I've never seen. One, the largest, appears to be a woman smiling down from the heavens. I look away, and my cheeks flush. Committee Member Trumble once told me my biological mother had tried to set herself above God. I didn't realize he'd meant Allarice had literally stuck her face in the sky. Seriously, how conceited do you have to be to make a constellation of yourself?

A few boxes remain in the truck, but most of the potential customers have left. Fin-head and his men clear their site, close the gate, and climb in the cab. I sit between one man with scales and another with gills. I hold my arms tight to my sides and press my knees together, but I still bounce into one of them. Gross.

The road curves along a ridge. We leave the woods. Below are streets lined with houses. Buildings as tall as the sandstone cliffs, filled with light, stand at city center. More people probably live in this one city than half of Old Lithisle. We drive to the outskirts and park in front of a huge square shop surrounded by pavement.

Fin-head taps his controller into the controller of the man in the passenger seat. "There's four hundred credits. Do you think that'll be enough?"

The men cheer and share high-fives and fist bumps.

"No worries for a few weeks, anyway," says Fin-head. The three men leave the truck and walk to the building. For the first time I notice how their clothes hang loose on their bodies. Maybe Fin-head's ridge is less fin and more near-starvation. I'm not sure. Even his fingers are bony.

He looks at me in the rear-view mirror. "Are you hungry?"

My stomach hurts as if it's eating itself. I nod.

Fin-head puts the truck in first and eases off the clutch. We drive a block and pull up next to a giant hotdog. A woman's voice comes from the speaker. He orders burgers, fries, and shakes.

We roll up to the window. Fin-head taps his controller again and they hand him two paper sacks. He tosses one to me over the seat and parks with a view through big glass windows into the restaurant. Customers sit at red tables with natural finish chairs.

"I can't go in." He opens his bag and eats a fry. He chews and chews and chews. I guess he has to with those tiny little teeth. "Alterations go right and they put you on the network, make you a star. Things go bad, and you're lucky to not die in a work camp."

He is genetically modified. That doesn't mean I want to talk about it. I pull the meat patty off the burger, *yuck*, drop it in the bag, then fill my mouth with bun, lettuce, tomato, and onion. I don't normally eat anything that's touched dead animal, but I'm starving.

When we're done Fin-head turns the key in the ignition, but we don't head back to the shopping center. He drives the opposite direction. After a few blocks the street narrows. Broken lights leave much of the way dark. Iron gates cover windows and doors. The truck stops in front of a

17

four-story building of steel and glass. Light blue curtains, floor to ceiling, can be seen through the windows. The sign flickers, *Petrich Mission.*

"Get out," says Fin-head.

I step onto the sidewalk. The air smells like the tannery back home, rotten and full of lye.

"So." I try to sound casual. "What are we doing here?" I hope the stop has nothing to do with me, but I doubt I'd have such luck.

Fin-head says nothing. He walks to the front door. My skin beneath the bracelet tingles. I hurry after him. Inside, a man, quite normal looking at first glance, sits behind a long, low counter. The lights overhead cast a pink tone.

"I've got one." Fin-head pushes me forward.

CHAPTER THREE
Tethered

The man behind the counter looks at me, his gaze moving from my feet to my head. "Her hair's brown and her skin is too white."

"Just get me whoever can transfer the credits."

"He's not going to give you anything for her."

Fin-head curls his upper lip. The light shines off his spiky teeth. "Get him."

"All right." The man walks to the wall. "If you insist." He presses a black button the size of his palm. A loud buzz echoes down the hall.

A door on the second floor creaks and heavy steps shuffle toward the stairs.

"There's a Barracuda here," says the man behind the counter. "He's got a girl."

The man on the stairs wears paisley silk pajamas, a dark blue velour robe, and leather slippers. His short silver hair and beard are flecked with strands of black. His skin is a deep golden brown, the color of acorns in the fall, like Suzanne's.

He stops. "She's not one of ours."

"She doesn't have an ID," says Fin-head.

"Are you sure?" The man comes down and holds his controller to my forehead. He raises an eyebrow as he looks at the display. "What region are you from? Who are your parents?"

I say nothing. No answers have to be better than wrong ones.

The man shakes his head and walks back to the stairs.

"She's from your group," says Fin-head. "Who else in New Lithisle could have no ID?"

"You'll have to ask her."

Fin-head grabs him by the arm. "Give me my reward."

"I'm not giving you credits for someone who's not ours."

"She'll bring a lot more than five thousand elsewhere."

There are quiet footsteps. A petite woman comes from the hall beyond the lobby. Her black hair, pulled back and tied beneath a scarf, falls to her waist. Her skirt, golden-yellow and embroidered with red swirls, glides across the marble floor. "What's going on?"

The man from upstairs bows to her. "It's a trick." He points to Fin-head's wrist. "He wears a tether to keep her. She'll run the minute it's gone and we'll have nothing."

The woman looks in my face. She lifts her hand to my hair and rolls a few strands between her fingers. The corners of her mouth curve upward. A chill runs down my spine. She knows who I am. I can see it in her eyes. I pull away. I have no idea how she figured it out so quickly.

I lean to Fin-head. "Don't leave me here. I can help you scavenge. The haul from the welcome center was nothing."

He ignores me.

"We'll take the girl," says the woman. "And the tether."

"Please." My voice falls to a panicked whisper. "You can't let her take me."

Fin-head holds out his controller. "Who's going to pay?"

"Give this gentleman the five thousand credits," says the woman.

The man from upstairs doesn't move. "Nasira, are you sure?"

"Do you want me to call Elder Binyamin?"

The man frowns. "No need." He comes down and taps his controller into Fin-head's.

Fin-head runs his controller over his bracelet. The metal loosens and he hands it to Nasira.

I gasp. The bracelets are computerized. Maybe I can hack into mine and free myself. He leaves without a glance and the door snaps shut.

Nasira takes small, quick steps to the hall. I scurry after her. She opens a door. A man sits on the second of two beds, his eyes fixed on his controller. He's in nightclothes, like the man from upstairs, but he also wears a short, round knit cap on his head. Suitcases are stacked in a corner. There's a wardrobe and a door to a bath.

"What trouble did you find for me this time?" he asks. He doesn't look up.

Nasira takes his controller, taps it several times and hands it back to him. His focus shifts from the screen to me, then back to the screen. "I don't care how much she looks like one of Allarice's daughters. I'm not taking another girl to the Ministry of Culture."

My throat tightens. I hadn't thought about the others. Nasira must have recognized me because I look enough like them, even though any bond we might have shared, twelve identical embryos implanted in twelve surrogates, was broken when they were genetically altered.

"We'll get the blood work done first this time."

"Nasira."

"Her father set off the aegis alarm three months ago. Now she's here. Do you think it's only a coincidence?"

No, of course it's not. Gilchrist should have never even tried to enter New Lithisle, he was banished along with the others for his refusal to get the pig genes, and he still has the quarantine ID buried deep in his brain, but apparently he'd tried. And failed. But, oddly, it does make me feel a little better about him pushing me through the wall. At least I hadn't been a total guinea pig.

"That was a hoax," the man says. "No one could have survived out there. He's been dead for years, along with Hannah, the child she was carrying, and everyone else who went with them."

Hannah. They even know who Mama is.

"Foolishness." Nasira's gaze meets mine. "Your father brought you and your surrogate back in, didn't he child?"

Sweat dampens my palms. I can't believe they don't know what happened. Do they really think no one is alive beyond the aegis? I'm not going to be the one to educate them.

"She's just another runaway," he says.

"I guess we'll find out," says Nasira.

Not if I can help it. I wriggle like a four-year-old and inch to the bath. Maybe while they argue I can hack the bracelet. "I need to use the toilet."

Nasira steps between me and the bath. "Not without supervision, and take off your backpack."

I drop it to the floor.

Nasira doesn't leave when I sit on the toilet. She turns the spigot in the tub. Water the color of tea spurts out. The steam stinks like an egg the hen has sat on too long. I let the warm water trickle over my fingertips. Even Suzanne doesn't have running hot water at her house. Mama and I are really old fashioned. We have to pump water at the kitchen sink.

"You act like you've never seen water before." Nasira adjusts the spigot.

"You certainly look like you haven't. You're filthy and those clothes are horrid. Take them off and get in. I'll have to find you something decent to wear."

At last Nasira leaves.

I feel the doorknob but the lock swivels around and around. I look at the frame. There's no latch. I won't be able to work on the bracelet now. Nasira could walk in on me. I take my controller and slip it between the folds of the towels by the sink. I'll come back when they're asleep.

I pull my fleece over my head and shimmy out of my pants. I poke a toe in the water. It feels like the pond in late summer. I sit in the tub. I splash water over my shoulders. It drips down my back. I'd like to lounge but I don't want to be naked when Nasira comes back. I'm dripping with a towel around me when she barges in.

She carries a long blue tunic. "This will do for now."

I dry off and dress. The fabric is smooth and light against my skin. I peek from the bath. The man kneels by the window, his head bowed. He looks like he's praying, but he can't be. He's an abomination.

"Are there under things?" I whisper.

"I'm not giving you mine." She gestures to my hips. "They wouldn't fit anyway. I'll order new things in Vlas tomorrow."

I remember the address on Gilchrist's undelivered message, *greycat40@vlas.net*. I take soft steps to the empty bed and scoot under the covers. "Is this Vlas?"

"No, we're in Petrich. Vlas is two hours north by rail. Try to sleep. Elder Binyamin has arranged transportation. We leave in a few hours."

I pull the blankets over my head. I must already be over a hundred miles from Gilchrist. I can't afford to be taken further away. Nasira speaks to the man, he must be Elder Binyamin, in soft, low tones. Their conversation slows, then stops. I sit. They don't stir.

The thick carpet sinks beneath my feet. I enter the bath and slip my hand inside the towels. I feel only rough cotton. I pat through more folds. Nothing. I flip on the light and shake each towel.

Nasira flings the door open. "Looking for something?"

"My hair was still wet."

"Don't worry, you'll get your things back, eventually. The controller is safe with your pack. Now to bed."

That's not what I wanted to hear.

I follow Nasira out of the bath. I don't see the backpack with the suitcases or on the dresser. I wait for Nasira and Elder Binyamin to fall asleep again, but now, while one has their eyes closed, the other watches me. I turn my back to Nasira and bury my head in the pillow. They're not going to give me a chance to use my controller tonight. Tears well.

God, keep Gilchrist alive, and get me back to him.

Nasira shakes me. The sky outside the window is still dark. I fell asleep. Elder Binyamin is gone. The corner where the suitcases sat is empty. "Get up. We've got to make it to the station before dawn."

My feet hit the floor. "Where are my clothes?"

"I got rid of them. Keep what you have on."

"This isn't enough."

"You're fine."

I pull the blanket off the bed and wrap it around my shoulders.

Nasira pulls it from me. "The bedding belongs to the Mission. Now hurry. Elder Binyamin will be back soon, and we need to be downstairs."

We walk to the lobby. Elder Binyamin is at the counter talking with the man who paid for me last night.

"Done already?" asks Nasira.

"Elder Daniel helped load our baggage."

Nasira's eyes narrow. "You didn't tell me he'd be along."

"The coach belongs to him. We'd look suspicious traveling in it without him."

Nasira grunts and straightens her skirt.

Elder Binyamin takes off at a brisk pace. Nasira and I follow him to the empty street. We quickly fall behind. This is like walking with Gilchrist. The cold whips through the tunic. I pull it close, but goose bumps rise on my arms.

Smoke swirls from a barrel on the corner. Men dressed in torn pants and ragged shirts hold their hands over the flames.

"Keep your face from them," says Nasira.

I tilt my head down.

The next street is filled with boarded fronts. We cross a vacant lot, bricks and glass scattered across the dirt. The night projection fills the sky, but the real sun lights the east. We cross row after row of railroad tracks. A building of stone with tall arched windows is on the far side of a long covered platform. We stop.

"Where's Elder Daniel?" asks Nasira.

Elder Binyamin steps on the back of an antique passenger car. "He went back to bed."

"He couldn't even greet us?" Nasira stays on the track.

"He gave me the entry code." Elder Binyamin unlocks the back door. Inside is a hall lined with cherry wood. Beyond are golden brocade curtains tied with long ivory tassels, the corner of a mahogany desk, and a leather chair. "I didn't think you were eager to see him."

"I'm not, but going to bed when one has guests is beyond rude."

"His brother woke him at two in the morning and sent him to the station. Give him a little grace."

Nasira pushes me ahead of her. I stumble up the steps. "When he extends it to me."

Elder Binyamin opens the first door off the hall to a narrow bedroom with one full bed. Nasira drags me in and shuts the door.

She tosses me a blanket and pillow. "Get some rest."

I spread the blanket on the floor and lay down. Elder Binyamin and Nasira whisper, but I can't hear what they say. There is a nightstand and a closet. I don't see the luggage or my backpack.

I toss on the floor for hours but Nasira's gaze never leaves me. Day shines bright from the window. Whistles and shouts ring through the station. A low rumble grows. The car rocks.

I sit. "What was that?"

"We're coupling to the train."

Steel grinds against steel. There is a whoosh of steam and the car rolls forward. My heart races. How am I ever going to get back to Gilchrist now?

CHAPTER FOUR
Elder Daniel

The train pulls from the station and gathers speed until the trees become nothing but a blur. At last Nasira yawns, pulls the curtains over the window, lies at Elder Binyamin's side, and closes her eyes.

The clock ticks. I count the seconds. Five, ten, fifteen minutes. I lift on my elbow. No matter how far they take me, my first step is still to get rid of the tether.

I crawl to the closet. Nasira's cloak hangs on one of the brass hooks. I shimmy across the smooth wooden floor and lift the bed skirt. Dust tickles my nose, and I have to pinch it tight to keep from sneezing. My backpack isn't in here.

At the door I examine the electronic lock. Plastic isn't going to be enough to keep me in. I lift a pen from the jacket Elder Binyamin tossed over a chair, and force the point between the joint of the lock's casing. It pops.

Nasira rolls on the mattress. Her eyes stay closed.

I remove the batteries, hold the reset button and then replace the batteries. I count to fifteen. There is a sharp beep.

I freeze.

Elder Binyamin snores.

I slip the casing back in place then turn the lock. The bolt slides and the door opens.

The hallway is quiet except for the rhythmic clanking of the wheels against the tracks. In the study, the desk catches my attention. I don't necessarily need my controller to hack into the tether, someone else's might do. I slide the top middle drawer open. The strong smell of wintergreen wafts toward me, but the package of gum I find is empty. Then I see it, beneath a large, yellow envelope. A tablet. The screen lights as I lift the orange cover. A login appears. I force a restart, wait for the settings options, and select *command prompt*. I type in a line of symbols, strophes for "reveal hidden files", and hit enter.

Command not recognized.

Maybe I mistyped the code. I try again.

Command not recognized.

This time I'm sure I put it in right. I test half a dozen sequences. None of the codes Gilchrist taught me work. My fingers fly over the entry pad. The programming language is full of nonsensical letters and numbers. I don't even recognize the operating system. The tablet is totally useless. I toss it back in the desk.

A few steps beyond the study is a kitchen. Tall oak cabinets and a granite counter line the wall. Maybe I don't need my controller or the tablet. I slide open a drawer. Smooth and serrated knives gleam alongside forks and spoons. I take a knife, put my foot on the table, and saw at the bracelet. The teeth grind to nothing, but the bracelet has little more than a scratch. I try a second knife, then a third. The laser on my controller worked better. I toss the knives in the trash.

The train sways. A wave of nausea sweeps over me. I am so hungry. I open cabinet doors. There are white and blue toile patterned china plates, glasses, pots and pans. Most of the shelves are empty. I climb to look higher.

"May I help you?" The voice is too low and polite to be Nasira's but it's not Elder Binyamin, either. I turn.

A boy, dressed in a navy suit with a crisp blue shirt and red tie, stands behind me. His sandy blond hair is parted neatly to the side. His deep green eyes sparkle like dew in the morning grass.

My heart stops. He's gorgeous.

No.

He's part pig. The fact he's hot instead of having a snout and tusks doesn't change the fact he has no soul.

But still. Heat flushes my cheeks.

"You're her, aren't you?" He sounds nervous, but excited. "Of course you are, Allarice's missing daughter."

I didn't know I was missing, but his mention of Allarice pretty much dampens any attraction. "My name is Amy," I say in a flat tone.

"Oh, no, Seventh Daughter. I would never presume to call you by anything but your title."

I stiffen. I'm not a number. I open my mouth to tell him as much, but yelling won't help me get the tether off. "Please, call me Amy."

"Are you sure?" he asks.

"Very." I look for a graceful way to the floor. There is none.

"All right." He hesitates. "I'm Elder Daniel, but you can call me Daniel."

I must not have heard right. "Elder Daniel?" I would have thought an elder would be, well, older. "This coach belongs to you?"

"To my region."

I'm not sure what a region is, or why it's his, but he sounds important, and rich. I try not to be impressed. I could take a clip of him, label it *sus scrofa domesticus Male-1*, and put him in my zoo.

I reach my hand to him. "Could you help me down?"

"Of course." Daniel glances down the hall, then takes my hand. I wrap my fingers around his. He smiles. I jump. His arm doesn't waver. I totter. He steadies me. I look into his eyes. His lashes are long, dark, and curled. Beautiful.

Just like the boars.

I pull my hand from his. "I was looking for something to eat."

"I bought a few things at the coffee house in Petrich." He points to a large white paper sack that sits on the table.

"I swear," I say. "That wasn't there a minute ago."

He smiles. "No, I had it with me." He takes a plate from the cupboard then piles it high with bagels, donuts, and pastries.

My mouth waters.

He pulls out a chair for me at the table. We sit, and I take an onion bagel from the plate. I tear off a huge chunk and cram it in my mouth.

Daniel stares.

I must look like a chipmunk. I swallow bits of half chewed bagel to empty my cheeks.

He still looks appalled.

"Is there something on my face?" I wipe my chin.

"No." He pauses. "We should have grace."

I choke. Maybe Elder Binyamin was praying last night.

Daniel bows his head. "Dear God..."

I look out the window. Surely a genetically altered abomination praying is blasphemy, but there's no lightening. I listen. No thunder, either. You'd think God would be offended, but I guess he doesn't bother with rehearsed prose from less-than-humans.

I mouth my own prayer, some soulless boy isn't going to out-religion me. Then I finish the bagel. Daniel makes polite conversation, something about how pretty I look without makeup, and he wonders why my sisters wear so much of it. I down a cheesecake pastry and three doughnuts, one glazed, one jelly-filled, and one cream, while he talks. I lick a dollop of cream from the corner of my mouth and reach for another pastry.

Daniel's eyes follow my hand. "You must have been very hungry." He's still working on his first bagel.

"I'm sorry." I leave the pastry untouched.

"No, please, take it." He rearranges the meager remains on the plate. "Elder Binyamin and Nasira are still asleep. They'll never know what they missed."

"You must think I'm a pig." Shoot. A pig reference. "Not that pigs are gluttonous or anything. I'm actually quite fond of them, at least the wild boars. I've never seen a domestic pig. They're banned back home."

Daniel raises an eyebrow.

I'm chattering like a squirrel. I take a deep breath. "My father and I were traveling. I haven't had much to eat lately."

"Then we'll have to order takeout when we get to Vlas. I was thinking of fettuccini for lunch. Do you like pasta?"

"I love canned spaghettis."

His expression is blank.

"You know, the little round ones with the orange tomato sauce?"

"I'm sure they're tasty, but I think we can do better than canned spaghetti in Vlas."

I doubt it, but he finishes his bagel, and pushes away from the table. "If you'll excuse me, my class is about to start." He walks backward to the study. He waves, even though he can't be ten feet away.

The tablet.

I drag a chair from the kitchen and sit next to him at the desk. "What are you taking?"

He lifts the tablet from the middle drawer. "Trig. Have you taken it yet? I mean, I know most sixteen-year olds haven't, but you must be really smart, with who your parents are, and all."

He knows my age, of course he does, because of the others, but somehow, his knowledge irritates me. Or maybe it was the mention of my biological parents. "You mean the mad scientists?"

Daniel flashes an uncertain half-smile, like he's not sure if I'm joking or not.

I'm not. "So trig?" I say, bringing the conversation back to where it needs to be, distracting banter. "My best friend, Suzanne, is a year older than me, and I've helped her with it, some." I lean over Daniel's shoulder, to see what passcode he might type in.

He tilts the tablet from my sight and taps. "So. You are smart."

"Sometimes, I guess." I scoot closer. A room filled with desks appears on screen. A man stands behind a podium, his face hidden behind his tablet.

Daniel's display goes black. A problem that looks like it was written in neon green chalk appears. Daniel does nothing. His eyes, wide and full of wonder, are focused on me.

I sigh. He's looking at me the way I've always wanted a boy to, the way William Davis did, once, at Suzanne's cotillion, until his father pulled him aside and whispered in his ear. Then William glared at me like I was the spawn of the devil, which, I suppose, isn't far from the truth.

I'd rather be hated for being Allarice's daughter than be liked for it.

"Daniel." I wave my hand in front of his face. "Are you going to solve the equation or not?"

Daniel starts. "Yes, of course. I didn't realize it was there." He writes on the screen with his finger, but less than a minute in he forgets to convert a polynomial.

I turn away. His assignment is none of my business. I count to one hundred and peek back. He smiles at me.

"Mr. Brennan." Daniel's instructor pops up in a window at the bottom of the screen. "Are you feeling all right today?"

"Fantastic."

"Then start over."

"What?" Daniel examines his numbers. His cheeks redden and he puts his thumb over the tablet's eye. "I don't normally mess up like this," he whispers to me.

"I'm sure." I nod, but a smirk lifts the corner of my mouth.

"Mr. Brennan."

Daniel doesn't answer. He's looking at me again.

This is ridiculous. I reach over Daniel and drag my finger across the screen. Daniel's work disappears.

"What are you doing?" Daniel pulls the tablet away.

I grab it. "I can help."

"Thank you for your concern but—" He tugs on the tablet.

I hold tight and swivel. His arm wraps around me as I turn. His chair creaks and he falls back. There is a thud.

Daniel is rumpled on the floor. His hair hangs in his eyes.

I laugh.

He smiles.

"It's okay, I've got it." I rework the equation. "There." I hand him his tablet.

I freeze. I had a functioning tablet in my hands and all I did was math.

"Good job, Mr. Brennan," says his professor. "That's more like it."

Daniel examines my work. "Yes, it is." Another problem comes on. For the second time he doesn't see it.

I point to his tablet. "You need to get back to your class."

"I do." He moves to the sofa. "Come sit with me."

I shouldn't.

I do anyway, because of the tether. Right? I have to get it off.

We start a cushion apart. By the time the class ends we're so close his elbow brushes against my arm.

Something in my gut quivers, like beach roses caught in a gust from the lake. A smile floats to my face.

The coach dips into darkness. I jump.

Boom. Crash. Burn.

I haven't thought of the coming destruction, or Gilchrist, in over an hour.

"We're in Vlas," says Daniel. "The station is underground."

I kneel on the sofa and look out the window. Light sprinkles into the concrete tunnel then pours. The walls are laid in brown, blue, and green tiles. They form scenes of farmer's fields, mountain peaks, city skylines, and ocean shores.

"Are you still interested in takeout?" Daniel asks.

I am still hungry. "Very."

He looks up menus. The green and black engine pulls the coach onto a side rail. The walls quake as it detaches.

Daniel recommends the pasta primavera, with garden salad and bread sticks, but he promises he'll stop by a grocery to see if he can find canned spaghettis, too.

The engine shoots a cloud of black smoke and chugs away.

"Is there anything else I can get you?" Daniel stands and tucks the tablet under his arm.

I stare at it. Elder Binyamin and Nasira aren't up yet. With Daniel's tablet I could hack into the tether and be gone before he gets back. My mouth falls open, but nothing comes out.

His eyes follow my gaze. "Would you like to borrow it while I'm gone?"

I take a deep breath. I shouldn't have this much trouble saying yes.

"I'm still logged on." He puts it in my hands. "Do you know how to use it?"

I angle the tablet from him, slide to unlock, and double tap the control panel icon. I search for attached devices. *Tether I* and *Tether II* pop on screen. I hold it to my chest. "Yes, thank you. I do."

"All right, then." He presses his thumb to the rear lock. A violet light shimmers. "I'll see you soon."

But if my plan works I'll never see him again.

CHAPTER FIVE
Doomed

Daniel opens the door.

Skull-piercing mechanical shrieks fill the air.

Nasira will wake. I clear the tablet, run with it to the study, and shove it in the drawer.

"She's gone!" Nasira cries from the bedroom.

My ankle stings like I've been bitten by a giant bee. I slap and hit a strip of metal. My leg spasms. The rest of me follows. I'm a marionette, twisting and jerking. I fall to the floor and writhe.

"Amy." Daniel is at my side. He scoops me in his arms. The shocks pulse through him as well as me. His face contorts with each jolt, but there is strength in his eyes.

Nasira stands above us.

"You t-t-tethered her?" Daniel asks, his voice loud and angry.

"She came that way."

The convulsions stop. I collapse into Daniel. He trembles, but holds me tight.

Elder Binyamin steps from the bedroom. "Nasira?"

"I had to activate the tether," she says. "I didn't know where she was. She could have been the one at the door."

"She could have died." Daniel turns to Elder Binyamin. "I want the tether off, now!"

"It's staying on." Nasira's eyes narrow.

"It's illegal," says Daniel.

"Your brother approved," counters Nasira.

"Well," says Elder Binyamin. "I told him about it and he didn't say no."

Daniel pulls a controller from his pocket. He double taps. Ring tones are cut short by a recording. He doesn't leave a message.

"Are you strong enough to get up?" Daniel asks.

I try to stand, but I shake.

"Don't worry." Daniel lifts me from the floor. "I've got you."

I rest my head against his chest. His heart races. Is it from the tether, or holding me? I don't know, but for a moment I feel safe, which is totally ridiculous. He can't even save himself from the coming aegis collapse, never mind me.

"What is this?" asks Nasira.

"I'm bringing her to my quarters to rest." Daniel walks toward his room.

"That's not what I'm talking about." Nasira takes hold of his arm. "She's a girl. Give her to me."

Daniel hesitates. He looks at Nasira, Elder Binyamin, then me. He holds me closer and keeps on down the hall.

"Elder." Nasira turns to her husband. "Stop him."

Elder Binyamin shrugs, looks back at his controller, and steps from the hall.

Daniel swivels sideways to get me through his door. A chandelier hangs from the ceiling. The bed is so big it could fit five people and a fat cat. The spread is blue satin brocade, pulled tight, without a bump or wrinkle.

Daniel lays me down. "My brother is their lawyer. He's probably in court. I should go downtown and find him. He'll get the tether off." He pushes the hair from my forehead. I can't see beyond his eyes. "Unless you'd rather I stay."

I don't want him to leave, ever.

"You should go." I stumble over my words. "Take your time. Pick up lunch. I'll be fine."

"Are you sure?"

Nasira pushes into the bedroom, a pillow and blanket under her arm. "I'm not about to let a seventeen-year-old boy stay in a bedroom with a sixteen-year-old girl." She drops the bedding in the chair. "Get out."

"I'll go," says Daniel. He turns to me and smiles. "We'll get the tether off. I promise."

"Good luck with that," says Nasira. She shoves him out the door, shuts it, then turns the lock.

He's gone.

My heart drops to the pit in my stomach. I almost hope I don't figure out a way to get out of here before he gets back.

Nasira drags the chair to the side of the bed then settles on the cushion. "Don't let Elder Daniel fool you. He may act like he cares, but his brother is going to get a huge chunk of the reward money." She grimaces. "More than he should, for the work he's doing."

There's a reward. I should have known, but money can't be the reason Daniel held me through those shocks. They must have hurt him as much as they did me. "He's not like you."

Nasira rolls her eyes then pulls out her controller.

I shift my back to her. She is right about one thing. I can't let Daniel fool me. He's handsome, sweet, and kind— but not entirely human. I can't waste energy thinking about him. I have to plan my escape.

I look around the room. Behind heavy curtains are four windows, good options for exit once I get the tether off. There's a picture on the wall above the bed. Daniel stands with his arm around a petite, middle-aged woman. She must be his mother. Worn books are piled on his nightstand. He reads the classics. On the far side of the room a door is half open. Daniel's under shorts lie on the bathroom floor. He's not perfect. Good. Neither am I.

What is wrong with me?

My eyes well. It's Cowboy, all over again. I should have known better, to get attached, but who can say no to a black and white baby goat with big blue eyes? I certainly couldn't. Cowboy's mother had died a few days after she'd given birth. I'd raised him on the bottle and he'd never quite figured out he wasn't a person. Cowboy stuck closer than Golden Star all summer. He waited at the garden gate, outside the outhouse, followed me to the porch and butted the door until I let him in. His affection didn't change the fact we already had a buck and didn't need two. No matter how I begged, when the butcher came that fall, Cowboy became stew. I went hungry. Mama chided.

Daniel is going to die.

My stomach cramps like I'm going to hurl everything I've just eaten.

I have to get out of here, before he gets back, before I have to see him again.

I sit and put my legs over the side of the bed.

Nasira holds the display of her controller to my face. "We need to find you something appropriate to wear to the Ministry of Culture tomorrow. Is there one you like?"

She scrolls through a dozen clips of dresses, as if I care.

"Well," she says. "Tell me what you like or I'll pick something myself."

Daniel's tablet.

"The screen is so small," I say. "I can't see anything."

"This is what we have."

"Daniel left his tablet in the other room. He said I could use it."

"Don't be so familiar," says Nasira. "He's Elder Daniel to you." She opens the door and calls to her husband. "Elder Binyamin!" He appears at the door a few moments later. I tell him where the tablet is. He brings it to Nasira. She accesses the network and shows me the dresses again.

"I don't like any of them," I say. "Can I see more?"

We browse dresses for a half an hour before Nasira finally sighs, hands me the tablet, and tells me to search on my own. She leans back in the chair and continues with her controller. I tilt away, minimize the dresses, find the attached devices again, and right click *Tether I* and *Tether II*. The program asks for a password. I don't even bother trying strophes again. I open a third window and search for information on the tablet's programming language. I download a cross-reference and start to piece together code. I enter a wrong phrase. I delete it. I enter it a second time. Wrong again.

I can't think straight.

Boom. Crash. Burn.

Daniel.

I glance at Nasira. She's still busy with her controller.

I run a new search, this time for the aegis. I follow a dozen links but there is only praise for the dome, no discussion of the electromagnetic pulse studies, solar storms, or the coming summer solstice. It's like no one in New Lithisle knows what's going to happen, until I land on Ander Smith's site. I mute the sound and read the closed captions.

"I have proof." Ander Smith sits at a desk in front of a wall of monitors and speaks into a silver microphone. "They deny it's unstable. They deny it's vulnerable. But the elite are collecting the nation's valuables for storage in a bunker they've built under Mount Paul." Pictures flash on screen of dump trucks and track hoes working among rocks and trees. "That's what they care about, themselves and their things, not you. To them you're nothing but a herd of cattle waiting for slaughter."

Not that all of the elite's digging and building will save them. If the toxic fumes don't get them the electromagnetic pulse will kill all of their electronics and turn their bunker into a tomb.

But Daniel's an elder. What if he's part of the elite?

I slam the tablet on the bed. Stupid Gilchrist for pushing me through the wall. Stupid Committee for sending me on the trip with him in the first place. And shoot, I don't want to blame God, but isn't he the one who's really responsible?

No.

This is all Allarice's fault. She's the one who made this mess. I guess it's fitting I have to deal with it. Probably die here in this dome, with all of her abominations. It would be poetic justice.

"What is wrong with you?" says Nasira.

"Nothing." I exit from the aegis search and close the attached devices. I pull a dress back up. "This one will do."

She takes the tablet. "That's one of the first ones I showed you."

I shrug.

Nasira calls Elder Binyamin. He takes her place in the chair. She disappears into their bedroom.

"Can I have the tablet back?" I ask.

"She let you have the tablet?"

"Yes."

"She shouldn't have."

"I'm bored."

Elder Binyamin points to Daniel's nightstand. "Read a book."

I take one and open it, but I don't read. I blew it. Maybe I will be here when the aegis collapses. What would it feel like? Quick torture, or prolonged suffering? At least no one else here has a soul. There is some comfort in that. Daniel might burn for a few minutes, but then he'll be at peace.

Over an hour passes.

A bell rings. I leap from the bed and run to the bedroom door. Daniel must be back.

Elder Binyamin steps in front of me. I peek around him, but the man talking to Nasira isn't Daniel. He's older, at least in his early thirties, short with thinning hair, a big nose, and weak chin. He hands Nasira several bags, but he can't be a courier. He wears a grey suit with a blue silk handkerchief folded neatly in the breast pocket.

He leaves, and Nasira comes to me. "These are your clothes. Change into the slacks and come to the kitchen for lunch.

"Daniel was going to bring me lunch."

"Elder Daniel," corrects Nasira. "And he won't be coming back. That was his brother. He brought you what you wanted."

Elder Binyamin winks at me. "I think she wanted Elder Daniel."

My face flushes hot, I can't believe he said that, but Daniel and his brother don't look anything alike. "That was his brother?"

"Elder Daniel doesn't look the way he does by accident," says Nasira.

I don't want to think about what she means, but I do. Genetic alterations.

"When is Daniel coming?" I ask.

"Elder Daniel," says Nasira. "And he isn't."

"You're a little too tempting for him," says Elder Binyamin. "Nasira and I decided it best he not come back."

Daniel liked me. I knew it. My heart warms, even though I don't want it to. He's soulless. I can be glad I don't have to see him again.

After lunch I am sent back to Daniel's bedroom. Elder Binyamin and Nasira take turns watching me. They keep the controllers and tablet away. At bedtime I am sure they are going to lock me with them in their bedroom, but instead Nasira kisses Elder Binyamin goodnight.

Elder Binyamin closes the door to Daniel's bedroom, pushes the chair against it and turns off the lights. He reclines and pulls his cap over his eyes.

I wait.

Elder Binyamin's breathing slows. His lips flutter. He doesn't snore. He should sleep sitting all the time.

I slip off the bed, put my hands on the chair and push. It slides across the floor. I reach for the doorknob.

Elder Binyamin grabs my wrist. "What are you doing?"

"I'm still hungry," I say.

He grumps, but brings me the plate of leftover pastries. He sits and plays with his controller. I nibble like a mouse on a cold, stiff raspberry tart. Elder Binyamin's head nods. I drop the tart, step beside him, and grip his controller with my fingers. I pull.

He grabs my wrist again. "When are you going to give me a break?" He slips his controller down his front chest pocket and settles back in the chair "Take my advice. You've got a big day ahead of you tomorrow. Get some rest."

I crawl back in bed, but I'm not planning on giving him a break, or getting some rest. I don't care if it takes all night, I have to get out of this horrible place, make it back to Gilchrist, and home, where everything, like abominations having to die, makes sense.

CHAPTER SIX

Escape

A faint ping wakes me. Elder Binyamin is slumped in the chair.
There is another ping. It comes from the window. I pull aside the curtain
to see a pebble fly to the glass. I wipe away the tiny drops of condensation.
Daniel stands in the dim light from the platform. He lifts a paper sack and
grins.

I wave to him. I smile so big my face hurts. How embarrassing. I tone
it down.

Daniel climbs the side of the coach. There is a clatter in the bath. I
spring from bed.

Elder Binyamin startles. "Where are you going?" His voice is groggy.

I grab my gut. "Bathroom. Too many donuts."

I slam the door and flush the toilet.

Daniel is sprawled in the tub. "I'm getting too big for this."

Above the tile surrounding the tub is a long, narrow window.

"I can't believe you fit through that," I whisper.

"Barely." He points to his room. "Is Nasira asleep?"

"I don't know. She sent Elder Binyamin to watch me."

"Oh." He keeps his voice at a whisper. "I doubt he'll check on you in
the bath."

I'm not so sure, but I take the sack and help Daniel to his feet.

His gaze moves to his under things on the floor. His face turns red
and he kicks them under the sink. "We don't have much time." He lays a
folded towel on the edge of the tub. "Sit."

The towel is thick and fluffy beneath me. Daniel kneels at my side,
pulls his controller from his pocket, and lifts the hem of my pants. He
runs his controller over the tether. The metal unwraps like a wound
bandage, and falls to the floor.

I gasp. I'm free.

"They're so dangerous," he whispers. "Nasira might be willing to take her chances, but I'm not."

I rub where the metal hugged my ankle. The skin where the tether touched is half a dozen shades darker than the rest of my leg.

He hands me the sack. "I can't stay but I found you canned spaghettis." He stands. "It was a pleasure meeting you, Amy."

"You're going?" I drop the sack. The can rolls in the tub.

"I have to."

"Now?"

"I shouldn't be here at all."

"Then let me come with you." I can't believe I just said that, but I did.

Daniel hesitates. "You really need to stay. I know Nasira is stressing, but she and Elder Binyamin are good people. They'll keep you safe."

"I don't want to be safe. I want to be with you." But I can't really mean that. Safe is outside the aegis.

He pulls himself up, turns his face to mine and smiles. "Good bye, Amy." He slides through the window and it flaps shut on its hinges behind him.

I scramble up the side of the tub and push my head out. I call. My voice echoes over the concrete walls. A lamp glows on the platform. The tracks are empty.

There's a knock on the door. I drop to the tub.

"What are you doing?" Elder Binyamin asks. "Come out or I'm getting Nasira."

I flush the toilet again. "One minute."

I don't have time to worry about Daniel. I climb back to the window and pull myself through. I hang half a dozen feet above the ground. I close my eyes and let go. I land on my feet, but topple to my backside. Something gleams in the dirt. I crawl toward the lit screen. Daniel's controller. He must have dropped it.

Or left it for me.

I grip it in my hand and run.

CHAPTER SEVEN

Vlas

The shadow of a train hides me as I crouch on the distant side of the station. I glance back at Daniel's coach. Light streams from the windows. Dark figures move inside.

My fingers fumble as I rush through the apps on Daniel's controller. Tracking devices are standard. I want the controller, but not to be followed. I uninstall the tracking app and block the positioning system.

A siren blares. A broad beam of light moves between the trains. Men in uniform, rifles strapped to their backs, approach Daniel's coach. My stomach tightens.

Steam hisses. A whistle blows. An engine's gears turn, and a train a few hundred yards away rolls forward. I run across the tracks, grab the ladder of a car, and pull myself up. The wheels gather speed. We approach the switch. The train shifts north. Great. Even further from Gilchrist. I'll have to jump as soon as I'm safe.

Darkness covers me as we enter the tunnel. The tracks ascend, and the train rumbles above ground. I close my eyes, count to three, and leap. I hit the ground and tumble. I slam into something hard. Everything is pain and gasping for air.

The first breath comes. My heart slows and my head clears. I've got to get out of here, now, before the police or soldiers or whoever they were realize I've left the station and they move their search to the tracks. I sit against the concrete barrier and reach to where pain radiates from my backside. Blood drips from my leg. I rip a sleeve from my shirt, fold it, and apply pressure to the wound. Nausea sweeps over me. I'm forced to the ground again. The moon is in the middle of the aegis. If it works like their sun, it's midnight. The moon blurs, clears, then blurs again, but this time it's not the projection, it's my eyes.

Panic builds in my chest. How am I supposed to out-maneuver a unit of armed men and find my way back to Petrich when I can't even see straight?

I pull out Daniel's controller. The screen lights when I touch it with my finger. I stare at the icons, then put the controller away.

I can do this. By myself. I have to.

I crawl to my feet and climb over the divider. More blood runs down my leg. I take the sleeve, and tie it tight above the cut in my leg. The blood stops, for now. I walk from the tracks. My leg grows numb. I stumble. I grit my teeth, and keep on.

The controller sings. *Elder Daniel Brennan* flashes on screen.

My fortitude crumbles. I reach to accept the call.

I stop.

No.

I can't let my imagination make Daniel what I want him to be just because he's gorgeous and looked at me all starry-eyed. I don't really know him. He's as likely to send the men with rifles after me as help me, and there is the matter of the reward. He could have set me loose to capture me himself. My heart tells me no, but Mama says a child's heart is filled with foolishness. Now isn't the time to trust it. I mute the sound on the controller. It vibrates instead. I try to turn that off, too, but when I can't figure it out I ignore it and head towards brick smokestacks and steel skyscrapers.

I limp through shadows of burnt-out warehouses. Beyond tiny houses stand with fenced yards. Toys lay on front porches and swings hang from trees. An occasional house has its lights on. The controller vibrates again and again. I almost stop noticing.

The moon continues in its path across the sky. The houses on small lots give way to side-by-side brownstones. Notes from a harmonica drift through the air. A mellow voice joins in. A group of men sit on the wide, flat steps of a row house.

Footsteps shuffle behind me. I try to move faster, but I sway. I dive behind an ivy hedge, and collapse. Through the leaves I see a man, thin and bent, dressed in a long, dark overcoat. I hold my breath. He stumbles. A bottle wrapped in brown paper sticks from his pocket. He stops at a trash can a few feet from me. He rummages through then moves on.

I roll to my side. The sidewalk is wet. Blood stains my fingertips. I'm bleeding, again. I tighten the strip of cloth on my thigh. Black spots float in front of my eyes.

The controller buzzes again. *Elder Daniel Brennan.* Maybe I should answer. It couldn't hurt to just talk to him.

It could, but I tap the screen anyway.

"Amy?" Daniel is breathless. "Is that you?"

"Yes."

"Thank God. I've been so worried. Where are you? We've got to get you back to Elder Binyamin and Nasira."

He said exactly what I didn't want him to. I should disconnect. I don't.

"I'm not going back."

"You're not safe on your own."

"I'm fine," I say. The pain flares. A cry escapes my lips.

"You don't sound fine."

"I'm hurt, a little."

He sighs. "Tell me where you are. I'm sure I can talk my brother into letting me come for you myself."

"I'm not coming with anyone. I only wanted to tell you I appreciate your concern and I will do my best to get your controller back to you someday." I disconnect.

The controller buzzes again. I answer.

"What if I don't tell anyone I know where you are until we've had a chance to talk about it?"

I hesitate. This is why I shouldn't have talked to him. "You promise?"

"I do."

"Deal," I say.

"Great. Now tell me where you are."

I peek around the hedge. "I don't know. Do you want me to turn the tracking app back on?"

"No. Whatever you do, don't do that. Can you see a landmark? The Capital Building? The Congressional Library?"

"There's a bunch of brownstones around me."

"That could be anywhere. Can you find a street sign?"

I pull myself to the sidewalk, stand tall and take a brisk step. My leg crumples. I catch a lamppost and manage to not fall. I slow, and limp down the street.

"I'm at the corner of Eighth and Thirty-fourth."

"That's perfect. You're almost to the park. Can you see the white building that looks like someone twisted it?"

"Yes."

"That's my apartment building. The parking garage entrance is on the west. My limo is parked in space one-eleven. I'll meet you there."

"Okay."

"Amy?"

"Yes."

"Don't disconnect. I need to know you're all right."

Daniel talks to me as I walk along the cobblestone path, past fountains and trees. My leg doesn't feel as bad, but blood drips down my thigh and calf. I tell him what I'm seeing and he tells me what it is, the Museum of Natural History, the Presidential Memorial, the National Archives.

I reach the garage. Daniel didn't have to tell me what space his car was parked in. Few spots are filled, and it's the only limousine.

"I can't make it down right away," he says. "Ezekiel's still here." The locks slide and I open the back door. I swear, it's bigger inside than my bedroom.

"Don't get in yet," he says. "The seats on the back right open to a bed. Stand clear." With that the seats grind and fold out.

"All right," he says. "What else do you need?"

I crawl on the bed. For the first time in hours, my body relaxes. "I'm bleeding, my clothes are torn, and I'm cold."

The engine turns. I sit.

"It'll take a minute for the car to warm up. I'll come when I can." Daniel says something else and disconnects, but I feel only the pounding from under the hood. The car is running. I leave the bed, slide into the driver's seat and investigate the instrument panel. The tank is full. Petrich can't be further away by road then it is by rail. If I don't run out of gas I could make it all the way to the abandoned welcome center.

My heart races. I don't want to steal a car, especially not from Daniel, just to save myself, but I don't have a choice. And it's only borrowing. I'll leave it locked in the parking lot with his controller inside.

I put my foot on the brake and move it into reverse. I back up and take a loop around the garage. No problem. I pull to the arm at the exit. It lifts. I rev the engine and turn onto the street.

I've never seen pavement so black or smooth. The traffic lines are painted a fresh, bright yellow. There are no other vehicles. I hope I'm not breaking some sort of curfew. I come to a full and complete stop at every stop sign, keep my speed exactly at the limit, and yield even though there's no one to yield to. Lights sparkle over the city. I cruise past half a dozen monuments to freedom, relics from the Lithisle Republic.

The controller signals again. It's Daniel. He's probably in the garage, in a panic. I can't answer.

I do anyway. "Hello?"

"I forgot to tell you there's a mini-fridge under the counter in the front. There's not a lot in it, but take whatever you want."

"Thanks."

"I've got bandages and I found a few clothes that might fit."

"Sounds good."

"I think Ezekiel's about to leave for the station to meet with Elder Binyamin and Nasira. I should be able to come down then."

"Thanks, Daniel."

"I'll see you soon." He disconnects.

I come to an intersection and stop. The Presidential Memorial soars above me. I crane my neck to see the marble and granite arch gracefully across the night aegis.

Boom. Crash. Burn.

The elite won't be able to put that on a semi and haul it to safety.

Daniel. I can't just leave him. Can I?

Me and my foolish heart.

The light turns green. I hit the gas, make a U-turn, and tear back to the parking garage. I pull into space one-eleven and scramble onto the bed.

Daniel opens the door, his face red. "Where were you? I came down and you were gone."

"I took it for a little spin." I try to make my voice bubble the way Suzanne's does when she talks to boys, but my tone deflates with every word. "They say the heater warms up faster when you're moving."

He doesn't smile. He knows I'm lying.

My eyes fill.

Daniel drops a cardboard box. A roll of gauze bounces out. He sits on the bed beside me. "It's okay. We'll get you fixed up."

I nod, and roll to my side.

Daniel gasps. "I think you need stitches."

"I can't go to a doctor." I try to look where the back of my thigh throbs but I only see blood. "Did you bring tape?"

He rifles through the box. "Bandage tape."

"Perfect." I tell him how to push the center of the wound together, the way Gilchrist taught me, and tape it in place.

"What if there's a vein or artery cut?" he asks.

"I don't think I would have made it this far."

"Good point."

I clench my jaw as he closes the laceration and wraps it in gauze.

"The bleeding's stopped, but I still think you should go to a doctor. The wound could get infected."

"I'll be fine," I say. I rest my hand on his. "Thanks."

He runs his fingers along the tattered bandage Gilchrist wrapped. The gauze is worn and grey with dirt. "What happened here?"

"I burned myself."

"It looks like it could stand a change too." I agree and he cuts away the bandage, washes my hand with bottled water from the min-fridge, over the ice bucket, and redresses it. When he's done he doesn't let go.

I fidget. "I should get dressed."

He keeps his fingers around mine and pulls the box closer with his foot. "Ezekiel's lost and found."

There are pink socks, several shirts, and a couple pair of pants, all women's. I pick up a shirt. "Ezekiel's lost and found?"

"From his lady friends."

Ezekiel was short, bald, and homely. He has lady friends, plural? I grimace and drop the shirt back in the box.

"Everything's been washed." He holds up a pair of jeans.

I take them and sniff. They do smell fresh, like Mama's flower garden after a rain. Daniel turns his back. I bite my lip and try not to cry as I wiggle into the tight jeans.

"What about you?" I ask.

"What about me?"

"Do you have lady friends?"

"No." He sounds offended, but I smile to hear it.

I button the jeans, replace my dirty shirt with a fitted white tee and sit next to him. "What does that make me?"

He turns. "Different."

"Is that good or bad?"

"Very good."

I move closer. Daniel's dark green hoodie looks warm. I'm still cold, even with the heater on. I pull at the sleeve. "I want it."

Daniel's face turns red. He scoots away.

What did he think I was asking for? I giggle. "Your hoodie, Daniel."

He sighs. "Oh." He pulls it off, he still has a tee on underneath, and hands it to me.

I slip it on. I breathe in his spicy scent.

The corner of his mouth curls up. "I like it on you."

I put the torn and bloody clothes in the box. "You can start your own Daniel's lost and found."

"I don't think so."

We laugh. The warmth in his voice gives me courage.

"There's been a misunderstanding."

"Did I do something wrong?"

I shake my head. "I need to get back to Petrich, before dawn." I tell him how Gilchrist was hurt, how I went to look for water and food, but was abducted by Fin-head.

He listens without a word. I wait for an answer.

"You're coming back, aren't you?" he asks.

"It depends on what shape he's in. I can't just leave him."

"What about Elder Binyamin and Nasira?"

"I have to get to my father. I can't think beyond that."

Daniel reaches for the controller. "I need to talk to Ezekiel."

I hold his arm. "We could take the car." Did I just say we?

"I can't call in my chauffer this time of the night. Besides, I've got school in the morning."

"I can drive." I pass him and sit behind the steering wheel.

"I mean neither of us is old enough to have a license."

I hadn't thought of that. I look at Daniel in the rear view mirror. I don't want him to get in trouble. He needs to be able to blame everything on me.

I fling the car into reverse. Daniel flies across the back, hits the wall and lands on the bed. I speed to the exit, driving backwards, and crash through the arm, onto the road.

"Amy! Stop."

I do, long enough to put the car in drive. We lunge forward. I don't obey any signs and I run the red light.

"They have recording eyes at intersections." Daniel grips the bed. "You're going to get me a ticket."

"Maybe I can hack into the system and delete the records."

"Don't even talk like that. Just stop."

I ignore him. I speed past monuments and memorials. I swerve onto the highway. The car bounces over the on-ramp.

"What am I going to tell Ezekiel?"

"I kidnapped you, and you didn't have a choice."

Daniel buckles himself in. "At least put on your seat belt."

I reach across, click it in place, then press cruise control. We settle in at seventy-four miles per hour.

I glance back at Daniel. He frowns. "Keep your eyes on the road."

I look to the highway. "I really appreciate this," I say. "I didn't want to go by myself."

In the rear-view mirror I see him smile.

CHAPTER EIGHT
The Borderlands

I talk while I drive. Daniel tells me to be quiet and pay attention
to traffic, even though there is none.

"Then you talk," I say. "It'll help keep me awake."

"You're not sleepy, are you?" Daniel leans forward, his eyes wide.

"Just talk."

He hesitates. "What about?"

"You." The word comes a little too quickly, but I'm dying of curiosity.

"Me?" Daniel's voice cracks. "There isn't much to say."

"You don't have to tell me anything personal." Although I did already
ask him if he had lady friends. "What's an elder, and why are you one?"

"You're kidding."

"I wouldn't ask if I knew."

"You really were raised in secret, weren't you?"

I shoot him an irritated glance. "We're talking about you, remember?"

Daniel explains. New Lithisle was divided into ten regions after the
pandemic. Secular authorities were appointed for each region, but
Believers came together and organized too.

"Believers in what?" I readjust the rearview mirror to get a better view
of him.

"God," he says. "What else?"

I don't know, but the Committee made a big point about the people
of New Lithisle not believing in anything. I look west. Far beyond the
expressway, the aegis glows.

I shudder.

I sure don't think I would care so much about religion if I didn't have
an afterlife to worry about.

Daniel goes on. "I was eight when the elder for our region passed.
They cast lots and it fell on me."

"Cast lots? Like a lottery?" What an odd way to pick a spiritual leader.

"No, God chose me." He speaks with confidence.

I'm not so sure. "God chose you?"

Daniel turns to the window. His face reflects in the darkened glass. "Not that anything involving money and power is ever that simple."

I squirm. "Oh."

His tone lightens. "You know, I've never said that to anyone before."

"That God chose you?" I try to not sound so skeptical.

He shakes his head. "That maybe he didn't. But it's the truth. My father wanted this more than he should have, and I don't think he was beyond bribes and back room deals." He looks back at me. "Are you shocked?"

"Not really." They are pig people.

"I just thought you'd understand," says Daniel. "About having a parent's life overshadow your own."

My throat tightens. Allarice. Maybe I'm not so different from him. "I do."

Daniel falls silent.

I drum my thumbs on the steering wheel. "Hey. What other places are there to eat in Vlas?" Talking about food has got to be better than the awful quiet.

Daniel answers, his mood lighter.

The more Daniel talks the less he pays attention to my driving. I drive faster. We stop for gas once. Daniel says there are recording eyes at filling stations, too. He calls me instructions on how to use the pump from the back seat.

I get a little confused in Petrich. Daniel uses his controller to find our way up the ridge. I park at the welcome center five hours from the time we left Vlas.

Daniel is asleep on the bed. He doesn't snore. Good.

"Daniel."

He sits, his hair tussled.

I smile. He's so beautiful, especially tussled.

"We're here," I say.

Daniel reaches to the mini-fridge. I crawl over the seat and he hands me a bottle of orange-pineapple juice. I've seen pineapples growing in the conservatory at Suzanne's house, but it takes years for the plants to produce the golden brown fruit, and they'd never waste any on me. I take a cautious swig. The juice is sweet and fruity, but I wouldn't say it's better than apple cider.

"Where are we?" he asks.

"This is where Fin-head grabbed me." I pull up a map.

Orange-pineapple sprays from Daniel's lips. "We're in the Borderlands!"

"The what?" I wipe yellow drops off his chin.

He smiles a dazed smile before he looks at the map again. "The Borderlands, between New Lithisle and the Wilds. It's against the law to trespass."

"Tell that to Fin-head and his little school of Barracuda."

"No wonder you got abducted. There's no law out here. You can be glad it was by someone who only brought you to Elder Binyamin and Nasira."

"Then maybe we should bring along a weapon." I take a pillow from the bed, pull off the case and fill it with drinks from the mini-fridge. I tie it off and open the door. "Do you have a hand gun or anything?"

"A gun? I'm not undercover Guard." He closes the door. "We're heading back to Petrich, now."

I open it again and step out. "How about a knife?"

"Get back in." His voice is firm.

I toss the pillowcase over my shoulder. "Can you get the bandages for me?"

"No."

"I can't carry everything."

"We aren't going."

"I am." I walk toward the path that leads to the interior aegis wall. "Are you coming with me or not?"

The door slams. I wait for the engine to start. It doesn't. Instead I hear footsteps running on the pavement. Thank goodness.

I wait for him. "You're sweet."

"I'm insane."

Every time I try to speak Daniel shushes me. "We have to listen for drifters and gangs," he says.

The closer we get to the aegis the faster I walk. When the trees gnarl and twist, I run.

Daniel holds me back. "Where exactly did you leave your father?"

"We're almost there."

"We shouldn't go any further." He points to a sign, bright yellow with the words, Caution, High Voltage written in bold black letters. Below it a second sign reads, No Trespassing. Funny, I hadn't noticed them on the way out.

I dash ahead. The trees clear. I drop the pillowcase. "This is it."

The aegis rumbles. Strong hands push me to the ground. A body shields me.

Daniel. On top of me. Heat flushes my cheeks, and I push him off. "It's okay," I stammer. "The aegis makes noise like that all the time. There's nothing to worry about."

"We need to go back." He trembles. "We're not safe."

I stand, and brush the dirt from my jeans. "I waited here two and a half days before I left." I don't mention I was passed out most of the time. "We'll be fine."

I walk into the clearing. Daniel stays behind. At first I'm not sure I'm in the right spot. There's only dirt. Then I see the note I left in the dust, half trampled. Someone swiped my SOS. I look through the aegis. Gilchrist's tent stands at the edge of the trees. My heart races. I call to him.

There's nothing.

"Gilchrist! Answer me."

He doesn't.

I have to get through the wall and find out what happened to him. I turn to get Daniel, but he's already followed me.

"Your father went out there?"

"Yes."

He puts his hand on my shoulder. "I'm sorry, Amy, but I don't think he's coming back."

"He could still be in the tent," I say. "Do you know how to get through? Do you know anyone who might?"

"Come with me back to Vlas," says Daniel. "We have a guest bed at the apartment. I'm sure once we explain the situation to Ezekiel, he'll let you rest a few days before you make any decisions."

"I'm not leaving until I find my father."

"You can't go out there."

"Ander Smith." I pull out the controller. "He'll know." I browse to his aegis research page, and follow the links I didn't have time to explore earlier.

"I'm not letting you go out there," says Daniel. "Even if you figure out how."

A picture of a little black box like the one Gilchrist left in his backpack flashes on screen.

"That's it," I say. "A magamp." I read the brief description. No wonder I barely made it through the first time. The device, designed to create a portal through the wall, should have been tight to my body instead of loose in the pack. I'd also pushed against Gilchrist while he'd pushed against me, and I'd gone through too slow.

I hand the controller with the picture of the magamp to Daniel. "We need to find this." I crawl through the dirt. "I left it in a bright spot."

Daniel scrolls down the page. "Was your father into this? Conspiracy theories?"

"Just find it."

Daniel squats next to me. "Let's go back to the car. I'm sure we can catch an auto train to Vlas sometime today."

"I told you, I'm not-."

"He's dead, Amy." His voice is soft and sympathetic. "No one has survived outside the aegis for more than a few hours since the pandemic."

I sit on my heels. "You honestly believe that?"

"Why wouldn't I?"

The more important question is why someone would tell everyone in New Lithisle they can't go on the outside or they'll die, although that belief has kept me safe all these years, and, I suppose, everyone else in Old Lithisle.

I spot a shining fleck of black in the corner of my eye. I turn and see the familiar honeycomb of solar cells. I stand and run.

Daniel dives ahead of me and grabs the magamp.

"Give it to me." I put out my hand.

Daniel holds it above his head. A tiny light shines green. The sun must have been able to charge the magamp through the aegis after all.

I jump up and down. "No fair. You're taller than me."

"Don't even think about it," he says. "I'm also stronger, and faster."

But he's not smarter. I tickle his gut and he doubles down. I almost grab the box before he slides it down his front pant pocket.

"Don't fight dirty." Daniel frowns. "I'm only trying to help. Ander Smith is a nut case. I'm not letting you risk your life on a bunch of hooey."

"Ander Smith is the only person in New Lithisle who makes any sense."
I hold out my hand.

"Things aren't always as they seem," says Daniel. "Especially when the situation is so emotional."

"Please," I say.

"It's not that I don't believe you."

But obviously he doesn't. I drop my arm to my side and walk back to the aegis. I wait for the orange and red swirls to pass and look at the tent. If Daniel would just cooperate I could find Gilchrist and go home.

But Daniel would be stuck here.

For a second I can't think. In my mind I see fire. And Daniel.

"I really am sorry, Amy." Daniel is behind me. "To have your father with you one day and gone the next, I can only imagine how horrible this is for you."

Horrible doesn't begin to describe it, but I have to forget what may have happened to Gilchrist, and what will happen to Daniel. I need the magamp. There has to be a way to talk him into giving it to me. I imagine what Suzanne would do, boys are always eager to please her, and take a deep breath.

"Thank you, Daniel." I slip my arms around his waist. "I'm glad I'm not alone."

He smiles.

I press my body to his.

He trembles, and lifts his hand to my cheek.

I drag him with me into the flames.

CHAPTER NINE
In the Wilds

Momentum is on my side. Daniel loses his balance and crashes with me through the wall. Pain rips through me, but not as bad as the first time.

Daniel doesn't move. I pat his cheek. His eyes flash open. He gasps. "W-w-why?"

I shouldn't, but he's so pretty, and somewhat disoriented, so I lift my hand to his brow, and stroke his hair. "You'll be all right, I promise. I'll check for my father and we'll get you right back through."

He pushes my arm away. "S-s-stupid. S-s-selfish." His focus shifts from my eyes to the sky. Grey storm clouds billow.

I wipe my eyes. He's the one who wouldn't give me the magamp. I move away. "I'm going to look for my father."

I walk across the field. The aegis hisses. A gust of wind rustles the leaves. The antenna is toppled. Gilchrist's rolled sleeping bag sits where he rested his foot on it.

"Gilchrist," I whisper.

There's no answer.

I hold my breath and lift the tent flap.

Light shines through the empty space.

He's not here.

But my backpack is, unzipped. The night Gilchrist pushed me through I'd left it leaned against a tree.

I run to Daniel. "He was here after the accident. He moved my backpack. He's got to be alive."

"G-g-good." His voice is stronger. "He's probably back in the aegis, safe and sound, like we should be."

Daniel won't look me in the eyes. His words are curt. He has every right to be angry with me.

"I think he must have tried to climb the ridge," I say. "I'm going to follow him."

"That's not what he'd want. He'd want you s-s-safe."

I don't answer. I leave Daniel on the ground, go to the tent and put on my backpack. I nibble on a lemon bar and bring one to Daniel. He's managed to sit up.

I toss the lemon bar to him. "You have the magamp in your pocket. Just make sure the light is green before you go through, and run. You'll be fine."

"I'm not going to do that. If you don't f-f-find your f-f-father you'll never be able to get back in. You'll die."

"You're sweet, Daniel, and I appreciate everything you've done for me, honest, but you really don't understand everything, okay? You're just going to have to believe me. I'll be fine."

I don't give him the chance to answer. I run. I glance over my shoulder. He stands, but falls to one knee.

My stomach sickens. He's so worried something bad will happen to me, but I'm the one sending him back into the aegis to die.

I run until my chest aches. I slow. Drops of rain fall and explode in the dirt. They evaporate on my face and hands. I reach the rocks at the top of the ridge. The aegis steams in the storm. Waves of heat and mist swirl in my face.

I cross the rocks and continue west. The rain comes in sheets. Daniel's hoodie soaks to my skin. I can't smell him anymore.

I stop. I shouldn't have left him, not without making sure he got back into New Lithisle safely. What an oxymoron, but still, I imagine him writhing in the grip of the wall. I run back to the top of the ridge.

A tall, slim figure is silhouetted against the aegis.

"Daniel!" The wind and water carry my words away.

I'm at his side before he turns.

"Are you all right?" I ask.

"I'm c-c-coming with you."

"No, please. I'll bring you back."

"If we find your father I'll know you'll be all right." Even when he doesn't stutter his words are choppy and hesitant.

I should shoo him off, the way I'd sent Golden Star back to Mama the day Gilchrist and I had left Old Lithisle. *Bad dog,* I'd told him. *Go home. Bad dog.* He'd dropped his head, pulled his tail between his legs and turned back. But he wasn't being a bad dog. Golden Star is the best dog in the world.

Rain mingles with tears on my face. Bringing Daniel with me now won't change anything. Tomorrow, I'll have to bring him back, and leave him to die. But not today. Today, he'll be safe. "Thanks," I say.

The clouds break and the rain softens. We walk in silence to the valley. After an hour we leave the path and cross onto the road.

The satellites.

"Can I see your controller?" I ask.

Daniel hands it to me.

I try to log onto the New Lithisle network, but it says, *Connection Error*. I tap apps to see if one can connect me to any satellites, but I can't find anything. I'm not going to be able to communicate with Gilchrist, the Committee, or anyone, without my controller.

The rain clears. The little white farmhouse comes into view. Apple blossoms blow across the path. We reach the rusted mailbox. I run. I stumble across broken sod to the porch.

Daniel eyes the jumbled lawn.

"The boars have been rooting," I say.

"Boar? There are animals out here?"

"Of course." I take the front knob, smooth and worn, in my hand. The door glides over a golden pine floor. It wasn't locked. That's a good sign.

"Gilchrist?" I call.

There's no answer.

I step into the entry. Dust lays thick and cobwebs droop from the ceiling. A faded gingham sofa, plump and hardly worn, stands in a parlor next to an upright piano. Sheet music, half-way through a song, rests against the piano rack while a silent metronome waits beside a darkened lamp.

Daniel runs his fingers along the keys.

"Do you know how to play?" I ask.

He returns to the keys, this time with purpose. By the time he finishes my heart aches with the beauty of the sound. "You're good," I say, my words an inadequate complement.

He shrugs.

On the other side of the entry is the kitchen. A red and white dish-towel lies over a stack of bowls eternally drying in a wooden rack by the sink. A spider has woven her web in a light brown canvas jacket that hangs by the back door. Narrow wooden stairs lead to a second story. We follow them to a hall. A bedroom has a white canopy bed with ruffled pink curtains that flow to the floor. A little brown bear wearing an oversized blue bow sits guard over the lacey spread. A toy chest sits in the corner, overflowing with plush animals.

The bath is undisturbed. I swallow hard. This is where Gilchrist would have searched for medicine, and dressed his wounds. He wouldn't have left towels hanging neatly.

I run to the last room. Shirts, ties, and dresses hang behind an open closet door. A pair of boots, caked with hardened mud, lay in the middle of the floor. The bed is unmade.

"He's not here."

"Was he?" Daniel asks.

"No."

"What are you going to do?"

"Spend the night, for starters. We need to eat and dry off."

"And tomorrow?"

Go home, without him, but he doesn't have to know that yet. "Let's worry about it later," I say.

I go to the closet and shuffle through the shirts. I pull out an extra-large grey hoodie, *Green Hills Plumbing & Heating* embroidered on the back. I hold it to Daniel. "It's warm and dry."

He waves his hand in protest. "It's not mine."

"I don't think the owner will mind."

"How do you know?"

"He's dead."

"Or in New Lithisle."

"You're thinking too much."

I browse the woman's clothes. They definitely do not fit a sixteen-year-old. I take a pink, thick cotton robe and change in the bathroom.

When I come out Daniel has on PJ bottoms and the hoodie. *Leroy* is embroidered in red on the front. I giggle. "Hey, Leroy."

Daniel grimaces.

We bring our wet clothes downstairs to the family room, build a fire in the wood stove, and hang the clothes on a line made of paracord we find in a kitchen drawer. There are no canned spaghettis, but we eat our fill of soup and beans after grace. Daniel didn't even have to remind me. I said it for him.

My eyelids are heavy.

"Rest," says Daniel. "I'll keep watch."

He doesn't. He's asleep in front of the stove by the time I'm back from the bath. I lie on the sofa. The cushions are as soft as Mama's down pillow. I curl beneath a throw and fall asleep.

A loud crash wakes me. Metal clinks. The light from the window is soft and scattered. The spot by the stove where Daniel slept is empty.

I tie the robe tight and take quiet steps to the kitchen. There's a glint of the evening sun on a long, wide blade. A butcher knife trembles in Daniel's hand.

"What are you doing?"

He jumps, and the knife falls. He leaps aside as the blade clatters to the floor. "There's something out there."

"Where?"

He points to the yard. I pull the curtain aside. Dark shadows move across the grass.

I squeal. "A sow with piglets!" I hold out my hand. "Where's the controller?"

"You can't go out there. That thing is big and vicious, and loaded with germs."

I see the corner of the controller sticking from his pant pocket. I grab it. "She's not going to come on the porch."

"But germs can be airborne."

I take his hand and pull him to the door. His fingers wrap around mine. For a moment I forget the sow and her offspring. The mother snorts. I smile, and open the door just wide enough for Daniel and me to look out. "I do this all the time. It'll be fun."

I lift the controller, focus on the piglets, and tap record. The brown and beige striped babies run more than they eat, their little grunts notes of a happy song.

The light in the sky fades. The sow and her young wander to a distant patch of dirt. Daniel sits beside me on the porch steps. Together we watch the stars fill the sky.

"Mum used to tell me about the stars," he says. "I thought I understood but I didn't. There are so many."

"So you're not too angry with me?"

"Why would I be angry with you?"

"I dragged you through the aegis."

"I did fear for my life." Daniel kicks a stone at his foot. "But I don't blame you."

"You called me stupid and selfish."

"No." Daniel turns to me, his face earnest. "That was me. I'm stupid and selfish."

I jab him in the shoulder. "You are not."

"I have responsibilities." Daniel rests his hand on mine. My insides melt like butter on a hot skillet. "I'm missing school, and the baby dedication for the Charles triplets."

"You didn't have a choice. I kidnapped you."

"I let you kidnap me." Daniel leans to me, his breath warm on my face. Our noses touch. His lips brush against mine.

I want to pull him close, press my lips to his, and feel what it's like to share a real kiss, like the ones Suzanne's told me about.

Pig gene. Abomination.

I pull away.

Daniel's chin drops. "I'm sorry. I shouldn't have done that."

"I understand." I let go of his hand and slide until there is a good foot between us. "It's late. We're tired." Daniel doesn't answer. The chill of the night air steals his warmth from me. Silence creeps between us like a thick fog.

I stand. "I guess we should get to bed." My face flushes. "I mean sleep. We need to get to sleep. I'll take the family room. You should go to the barn."

"The barn?" He turns his face to the red and grey pole barn.

"It wouldn't be proper for us to spend the night under the same roof, would it? And I'm sure there will be hay or something for you to sleep on."

"All right." Daniel half-waves. "Good night."

"Good night to you, too." I try to sound cheerful. Normal, like we didn't just sort-of, almost kiss. I hurry to the family room without looking back. I lay on the sofa, plump the pillow beneath my head, and watch the fire flicker. I try not to think about Daniel, I have Gilchrist and getting home to worry about, but he consumes my thoughts anyway. If only I could fall asleep. At last my eyes close.

I dream I'm a princess. I run down the hill from Mama's cottage to the creek. Silk slippers beaded with pearls cover my feet, my skirt and bodice are blue taffeta. I wear long white silk gloves that reach above my elbows. The yellow marsh marigolds are in bloom, the sun glitters through the bare spring branches and the water gurgles over sand, pebbles, and rocks. I see my reflection. My hair is pinned and curled like Suzanne's, a diamond tiara on my head.

"Kiss me," Daniel says. I look but don't see him.

A green frog with brown spots hops to me. He puts one webbed foot on my slipper. "Kiss me, Amy," he says in Daniel's voice. "The wicked Allarice changed me from a handsome elder to this, but if you kiss me I'll get my penthouse and limousine back."

I know this story, the Frog Prince, and every word he says is true, so I pucker up. The kiss is cold and slimy, and I wipe my lips when I'm done.

"Much better," says Daniel. I look in the creek, and his tail swooshes in the water. He winks at me, scratches himself with his tusk, snorts, then buries his snout in the mud.

I wake with a start.

Bright light fills the room. Daniel is at the stove. He tosses two logs on the bed of orange coals.

I sit. Pain shoots through the cut on my leg. I yelp.

"I didn't wake you, did I?" Daniel asks. "I wanted to be sure you were warm." After I banished him to the barn. He probably shivered all night.

"Just the cut." I stand. And the contusions. Every muscle in my body is stiff. Each vertebrae in my spine aches.

"Are you all right?" He takes my arm and steadies me before I even realize I'm about to fall.

"A couple of aspirin and I'll be as good as new."

"Maybe you should rest a few days."

"Nonsense. We've got to get you home. Your brother has to be worried sick."

"I doubt it," says Daniel. "What about you?"

I've rehearsed my answer, not the truth, but not a lie either. "Is the offer to stay with you in Vlas still good?" He won't figure out I'm not coming with him until he's back through the wall, and I've left him behind.

"Absolutely." Daniel looks happy and relieved.

I feel a trickle of guilt.

In the kitchen, he's opened cans of peaches and put them in bowls on the table. Spoons rest on folded napkins.

The trickle becomes a cascade.

I've slurped down half of my peaches before I notice Daniel's bowl is still full.

I'm sure we had grace.

He pushes at the peaches with his spoon.

"Is there something wrong?" I ask.

Daniel keeps his focus on the fruit. "I want to apologize for my inappropriate behavior last night. I want you to know-."

"Don't worry about it." I'd rather not have any insight into what did or didn't happen. "It's fine."

"No, it's not." Daniel drops his spoon and it clinks against the ceramic. "I behaved like a common beast."

"You did not."

"It's like I can't control myself when I'm with you. My body reacts and I—"

"Stop right there." I don't want to hear about his body reacting.

Daniel finishes his peaches without another word.

After breakfast I wash and change in the bath. I hang the robe on the back of the door and pull on my jeans. The rough fabric presses against the cut. I'd better not have to scavenge too many houses on the way home before I find something more comfortable to wear. Stretchy leggings sound perfect.

I come down the stairs. Daniel is at the piano. The melody is soft and slow, drops of rain on the lake, but then it builds. Waves crash against the sandstone cliffs.

Tears blur my vision. I run to the drive and wait for the music to stop.

Daniel comes out. "You forgot your backpack." He wears it even though it's too small, and rides up his shoulders.

I'd wanted to leave it, I'll be back by night. But I wipe my tears and smile. "You look good in pink and brown camo."

"Not my first choice."

The walk across the valley is slow. Daniel listens to every ground squirrel chatter. He points to every bird.

A fat brown hen flies across the road.

Daniel jumps.

"Partridge don't bite," I tease. "You act like you've never seen one before."

Daniel shakes his head. "Of course I haven't."

I remember the quiet woods on my walk to the welcome center and the silent grasses that surrounded it. Allarice had all the pigs inside put down as part of quarantine measures, but maybe she had gone further. Are there any animals left in New Lithisle? I'm not sure how to ask Daniel without cluing him in to the fact I'm from out here.

A sick feeling rises in my stomach. Allarice must have ordered the extermination of all animals, killing birds, cats, and dogs as if they were bugs. It sounds like something she would do. Does God view Daniel the same way she must have viewed animals? As a threat that needed to be done away with? Daniel prays. He plays the piano. He's not ... what? An animal? A person? I don't know, but the world will be an emptier place without him.

I don't say anything for a mile.

Daniel comes to an abrupt stop. "Why would they say it's toxic out here when it isn't?"

"I don't know." I'm not sure who benefits, beside everyone in Old Lithisle. "Maybe for some people it is."

Daniel's face pales. "Am I going to get sick?"

"You'll be fine," I say, but I choke on my words. He'll be fine, until the aegis collapses.

I'm the cockroach.

We eat lunch on the rock overlooking the aegis. I wouldn't have thought to bring anything special, but Daniel packed garbanzos and blueberry pie filling. I tell him about hiking to the cliffs, where the pine trees grow, to pick blueberries. He tells me about eating blueberry pie before a wedding, and having purple teeth during the blessing. He'd been nine, and the bride had scolded him after the ceremony.

Daniel finishes a lemon bar. "It's so small," he says.

I look from lunch and follow his gaze to the aegis, as colossal as ever. "I don't think anyone else would describe it that way."

"My world," he says. "My world was so small." He's not just talking about the aegis. He's talking about me.

I've got to get this over with. I stand and walk ahead of him. "We've got to go."

He follows a few paces behind. Half an hour later we reach the base of the aegis.

I stop. "I guess it's time for the magamp."

Daniel pulls it from the pack. The light is still green, although not as bright as it had been. I should have left it in the sun while we walked, but it's a go. I slip it down the front of my shirt and lodge it the one place I know Daniel won't attempt to retrieve it. "You ready?" I ask.

"What do we do?"

"Stay close." I wrap my arms around him, it worked the first time, and hold my body to his.

But it's not like the first time. I'm bringing Daniel into the aegis to die.

He draws me closer and smiles, shy but happy. "I can't think when we're this close."

If only I could stop thinking, about pig genes and souls, but Daniel should never have been born. God willed that his parents, along with everyone else not naturally immune, die during the pandemic. The aegis collapse will only correct Allarice's meddling. My biological mother's meddling.

Daniel cradles my cheek with his hand. He leans toward me.

He's going to try to kiss me, again. I should shove him or turn my cheek or something.

I don't.

Daniel deserves something good, and while this isn't how I imagined my first real kiss, at least he'll have a pleasant memory to carry with him into eternal nothingness. I try not to think of the awful time Emil Spinelli tried to kiss me when I was thirteen and brace myself.

Daniel presses his lips to mine, soft and sweet and full of unspoken promises.

I can't breathe. Warmth spreads from my chest. My skin tingles. I lift onto my tiptoes. Daniel kisses me harder. The rapid beat of his heart echoes my own.

He's going to die.

I push away.

No. I won't let it happen. But what can I do? I can't spare him from the aegis only to have him spend a lifetime alone in the Wilds. Back home they'd slice his throat, drain his blood, then incinerate what was left of him.

Daniel's face flushes. "Amy, I'm so sorry. I shouldn't have done that. Honest, I never have with anyone else. I'm not even supposed to have a girlfriend."

"Daniel." I wrap my arms around him. "It's not that. I just feel so…"

Helpless, like when I was little and it had been my job to herd up not just Cowboy, but all the goats and chickens Mama raised for food. I would hold them in a stall and watch with tears in my eyes as the butcher did his work.

But I'm not a child anymore, and what fills my heart isn't foolishness.

"Never mind," I say. "Change of plans. We need to go to Vlas, get my controller from Elder Binyamin and Nasira, then come back here. I have to talk to my father."

There has to be a way to save Daniel. If there is, Gilchrist will know.

"Okay," says Daniel.

I smile. He holds me tight and we plunge into the fire.

CHAPTER TEN
The Barracuda

Mama hums in the kitchen. I smell broth and onions. There is a quick tap, tap, tap as she strikes the stirring spoon against the edge of the pot. Metal clinks against metal as she puts the lid back on. I breathe deep. Lentil stew for breakfast.

For breakfast? I open my eyes, but I'm not in my cedar bed, and the lump at my feet is a stray pillow, not Posey with her tail wrapped around her. Heavy calico curtains are drawn across a window above the bed. I peek out. A water wheel turns in the late afternoon sun and a thick, black power line drapes down the dirt street to little clapboard houses. A man hauls a cart by, women in long skirts chat in front of a mercantile, and children kick a white ball across a field.

At first I think I must be in Old Lithisle, but something is off. I can't quite figure out what.

I get out of bed. My head spins. I slow. I wear a white tee and my under things, but nothing else. I don't see the rest of my clothes. I pat the magamp, still tucked safe against my chest.

A cotton pad sticks to my backside. I pull. My leg stings. The cut. I walk to the mirror that hangs on the back of the door. The wound is about two inches long, a finger-breadth wide, and drains bloody fluid. The cut shouldn't look like that. Daniel taped it.

Daniel. If they figure out where he's from they'll kill him.

A dresser sits opposite the bed. I pull open drawers until I find a stack of pajama bottoms. I hold up a pink pair printed with fluffy white sheep. They're huge, but they'll have to do. I tie them double at the waist and roll the cuffs.

I stand on the bed, grip the window rail and lift. It opens. I stick one foot out and my skin tingles. I freeze. A flat metal bracelet dangles from my ankle. I'm tethered, again, and this isn't home. I'm in the Borderlands.

At least Daniel is probably safe, somewhere.

I close the window and move to the door. I turn the knob. At the end of a hall is a wood cook stove. The humming chef is nowhere in sight.

"Hello?" I call.

The humming stops. Footsteps patter across the wooden floor. A young woman, tall and thin, with an apron tied above her round, bulging belly, turns the corner. "You're awake."

"There was a boy traveling with me," I say. "Do you know where he is?"

She doesn't answer. She comes to me and puts her hand on my forehead. A flat metal bracelet slides from her wrist to elbow. "You shouldn't be up. You've been unconscious for days."

"You're tethered?" I ask.

"No. You are, to me."

I look at her for scales, gills, fur, any hint as to what group she might belong to, but her complexion is rosy and her skin smooth.

She puts her arm in mine and leads me to the bed. On the way she bends down and picks up the cotton pad I pulled from my wound. "You need to keep the bandage on, or it's going to get worse again." She drags a chair from the corner, sits near the bed, and pulls supplies from the nightstand. "Roll over so I can redress it."

I turn to my side.

She pokes and prods around the cut. "It was healing on the outside but infected underneath, so I had to open it." She flushes the wound with water from a small plastic bottle, packs it with long white strips of fabric, then finishes with a fresh bandage.

"The stew should be done." She leaves and comes back with a bowl.

Steam rises. I fill a spoon with potato, carrot, and lentils. "What about the boy?"

"He's fine," she says. "Back in Vlas."

"He left?"

"He didn't have a choice."

I suppose he didn't. I blow on the spoon. The stew ripples.

The young woman wrinkles her nose and puts her hand to her face. "Daddy said he was the young elder. Is that true?"

"I guess. He's young and he's an elder."

"Oh." Her voice lightens. She walks to the door. "Call me if you need anything. By the way, I'm Ruth."

She pauses, like I'm going to tell her who I am.

I don't think so.

She shrugs and leaves.

I eat.

The stew is warm and smooth sliding down my throat. I'm so hungry my stomach cramps. Finishing the stew takes forever, but when the bowl is empty seconds sound good. I slip from bed and look out the door. The kitchen is quiet. I tiptoe down the hall. The pot of stew simmers on the stove. There is a hand pump at the sink. A table is made of roughhewn planks. The young woman sits in a rocker. Her eyes are closed. I inch closer. Her head is leaned back, her hands cradle her belly. Beside her is a bucket of potatoes, a knife, peelings, and a pink, sparkly controller. I've never seen such a cute controller. Why couldn't Gilchrist have found me one like that?

I sneak across the floor, grab the controller and sprint back to the bedroom. I lock the door, tap the screen, then *Slide to Unlock*. An icon looks like a little tether. I tap it. Nothing. I right click and a menu appears. *Disengage*. The bracelet falls open. I'm free. I kick and the bracelet spins across the floor.

I pull a jacket from the closet, stuff the controller in the pocket, and look across the room for my boots. They aren't by the door or under the bed.

I sneak back to the kitchen. Ruth hasn't moved. Shoes line the wall of the entry. I don't see mine. I try on a pair of soft-soled moccasins. They slip off my heels with each step, but they're better than nothing. I lean over the kitchen sink and look out the window. The street is empty. I tug on the front door. It flies open.

I didn't pull that hard.

I take a step. Fin-head blocks my way.

"John!" He grabs my arm. I stumble behind him as he pulls me to the bedroom. "John!"

He pushes me to the bed and yells for John again.

Ruth runs into the bedroom, her face red. "He's out."

"He's supposed to be here." Fin-head's grip tightens. "Get the tether."

"What?"

"She took it off! Find the tether."

She drops to her hands and knees and crawls over the floor. She pulls it from under the dresser.

A second man steps in the bedroom. He has dark wavy hair, almond eyes, and a strong jaw, handsome, until I see the scales. He's a Barracuda. "What is Ruth doing on the floor, in her condition?"

Fin-head takes the tether and slaps it on my ankle. "You're the one who left her alone with the girl."

"She's been asleep for days," says Ruth. "He wanted to cut firewood. I told him to go."

Fin-head glares at the young man. "Your duty was to stay."

Ruth takes John's hand, pulls him close and gives him a quick kiss on the lips. "I'm fine, honey." She keeps her arms around him, but looks at Fin-head over her shoulder. "You worry too much, Daddy."

My stomach rolls. Fin-head is Ruth's father, and she's going to have a guppy. *Ick.* I shift my gaze from her protruding belly. A swirl of red on Fin-head's oversized grey hoodie catches my eye. *Leroy,* embroidered in silky strands.

I leap to my feet. "That was Daniel's."

They look at me with blank stares.

I point. "The sweatshirt."

"Actually, it's mine." Fin-head turns and shows me the back. "I did heating and plumbing in the valley before the pandemic. Elder Daniel insisted I keep it."

The conversation I heard from the back of the blue pick-up snaps to my mind, Fin-head getting in the front seat, the man on the path holding the box of ramen noodles.

Tell Ruth we'll be back in the morning, he'd said.

Sure thing, Leroy.

Fin-head's real name is Leroy. Daniel and I spent the night on the outside in Fin-head's old house.

"Where did you get it?" asks Fin-head. "Elder Daniel seemed a little forgetful, only said you'd given it to him."

"I love thrift shops," I say. "I thought it would fit him, he's so tall."

Fin-head raises a quizzical eyebrow, but he doesn't ask any more questions.

Thank goodness. "What are you going to do with me this time?"

"Nothing," says Fin-head. "The young elder is paying us to keep you here until he gets back."

"He's coming back?" My heart leaps.

"When he can."

I lift my leg to display the tether. The moccasin clops to the floor. "Daniel wouldn't approve."

Fin-head picks up the shoe and hands it to me. "No, he wouldn't, but we already almost lost you, and you had it on."

"Take it off and I'll know you're telling the truth."

"If he weren't paying for you, you'd be back at the mission." Fin-head pulls the jacket from my shoulders, digs through the pockets, pulls out the controller and tosses it to Ruth.

She catches it, and turns it over. Her jaw drops. "She stole my controller?" Her cheeks flush. "Sorry, Daddy."

"Don't let it happen again." He walks to the door. "It's time for supper. Come eat."

Fin-head, Ruth, and John leave. The smell of stew fills my nostrils. Was Fin-head talking to me? I never did get seconds. I follow them to the kitchen. There are four bowls set on the table. I guess for now I'm a Barracuda.

CHAPTER ELEVEN

Attack

The evening sun creeps across the floor. I stand at the kitchen table and slice green tops from plump strawberries, red juice running down my fingers. I look in the white plastic bucket. Only a dozen or so are left unhulled. I'm almost done.

Ruth sits in the rocker, her swollen feet propped on a stool. "You're good at this. I should hire you to make my preserves every year."

"No thanks. Your pay stinks."

"True." Ruth leans forward, snatches a handful of cleaned berries and pops them in her mouth one at a time. "You're paying me to do all my work."

I smile. "Daniel is." Gift-that-keeps-on-giving, Fin-head calls me. Day twenty-three with the Barracuda, and Daniel wires money to Petrich once a week. If only he'd send word.

"Elder Daniel," Ruth corrects. "Don't be so infor-" She grabs her abdomen and swears.

"Are you all right?" I ask. She's had too many contractions today for my comfort. It would be just like her to go into labor while Fin-head and John were gone.

"Do I look all right?" she screams. "Push!"

I drop the knife. "You need to push?"

She swears again. "No, you push! On my back!"

She rolls to her side and I press the small of her back. Ruth purses her lips and inhales, exhales. At last the muscles beneath my palm loosen. Ruth falls limp.

"Are you sure you don't want me to get Mrs. Merrick?" I ask. "The contractions are coming pretty fast." Fin-head took my tether off before he and John left for Petrich. He wanted to be sure I could fetch the midwife if I needed to. That's when he'd told me it'd never really been on, only in warning mode. I glance at my ankle. The skin where the bracelet was is the same creamy white as the rest of my leg.

"I've been having them for weeks now. They always go away."

"Until they don't." I go to the table and continue cutting. I dump the finished berries in the cast iron pot and set them on the stove. I mash, then add sugar.

"So I guess your mother taught you how to make preserves, too."

Ruth is obsessed with motherhood, I guess for a good reason. I try to humor her. "Yes, she did."

"Do you do it exactly the way she taught or do you improvise?"

"Improvise."

"Does it bother her?"

"She doesn't say."

"Would she? If she didn't like what you were doing would she tell you?"

I put the lid on the pot. It clanks a little too loud. "Ruth, you're going to be a good mother. I really don't think you have to worry about it."

"Easy for you to say. You have a role model."

"So do you."

"Daddy? He's a man."

"What difference does that make?"

"None, if I have a boy." She rubs her belly. "That's why he's got to be a boy. I wouldn't know how to raise a girl."

"You and John are going to be fine, no matter what the baby is."

She sighs. "Even a guppy?"

My cheeks flush hot. How does she know that's my nickname for the baby? I'm sure I've never said it out loud.

"Awful, isn't it? That's what my friends called him when they found out I was pregnant. Some friends, huh?"

About like me. I'm not going to be too hard on them. "I'm sure they'll feel differently once the baby's here."

"Are you kidding? I haven't seen any of them in months."

I have noticed Ruth hasn't had visitors, not even from the Barracuda village.

She takes my hand and holds it tight. "That's what's so great about you, Amy. You treat me, Daddy, and John the same. You're not prejudiced one way or the other."

I pull my hand from her grip. It's true. I treat them all like doomed abominations. Shoot. Being in New Lithisle is complicated.

Ruth moans. "Another one's coming."

I press her back.

She writhes. "Maybe when this one's over you can get Mrs. Merrick."

Ruth relaxes. I run to the street. If only I could remember exactly where the Merricks live. I knock on three doors before the petite woman with tattoos, spiked silver-green hair, and gills answers.

A siren blares. Great. Coyote attack.

"Bring her to the safe house." Mrs. Merrick grabs a worn, black doctor's bag by her door and lifts her long skirt. "I'll meet you there."

"But she's in labor."

"I'll meet you there." She steps out, shuts the door, and runs.

I hurry back to Ruth.

She puffs and pants in the rocker. "This had better be a drill."

"I'm afraid not." I pull. Ruth wobbles to her feet. We exit through the back door, cross the yard and enter the woods. We trample ferns and dodge trunks. Ruth doubles over twice. I press her back until the contractions pass. We move on.

Through low-slung hemlock branches I spy brick, remnants of the old town, a post office, bank, and bakery. Ruth and I climb the steps of the school. The Barracuda have exactly two shotguns. Guards on the roof hold them at the ready.

Mrs. Merrick waits at the front door. She puts her arm around Ruth. "This way."

I let go.

"You're coming with me, aren't you, Amy?"

I hesitate. I'm not eager to see anything born, especially not a guppy. Oops. I didn't mean to think of him as that again. "Of course."

Mrs. Merrick's arm shoots in front of me. "She should stay with the others."

"But I want her to come."

"I won't be in the way," I say. "I could even help."

Mrs. Merrick eyes me warily. "You're of no use to anyone."

I don't understand why these Barracuda are so negative. Do they think I'm a criminal or something? I don't have the tether on anymore.

"Don't listen to her," says Ruth.

I watch Mrs. Merrick lead her away.

"I'm sorry," I call. I wouldn't want to be alone during labor, but there's not much I can do. I stay in the entry until a guard pushes me down the hall. I wander to the library. The Barracuda not able to fight, the young, old, and women, sit and stand among the shelves, many with blankets and pillows. It's going to be a long night.

"Don't you worry," a grey-haired man says to a little boy on his lap. "Coyotes have fangs and claws, but we've got teeth like razors. We'll send them home with their tails between their legs. We always do."

I imagine men with bushy tails. I hope he's only being figurative.

I meander through the empty shelves and look for a book to get my mind off Ruth. Like everything in New Lithisle, the library was scavenged a long time ago. Apparently books made good fuel. There are few left to read and none in obvious places. The last time Ruth and I were here I found a volume pushed under a desk leg to keep it level.

I climb to the top of a shelf in an empty corner. A book, covered in cobwebs, sits atop another shelf on the far side of the room. A dozen Barracuda lounge beneath it. I crawl from shelf to shelf. I reach for the book.

"Who is that?" a woman asks.

"The crazy girl Leroy's been keeping in his house."

"Spy," hisses another. "We've had more Coyote attacks since she got here than we've ever had."

She's right, indirectly. The Coyote aren't coming because of me, but for the money Daniel's been sending, and the supplies the Barracuda have been buying with it.

I take my book back to the far side of the library and hide behind an overturned desk. A shirtless man, his hair long and flowing, shares a passionate embrace with a buxom woman on the cover. This type of book isn't my usual read, but maybe I can learn a thing or two. I don't want Daniel to think I don't know anything about kissing, which I don't, if he comes back and wants to try it again. He is coming back. He wouldn't be paying Fin-head to keep me safe if he weren't.

I'm three-quarters through the book when they signal the all clear. I put it down. I don't feel the need to finish. I learned a lot more than I counted on, but I'm not sure the information is accurate. If I tried some of that stuff on Daniel I'm sure he would burst out laughing.

"Where's Ruth?" I ask the guard at the door.

"They're closing up here, you need to go home."

"But I came with her."

He shoves me out. "Get along."

My heart stops. What if something went wrong? I abandoned her. "Is she all right?" I ask. "Did she have the baby?"

"She's here, and she won't be coming home any time soon." The guard slams the door in my face.

I rap on the door. "Ruth wanted me with her."

"Leave, or I'll do more than talk." He racks the slide on his shotgun.

The sound makes the hair on the back of my neck stand. I run to the edge of the woods and dive behind a tree.

My heart rate slows to normal. I peer across the yard. The schoolhouse is quiet. I lean against the tree. I'll wait here for Ruth, stay until she or Mrs. Merrick comes out. But hours pass, and no one comes or goes.

CHAPTER TWELVE
Arrival

A hand on my shoulder shakes me softly. My eyes fly open. Wispy clouds float through an azure sky. I'm still behind the tree across from the schoolhouse, my hair full of leaves.

"There you are," says Fin-head.

"They wouldn't let me in with Ruth. Is she all right? Did she have the baby?"

"Yes, she and the baby are both doing well, except for worrying about you." He takes my hand and pulls me to my feet. "There's someone at the house very anxious to see you."

Fin-heads steps are fast and long. I can't keep pace, but he pauses for me often. He never lets me get more than a yard or two behind.

In the kitchen I peer in the iron pot. The strawberries are gone. So is the white bucket on the table. I guess the Coyote will be having strawberries on their biscuits this morning.

"What else did they take?" I ask.

"They cleared out the pantry," says Fin-head. "But they didn't find our long-term storage."

It's hard to hate starving people who steal food, but I still feel bad for Fin-head. If he'd been home the Coyote wouldn't have dared come anywhere near his place.

Fin-head sticks his head in Ruth's doorway then waves me in.

She sits propped in bed, playing with a black, faded, and scratched controller that almost looks like...

John shoves a bundle of baby in my arms.

"Oh my," I say. I hate to admit it, but I'm looking for scales. "He's very handsome." He is, in a baby sort of way. And I don't see scales.

"Beautiful," says Ruth. "She's a girl, naturally."

"I knew it, the way you wanted a boy."

The baby opens her eyes and looks at me. They're big and grey, earnest. She searches my face, as if I'm the first person she's ever seen. Maybe I am.

"What's her name?"

"John Junior," Ruth says.

"Come on," I say.

"I wasn't thinking of girl names."

"Are you taking suggestions?" I ask.

"Hit me with your best shot."

I've actually given girl names quite a bit of thought. Someone had to. "Okay, your Dad is Leroy, right?"

"Yes."

"And your mom was Anne."

"Uh-huh."

"LeAnne. And for a middle name, Joy, after John's mother."

"LeAnne Joy," says Ruth. "I actually like it."

I smile with smug satisfaction. "I thought you might." I cuddle the baby closer. She opens her mouth and turns her face to my chest.

I hurry to Ruth. "I think she's wanting something I can't give her."

"We'll trade." Ruth takes the baby and tosses me the controller. "I'm done with it for now, anyway." She grins mischievously.

I catch. I gasp. "This is my controller. Where did you get it?"

"We meet up with Elder Daniel in Petrich," says John. "He brought it with him."

"You saw him?"

"Didn't you?" says Ruth. "He's in the yard, washing."

I spin and run out the door.

Ruth calls to me. "Amy, wait. There's something I want to ask you!"

I don't stop.

CHAPTER THIRTEEN
Stranger

I reach the yard. Daniel's shirt is off. He's bent under the pump, water splashing over his neck and back. He stands and shakes his hair, the way Golden Star does when he gets out of the lake. Water sprays around him and catches the light, like a halo. His gaze meets mine. He smiles.

I dive behind the wood stack. I'd forgotten how good-looking he was, much better looking than I am. There's no good reason for him to like me, and one very bad one, Allarice. I crawl around the backside of the pile. I can make it to my bedroom window before he sees me again.

"Amy?" Daniel says.

He followed me. I stand and turn. "Hi." I push a strand of greasy hair behind my ear. Pine needles fall out.

"It's me, Daniel." His voice is full of concern. "Don't you remember me?"

"Of course. I couldn't forget you." I try to laugh, but it comes out strained. "I'm sorry, I didn't mean to interrupt your bath." Of course I did. Ruth said he was in the yard washing.

He still doesn't have his shirt on. My focus falls from his face to his chiseled chest, down his washboard abs to where his jeans hang low on his hips. My heart races. Back home, Suzanne and I caught the boys swimming once, jumping off the cliffs into the lake with only their shorts on, but I've never been this close to one so undressed. What would Mama say?

"I was so worried about you," he says. "I couldn't wake you up."

"Yeah, about that. I'm not quite sure what happened there."

"You look really good now, though. You've put on weight." He lifts his gaze from my torso. "Healthy, I mean."

He was checking me out.

I can't help but feel a little pleased, but I cross my arms over my chest anyway.

"It's so strange to be together again after so long," he says. "Isn't it?"

More than strange. I kissed him. I kissed this handsome boy. *What was I thinking?*

He holds his hand to me. "Get out of the woodpile, Amy."

I giggle. I'm standing in a woodpile. I come to him. I take his hand. A flood of warmth rushes through me.

Is this how he feels about me? If he does, he's gotten the bad end of the deal.

He reaches his hand to my hair and pulls out a twig. "I hear you spent the night in the forest, like a wood nymph."

His words are so much nicer than saying, *You stink and your hair is full of sticks.* Which is true. I must smell awful. I slept in the dirt after picking strawberries all day.

"I'm sorry I was so slow," he says. "It took forever to track down your controller, then I had to get it out of storage without Ezekiel discovering me. By that time I only had a few days left in school. I figured I might as well finish my exams."

"You did great," I say. "Thank you so much."

He smiles, leans down, and kisses me. Just like that. I swear if he weren't holding me I'd be a puddle on the ground.

He pulls away. "I'm so sorry. I shouldn't have done that."

"You keep apologizing," I say. "But you keep doing it."

"I'm not sorry about the kissing. I took council with Elder John, and he only told me I shouldn't."

"So you shouldn't kiss me?"

"No, but he didn't say I couldn't. There's a huge difference. Shouldn't means doing it could cause me unnecessary difficulties, but it's not a sin."

"Okay." That makes sense. I guess.

Not really.

"We just have to be discreet. Some Believers might find it confusing to see an elder in what they may perceive as a compromising position."

He's talking in circles. Whatever. "A half-dressed elder," I say.

Daniel looks down at his chest. "My shirt." He glances around the yard. It hangs on a branch near the pump. He sighs. "They asked me to bless the baby. We can leave after that."

"We should be able to make it to the wall by evening," I say.

He pecks me on the cheek. "I'll see you soon." He looks left, then right, then strolls casually back to the pump.

I crawl over the woodpile to my window. I don't know why. I could have gone through the door and down the hall. I climb inside and flop on the bed. I touch my lips. He kissed me, and this time he didn't apologize for it, exactly.

But I can't lay here all day thinking about it. I need to wash. I pour water from the pitcher, take the cloth and give myself a good scrub. I brush through my hair then wash and rinse it over the basin. I set aside Ruth's old PJs and put on the only clothes I have that kind of fit, the ones Daniel gave me. I look at myself in the mirror. Suzanne says I've got a perky figure. I'm not quite sure what she means by that. Healthy, Daniel said. He doesn't seem to mind.

I pause at the door. Daniel talks in the kitchen. My heart swells. I want to run and throw myself in his arms. But I can't. We have to be discreet.

I walk down the hall and stop at the sink. "Breakfast looks good." I wait for Daniel to clue me in as to how we're supposed to act.

He smiles. "Come eat." He scoots over on the bench so there is room for me to sit next to him.

Not too discreet.

"Ruth was asking for you," says Fin-head. "Maybe you should see her first."

That's right. She called for me when I went to see Daniel. I excuse myself and go to her bedroom.

The baby is asleep in a white wicker cradle. Her little fists are clenched by her round face. I stroke the back of her hand. She is pretty adorable. May even have the piglets beat on the cuteness scale.

"Did you see your elder?" Ruth says. She smiles, but it's so fake.

I sit on the bed. "He's not my elder."

"That's not what it looked like from here." She points to the window. She has a perfect view to the woodpile. "You said you hardly knew him."

"Just because I hardly know him doesn't mean I can't kiss him." I force a laugh. "I mean, look at him. Wouldn't you?"

"You said you didn't know why he was paying us to keep you, that you kidnapped him while he was trying to help you."

"Isn't there some syndrome where you fall in love with your captor?"

I say. "Really Ruth, it's no big deal."

"You lied to me." The fire in Ruth's eyes fade. "I just thought..." Her lip quivers. "I just thought we had become, you know, we were...but you're not. You're a total stranger." She turns her back to me. "Just go."

"What are you talking about?" I ask, as if I don't know, but I do. Friends. She thinks of me as her friend.

Not that I can let myself think of her that way.

Ruth keeps her face to the wall.

Never mind. I walk to the kitchen.

"Did you say yes?" Fin-head asks.

"To what?"

"Ruth wanted you to be LeAnne's godmother."

Godmother? My breath grows short. Why would I want to be godmother to some fish baby? Some fish baby who is going to die.

My stomach turns. Bile rises in my throat.

There's a wail from the bedroom. It's not the baby. John scrambles from the table.

"I think she changed her mind," I say.

Fin-head pats my shoulder. "Women can be a little emotional after they deliver. Hormones, you know. I'm sure she'll come around."

"Thanks," I say, but I don't want her to come around.

Ruth is going to die, too. They all are.

I throw my napkin to the table, dash to my bedroom, and slam the door shut.

There's a slight tap. "Amy?" says Daniel. "Are you all right?"

"I'm fine." I wipe tears from my face. "Do what you have to and let's go."

CHAPTER FOURTEEN
Sympathizer

The sky grows dark. Daniel's fingers hold tight to mine. He's held my hand the entire dozen or so miles, making for a slow hike, but that doesn't mean I want him to let go. I need the support. In a few minutes we'll be at the wall. I'll signal Gilchrist and he'll tell me what to do. Everything will be all right.

Won't it?

Maybe for Daniel and me, but not for Ruth and little baby LeAnne.

I wasn't going to think about them anymore.

We reach the clearing. The aegis rumbles.

Daniel pulls me to a stop. "Are you sure you're going to be okay? Maybe I should go through alone."

"I'll be fine. Last time the magamp charge wasn't as strong as it could have been." I show him the light. "It's bright now. We'll be fine."

He pulls me close. "That would be nice, but what if you pass out again? What do you want me to do?"

I see the outline of Gilchrist's tent through the aegis. "Stick me in the tent until I wake up. If you have to get supplies I'll be fine."

"I wouldn't leave you," says Daniel. "And I brought plenty of food."

"You're prepared."

"I try." Daniel's embrace tightens. "Ready?"

I squeeze his hand. "Yes."

We plunge into the wall.

I feel like I'm going to explode.

The screaming in my body stops. I face-plant in the dirt. The sun, the real sun, shines on me. I can't breathe. Daniel is on top of me.

I spit out sand. "See? I didn't pass out at all."

Daniel doesn't move.

"Daniel?" I poke him in the side.

There's no reaction. I push and wiggle from under him. I roll him onto his back. I lay my head on his chest. His rib cage expands and contracts. His heart beats.

Light shines on his face. His lips are full and parted. I lean to him. I pull away. I don't want him to catch me kissing him if he wakes.

Did he want to kiss me when I was passed out? Did he?

I unstrap Daniel's backpack and put it in the tent. I drag him the same direction, but my arms shake. I stop halfway, sit, and log on to my controller. I open the satellite network. I expect messages from Gilchrist and the Committee to pile into my inbox.

There's nothing.

I signal Gilchrist. His ringtone plays and plays. I try not to listen. The slow, solemn notes had sounded funny when I'd picked them. Now they're just creepy. I disconnect. That's weird. Gilchrist might not always answer, but he never turns his voice mail off. I try again. The results are the same. I'll try again in a few minutes.

I drag Daniel the rest of the way to the tent. I put him inside, brush off the dirt then sweep out the tent. I kiss him, but only on the cheek.

Half an hour passes. I signal Gilchrist again.

There's no answer.

I scroll to Mama's ID. She never has her controller on, and it could be a week before she checks her messages. I can't signal the Committee. I'm a sympathizer now, like Gilchrist. I think.

There's always Suzanne. I'm not supposed to signal her from outside Old Lithisle, but the circumstances are extreme. I aim my controller's eye at Daniel and take a clip. I'll tell her I kissed him. She'll be shocked. Late bloomer, she calls me, but he's more handsome than any of the boys she's courted. I wipe a bit a drool from his mouth. I retake the clip. Better.

Suzanne answers right away. "Hello?"

"Suzanne it's me, A-."

"Hello?" she says again. "Hello?" She disconnects.

We must have had a bad connection. I signal her again.

She picks up before her ring tone plays.

"Wasn't that Am-?" I hear her mother say.

"No, it's a prankster." Suzanne speaks with force into the controller. "Don't call back, you."

But she's not talking to an anonymous signaler. She's talking to me.

My gut twists. Suzanne has been angry with me before, like when I wore my barn boots to the dance and she said I smelled like a manure pile, but no matter how I've embarrassed her, she's never refused to speak to me. Talking is her thing.

I lay my controller on the floor and scoot next to Daniel. Maybe it was bad timing. She'll signal me when she can. I close my eyes. Daniel is warm. The rhythm of his breath reminds me of waves lapping the lakeshore. For now he's safe. I'm safe.

But little baby LeAnne is going to die.

No. I wasn't going to think about her, or Ruth, or John, or Fin-head. They're fish people. There might be hope for Daniel, but I have to draw the line somewhere. I can't save everyone. I shouldn't. They're abominations. At least, that's what I've always been taught.

My palms dampen. I grab my controller and signal Mama.

"Hello," a man answers.

I disconnect. Mama does not entertain men.

My controller sings, with Mama's ringtones. I doubt it's Mama. The signal stops. The controller rings again.

I tap to answer. I don't say a word.

"Amy?" The man's voice is hesitant, earnest.

"Committee Member Trumble?"

"I can't believe it's really you." He sounds relieved.

I waver. He was always quick to smile, and kept his pockets full of peppermints for the boys and girls who sat still during revival, but he also raged from the pulpit against New Lithisle's abominations.

"Where's Mama?"

"She's fine, but I borrowed her controller for a few weeks, just in case."

"Just in case what?"

"You were still alive. Committee Member Harris told us you were deceased, but I couldn't give up hope."

"What?" I ask. I don't understand why Suzanne's father would tell the Committee I was dead.

"He said he saw you inside the aegis, motionless."

I suppose I could have looked pretty dead. Was that why Suzanne called me a prankster? Does she think I'm dead? No, a miraculous return from the grave would be more of a reason for her to talk to me, not less.

"Were you inside the aegis?" Committee Member Trumble asks.

I feel like I'm ten again, and he's giving me a scolding. I talk so fast I spit. "Gilchrist pushed me through. I told him not to. He did it anyway."

"Where have you been?"

I tell him everything. Everything but Daniel.

"Send your coordinates," he says. "We'll get the helicopter out. Your mother will be glad to see you."

My mouth hangs open. They can't come and find Daniel.

"Amy?" Committee Member Trumble asks. "Are you still there?"

"Yes," I say, searching for excuses. "But you don't need to send the helicopter. There's no need to waste so much kerosene. I can make it back on my own."

"Don't be ridiculous. You're very important to us. We were devastated when we thought we'd lost you. We won't let it happen again."

"No, really, I'll be fine."

"Amy, we're sending the helicopter." Irritation fills his voice. He's running out of patience.

"Okay." I have to sound like I'm on board. "Since you insist, thank you. I appreciate it." I lock onto the satellites and drop the coordinates in a file. I tap send. "How long do you think it will take?"

"We've got a patrol ready. A few hours at the most."

I have a few hours to get as far away as possible. I disconnect, and pat Daniel on the face. I shake his arm. "Wake up, sleeping beauty."

He sleeps on.

Chances are he's not going to pop up and run anytime soon. I need to come up with an alternate plan. Along the ridge are cliffs. There must be crags to hide in, but I'll have to figure a way to get Daniel up there. I could barely drag him along on the flat.

Outside the tent I see Gilchrist's sleeping bag. I loosen the ties and shake it out. The fabric is wet and smells of rot, but I bring it in the tent, unzip it, and roll Daniel over. I take fistfuls of the bag and pull. The bag, with Daniel on it, is still heavy, but it slides along the ground more easily than just Daniel. I head north in the light of the aegis. If I can drag him a few hundred yards before I head to the ridge, they'll be less likely to find us. I glance back. There's a rut in the dirt where the bag has been. The drag mark sort of looks like a huge arrow with the words, *She went this way*, written on it.

I sit and eye the tent and the clearing as if it were a blank slate.

I drag Daniel into the woods and lay him and his backpack beside a fallen tree. I camouflage him with leaves and twigs. I break off a maple branch and use it to wipe away our tracks. I leave the long, deep impression in the dirt from where I dragged him from the aegis to the tent. I yank at the tent, tear at it with my fingers. I stomp in the dirt along the tracks to the aegis. I pull out strands of hair and leave them.

Whoever comes with the helicopter had better be into fiction. I was waiting in the tent. I was attacked. I fought. They dragged me back into New Lithisle.

I go back to Daniel, lie at his side and wait. The time to rest isn't all bad. I hold his hand, then sleep. I run my fingers through his hair, then stretch my neck and upper back. I feel the stubble on his chin. I lean to his lips. I pull away.

I take out my controller. I scroll to Suzanne's name on my contact list. Does she really think I'm dead?

Daniel moans. His eyelids flicker.

"Welcome back," I say.

"How l-l-long?" he asks.

"Only a few hours."

He shakes his head.

The wind roars.

He sits.

I pull him down.

The treetops sway. Searchlights pierce the dark. A helicopter swoops over the ridge.

"W-w-what is that?" he says.

"Helicopter. We're hiding. Stay down."

"Why is it flying?"

"Isn't that what helicopters do?"

"Where are we?"

I don't have to tell him.

"There are people in the Wilds? People with h-h-helicopters?"

"They're here to take me home, but I don't want to go."

"Where exactly are you from?"

I couldn't answer if I wanted to. The wind steals my breath. The beat of the blades pounds in my ears. The helicopter tilts and touches the ground. The blades slow. The door opens. Half a dozen troops pile out, weapons aimed. A tall, dark man follows. He hurries to the tent.

I catch a glimpse of his profile.

The man is Suzanne's father.

My heart leaps. I leap with it.

Daniel pulls me down. "W-w-what are you doing?"

"I don't know," I say, but I do. I used to sit on Mr. Harris's lap while he read Suzanne and me nursery stories. He bought Mama yards of blue muslin when he saw I'd outgrown all my dresses, and she couldn't tear them up to recycle them one more time. Mr. Harris, not Gilchrist, had been the one who'd presented me as an adult to the church congregation on my thirteenth birthday.

But Suzanne wouldn't talk to me, Mr. Harris told the Committee I was dead, and now he's here.

Mr. Harris emerges from the tent. "She's not here."

"She can't be far," says Committee Member Trumble. "I talked to her only a few hours ago. Search the woods."

My throat tightens. That's exactly what they weren't supposed to do.

"There's drag marks to the aegis," calls one of the troops.

"The tent is torn," says another. "It looks like there was a fight."

"No one on the inside can get out," says Committee Member Trumble. "I made sure of that."

"On the inside she's extraordinarily valuable," says Suzanne's father. "People would risk a lot to get their hands on her."

I start. What does he know about that?

"We're not leaving without her," says Committee Member Trumble. "Get out there and look."

"Can you climb?" I ask Daniel.

"Like what?"

"A tree, now. Are you well enough to climb this tree?"

"I'll try."

I help him put on his pack and push him ahead of me.

"No, you first," he says.

"Just go."

Daniel stands on his toes and reaches the lowest branch with ease. Silent as a snake he works his way forty, fifty feet up the tree.

I jump. My fingertips are inches from the branch. Footsteps approach.

A light flashes. I jump again. I miss. White teeth smile in the darkness.

"Up you go," Suzanne's father says. He grips my legs and shoots me in the air like I'm still six and we're playing in the backyard. I catch the branch on the way down.

"Mr. Harris...."

"No," he whispers. "Stay hidden. Your father is in jail. Finish what he started." He takes a deep breath and calls. "I found something."

I've already cleared thirty feet.

I reach Daniel. His face glistens with sweat.

"Are you going to make it?" I whisper.

He nods.

I wrap my arms around him.

Committee Member Trumble is at the base of the tree. "A rotten sleeping bag?"

"And branches spread out for camouflage."

The red light from Committee Member Trumble's infrared heat detector flashes left then right. Not up.

Daniel slips. I hold tight. Flakes of bark flutter to the ground.

"Keep looking," says Committee Member Trumble. They wander off.

I exhale. Suzanne's father hums. I hear his baritone voice sing in my head, *Let all things now living, a song of thanksgiving, To God the creator triumphantly raise. Who fashioned and made us, protected and stayed us. Who still guides us on to the end of our days.*

He's a sympathizer. He has to be, like Gilchrist. Like me.

Poor Gilchrist. He obviously got home somehow, but then they must have charged him with treason. At least the burn on his arm would have been treated, and he's alive, for now.

Finish what he started, Mr. Harris said, but I don't know what that is. I need to talk to him again. I let go of Daniel and step down a branch. He slumps. I grab him.

"Sorry," he whispers.

I nod, but I won't be able to leave him alone, at least not fifty feet up.

More than an hour passes. My arms tremble, until I worry I might fall, and Daniel along with me. At last an engine turns. Blades spin. The helicopter lifts, soars over the ridge and is gone. So much for getting details on what I'm supposed to do.

Daniel and I head down the tree. His feet touch the dirt. He collapses.

I push the hair from his face. "You did good."

He grunts, curls beside the fallen log and closes his eyes.

I haul our backpacks to the tent. I come back and lie beside Daniel.

greycat40@vlas.net

Gilchrist was trying to send a file to someone in New Lithisle. Of course. I search my folders. The file is still there. I examine the coding and piece together the first few lines. It's a patch of some sort. For the aegis? What was he trying to do?

Terror seizes me.

Shut it down and let the abominations free.

Maybe Gilchrist does deserve the hangman's noose.

Daniel stirs. My heart stops. What if shutting down the aegis is the only way to save him?

My thoughts tangle. The Committee says not one person from New Lithisle can be allowed to escape destruction or eventually the soulless gene will pass from parent to child until no real people are left.

Would I want that first cursed child to be mine?

I take a deep breath. I'm overreacting. I don't know for sure what the file is. Mama says never assume. Suzanne's father thinks whatever Gilchrist had in mind is a good idea, and Mr. Harris has never been a radical. Except he's always been kind to me, Allarice's daughter, and he let Suzanne befriend me when all the other parents called their children away.

Maybe he and Gilchrist have been in on this from the beginning, like before I was born.

I tap Daniel. "May I borrow your controller?"

He grunts again. I take it as a yes. I pull it from his back pocket, link it to mine, make a copy of Gilchrist's file and transfer it to his controller. Whatever the file is, it's too important to not backup.

"We've got to go back in," I say. "My father has a contact in Vlas. I have to talk to him." But I won't send him the file, not until I'm sure what it is.

"Now?" he says. "I'm not sure I can."

"In the morning," I say. There's not much else I can do.

"Okay." He takes my hand and squeezes it.

I curl next to him, watch the stars, and listen to his breath as I fall asleep.

Heat presses against me.

My eyes fly open. I'm not anywhere I've ever been. Fire flames across an endless plain. Pain rages through my body. I push to my feet and try to run, but my legs are slow and heavy. I scream, but no sound comes from my lips.

I look for a landmark, anything familiar. Is this a vision of New Lithisle burning? Or a glimpse of what my eternity will hold if I spare it?

I force myself awake, it's only a dream, but my heart pounds against my chest.

Dawn lights the eastern sky. I shake Daniel. We gather our things, hold each other tight, and head back in.

CHAPTER FIFTEEN
The Contact

"Amy." Daniel's voice wakes me. I open my eyes. I expect light, mossy dirt, and trees but I'm in a dark room, my cheek against a satin pillow. Sheer fabric, draped from a canopy bed, encircles me.

I must have passed out. Before we stepped through the wall, I'd assured Daniel I'd be fine, sleep a couple of hours at the most, the way he had. Apparently not.

"You're awake," says Daniel. The mattress sinks as he sits next to me. "Can I get you breakfast?"

I look at the floor to ceiling windows that fill an entire wall. Lights twinkle against a black horizon. "It's morning?"

"Five-thirty. They called an emergency Elder's council at seven and my briefing starts at six." He's in a suit and tie.

"Breakfast sounds good."

Daniel ties the sheers back.

I pop from bed. "Gilchrist's contact. I need to get in touch with him."

"Breakfast first."

"Don't you dare...." I run after him to the door.

"You can't come out." The door shuts in my face. I raise my hand to knock, but let it fall to my side. I pace instead. Thick black carpet plumps between my toes. Cool air whooshes from a register. Daniel comes back with mixed fruit, juice, and a bowl of oatmeal.

"What's going on?" I ask.

Daniel ignores me and says grace. "Eat. It's been days."

I pluck a strawberry from the plate and pop it in my mouth. I cross my arms and wait.

"I wouldn't exactly call that eating," says Daniel.

I don't budge.

"I already tried to send a message."

"What do you mean, tried?"

"I found the file you put on my controller. I sent an inquiry to the intended recipient, *greycat40@vlas.net*."

"And?"

He shows me his screen. "There was a slight complication. The e-mail came back with a delivery error. Vlasnet sold out to Kastar six months ago. Most of the addresses are invalid."

"That's not slight."

"Don't worry. I've already taken care of it. A Believer in my region works at Kastar. He's getting me the old records. We should have the name and address of your father's contact in a few days."

"You're sure?"

"Maybe sooner."

I put the spoon in the oatmeal. "You could have told me before you tore off to the kitchen."

"I'm leaving any minute. I had to prioritize, and you eating came first."

"That's a little much, Daniel." I glare at him. "I don't need you to take care of me."

"Except when you're unconscious."

I have to give him that. I fill my mouth with oatmeal.

"This is very important." Daniel puts a piece of paper on the tray. "My brother has a fiduciary responsibility to Elder Binyamin and Nasira. If he figures out you're here, he has to send you back to them. These are the rules to keep that from happening."

I read the first few lines. No leaving the room, no talking to myself, no standing near the windows.

A voice calls from the hall. "Daniel, get a move on. We're going to be late."

"It's Ezekiel," whispers Daniel. "I won't be back until night." He kisses me, full on the lips. "I'll see you tomorrow."

"What am I supposed to do?"

"You could bathe." Daniel points to a door at the end of the room, beyond a loveseat and chair. "The bath is there."

"Daniel!" his brother yells.

Daniel squeezes my shoulder. "Bye." He disappears out the door.

I could bathe? I sniff my arm. I guess I do smell a little like the goat shed. I unfold the bedding. Discoloration the general shape of my body stains the sheets. *Eww.* I pull the sheets off and bring them to the bath.

The tub is round and carved from stone. The faucet pours from the ceiling like a waterfall. I float in warm bubbles. A few hours later I have everything scrubbed, wrung, and hung to dry. I wear Daniel's thick taupe robe. The hem trails behind me when I walk.

I sit on the sofa. I'm done bathing. I'm not tired. I can't leave the room. I take out my controller, it's so good to have it back, and open my contacts. I don't doubt Daniel but I have to double check. I connect to the New Lithisle network and run the program Gilchrist wrote to send e-mails.

Upload error.

Daniel's explanation for the failure makes as much sense as anything.

I browse the network. I end up back on Ander Smith's site. There's a three-hour documentary about the aegis, *Fiery Collapse, The Elite Want You Dead.* The title is little melodramatic, but it could help me figure out what Gilchrist meant to do with his file. I tap play. The first clip is of Patient Zero at the beginning of the pandemic. No wonder the documentary is three hours long. Someone needs to teach Ander Smith how to edit.

The middle section is about Allarice. I fast forward. I know what she did, betray all that was decent and good to splice animal genes into the human genome. I stop, tap rewind, and watch it anyway. I've never seen her pre-alterations. Her brown hair had streaks of gold, her dark eyes sparkled, her voice was soft and sweet. The strangest thing is watching her mannerisms. I don't think I look that much like her, but when she smiles or tilts her head it's like looking in a mirror. Weird.

At last a picture of the aegis generator with the engineers who built it flashes on screen. I look for Gilchrist's face.

The door to Daniel's suite opens. I jump. Rule number nine. I'm supposed to hide under the bed if someone comes in. I'm on the sofa. The door is between me and the bed. I dive into the closet. At least I thought it was the closet. The room is almost as big as Mama's whole cottage and looks more like a tailor's shop filled with clothes Daniel's size.

The light flicks on. "Amy?"

"Daniel?" I crawl from behind a row of pants. The hangers clink. "You scared me. I thought you said you wouldn't be back until late."

"They gave us a lunch break." He pulls me to my feet. "What's with the sheets?"

"They were soiled."

"I have a laundry service, you know." He opens a cabinet. There's a chute that drops into darkness. "You can put dirty things in here."

Of course he has a laundry service.

Daniel leads me out the door, despite the rules, down the hall to a kitchen. "What do you want to eat?"

"What do you have?"

"Everything."

The kitchen has tall cabinets, an island, a gas range, stove, and refrigerator but it doesn't look like it has everything. "Canned spaghettis?"

"Everything but that." He scrolls through a menu on his controller. "There's spaghetti with marinara, rotini and capers, fettuccine alfredo-."

"What do you have in potatoes?"

He reads a list. I pick twice-baked potatoes. I love them, but Mama says they're a waste of time. She only lets me make them on holidays. He taps and a whirring sound comes from the cabinet above the range. In five minutes it beeps. He opens the door. A potato mounded with cheese steams in an oval dish.

I stand on tiptoe to look inside the apparatus. A metal tube empties into a white plastic box. "How did you do that? Is it like takeout?"

"I can't believe you've never seen an autowaiter."

"You'd never seen a helicopter fly."

"Good point." Daniel explains the autowaiter takes dehydrated food, reconstitutes it, then heats or cools it as needed.

I take his controller and order lasagna, pot pie, a vegetable medley, and strawberry cheesecake. The food isn't the best I've ever eaten, but my stomach bulges. Being full feels so good. I slide the fork over the plate and squish the last bit of cheesecake between the tines. I lick it clean.

"You didn't eat much," I say.

"They had tons of food at the meeting."

"When do you have to be back?"

"Fifteen minutes ago."

"You'd better leave."

Daniel shrugs. "They make such a big deal about everyone being there, but they never listen to me anyway." He takes my dirty plates and puts them on the counter. "What do you want to do now?"

"I should wash them." I go to the sink and roll up the sleeves on the robe.

"That's the help's job."

Of course he has help.

He pulls me from the dishes and into his arms. I smile. He presses his lips to mine. Daniel, strawberries, and cheesecake. I have never tasted anything so delicious.

"I told my mother about you," he whispers.

"Your mother?" I squirm free, tie the robe tight and look to the far end of the apartment. "Where is she?"

"Not here. She doesn't live in Vlas." He takes my hands and kisses me again. "I just wanted you to know my intentions are serious. I care for you, Amy." His eyes are full of hope, and expectation.

I bite my lip. This is where I'm supposed to tell him I feel the same way, but I'm not sure how I feel. I don't want him dead. Is that what he wants to hear? I'm risking my life in this doomed dome because I care about him, but I'm not going to tell Mama about him or bring him home to her. Ever.

"What did your mother say?" I ask.

"That I was star-struck."

"Are you?"

His face turns red. "At first, I guess, but not now."

"What makes you so sure?"

"Star-struck is not being able to pay attention in trigonometry," says Daniel. "Serious is traipsing around in the Wilds and the Borderlands to be with you."

Warmth spreads from my heart. I sort of believe him. He likes me, not Allarice, or one of the others.

Daniel's controller beeps. He reads the message. "He found the old Vlasnet records. I'll transfer them to my tablet and we can look through them."

"Great," I say. We go back to his room. I open the file and run a search. I find *greycat40@vlas.net*. "There isn't a name but there's an address. 10 Pen Street, Vlas, New Lithisle."

Daniel grimaces. "10 Pen?"

"Yes."

"Don't you know what that is?"

My gut tightens. "No."

"The Prime Minister's residence."

CHAPTER SIXTEEN
Advertisement

"My father's contact is the Prime Minister?" I ask.

"I doubt it," says Daniel. "He has a staff of hundreds. The person your father knows might not even be there anymore."

"That's just great. Are we going to have to go back on the outside? I don't even know who I'd signal." Gilchrist is locked up, Suzanne hung up on me, and I certainly don't want Committee Member Trumble to answer for Mama again. There are only so many times I can expect him to believe I was abducted.

"Not necessarily," says Daniel. "You could put an ad in the Vlas Daily and ask *greycat40@vlas.net* to contact you, behind a pseudonym, of course."

"Do you think it would work?"

"It's worth a try."

Daniel takes the tablet. He uses his brother's corporate post office box to set up an e-mail account for me. I pick Golden Star as my user name.

"Golden Star?" he asks.

"He's my dog."

"You have a pet dog?" Daniel's mouth hangs open.

"Yes," I say cautiously, thinking of all the other animals Mama and I keep.

Daniel shakes his head. "You should use a name that will give Grey Cat a hint at who you are without everyone figuring it out."

"A reference to my father?"

"I was thinking about your mother."

"What does Mama have to do with this?"

"I'm not talking about your surrogate. I'm talking about your real mother."

My jaw tightens. "Mama carried me for nine months, gave birth to me, and raised me. That makes her pretty real in my book."

"That's not what I meant and you know it."

I glare at him.

Daniel takes my hand. "I'm sorry. I'm just saying since your biological mother is—"

"Dead." I yank my hand from his. "Allarice is dead and I never knew her. She's not my mother."

Daniel looks down at the tablet. "I'm sorry."

"Don't be."

Daniel is quiet for a minute. "Golden Star is fine." He types it in. Maybe he is star-struck and he doesn't even know it.

I watch while Daniel posts the ad. We double-check it on the network. He doesn't say anything else about Allarice.

"That should do it," says Daniel. "If he doesn't read the Daily someone he knows will."

Daniel's controller beeps again. "It's just my brother." He taps *ignore* then mutes the sound. "Do you want to go outside?"

"Can I?"

"In a way." He takes my hand and leads me past the kitchen. He presses a button on the wall. A door slides open to an elevator.

I shudder. "Do you have stairs?"

"Lifts are safe," says Daniel. "Do you know what they are?"

"Of course," I say. "And I'm not getting in."

"All right," says Daniel. He brings me to a stairwell. We climb one flight. The door opens to rosebushes, hedges and plots of thick grass.

"This is the roof?" I run my fingers along the smooth, round leaves of a tall, spear-shaped plant. I didn't think so much could grow on the top of a building.

"The elder before me liked to garden, not that he did any of the work. I didn't see a reason to get rid of it, or fire the gardener." He disappears into a hedge. I follow, but there are only leaves. He calls to me. I run. He's led me into a maze. I find him lying on thick moss beneath a weeping tree loaded with pink blossoms.

"You might not be tired," he says. "But I need a nap. I've hardly slept since the Wilds."

"You could have napped in your bed."

"Not with you." He pats the ground.

I lie next to him. "How did you get me here?"

"I carried you back to Leroy's. He drove us to Petrich. From there I smuggled you into the railway station in my suitcase."

I hesitate. I want to ask about Ruth and LeAnne. "You stuffed me in your suitcase?"

"My luggage is quite big," says Daniel. "And you're quite small."

"I'm not that tiny."

"Apparently you are." He rolls to his side and kisses me.

"You're not sleeping."

"Maybe I won't."

But he does, after another kiss. I lift his arm from my shoulder. I get up and wander the maze. I come to a bed of pebbles, tiny black and white stones raked in swirling patterns. I hop on the pavers. There's another hedge. I push it aside. A ledge drops to the street below. Half a dozen black cars roar down the street. They screech to a stop in front of Daniel's building.

I tromp over the pebbles and run into the maze. It's a dead end. I turn. I'm back at the entrance. Where is Daniel?

A hand grabs my arm.

"What's the matter?" Daniel asks.

"How often do evil-looking black cars surround your building?" I ask.

"What?"

I bring him to the edge of the roof.

An armored vehicle pulls behind the cars. The rear doors swing open. Troops with rifles slung over their shoulders climb out.

"Oh, man." Daniel takes his controller and taps.

"What are you doing?" I grab his arm. I don't like him making decisions without at least talking to me first.

"Getting my brother." Ringtones play then go to a message service. "Ezekiel, this is Daniel. Signal me now. I'm afraid I wasn't entirely honest with you, and we've got a huge problem."

I take the controller from him and disconnect. "We don't need to get him involved."

"Ezekiel is one of the top lawyers in New Lithisle. He can negotiate surrender. No one has to get hurt."

"What about *greycat40@vlas.net*?"

"I think he just found you. That's the Prime Minister's Guard."

"I don't understand. Why would my father's contact come after me with armed soldiers?"

"You tell me."

"Those men can't be from him. We've got to get out of here."

"Twelve stories up surrounded by the Guard? You don't understand this world, Amy. I'm trying to keep us alive."

"So am I."

"The Guard is nothing more than the Prime Minister's personal thugs, led by his son. They're ruthless."

"Then we don't have a lot of time, do we?"

Daniel sighs. "There is the laundry chute."

"The one that falls into darkness?"

"Only two stories."

I hesitate.

"I've done it before," says Daniel

I nod. "All right."

We hurry down the stairs and pause at the door. The apartment is quiet. In Daniel's bedroom I pull my clothes off the makeshift line. They're still wet. I toss them down the chute. I put my foot in after them.

"No, I'm going first," says Daniel.

"There is no way. I'm in a robe with nothing underneath."

Daniel's focus shifts from my eyes to where the robe forms a "v" on my chest. "Nothing?"

"I washed my under things too."

"But I need to be below you in case you fall. I can catch you."

Pounding echoes through the apartment. "Open up. This is the Prime Minister's Guard."

"You go." I step from the chute. As soon as he's in I climb after him. The cabinet flaps shut. I didn't need to worry about him seeing anything. The chute is darker than midnight. There are shouts and crashes above us. My foot bumps into Daniel a dozen times. I slip. He grabs me. We continue. Neither of us says a word.

At last Daniel drops. Metal and plastic clatter.

I reach the end of the chute. Below me Daniel stands, arms outstretched, in a bin full of dirty clothes. I let go, and he catches me. We're in a shining white laundry room. The smell of detergent fills my nose, and a quiet lub-lub-lub hums from a dryer as the clothes inside tumble.

"What now?" I whisper.

"We stay put until Ezekiel signals back."

"They're going to figure out where we went." I pull out my controller and open the Ander Smith website. "We need help."

"That's why I signaled Ezekiel."

I show Daniel the picture of Ander Smith on my controller. "I was thinking of him."

"Not the conspiracy theorist." He rolls his eyes.

"We have no idea what's going on with this Grey Cat person. I want a second opinion."

"And you think he'll be able to give it to you?"

"Why not?"

"He's crazy."

"He was right about the magamp."

Daniel's controller sings, a soft lullaby I've never heard. Daniel digs into his pocket and taps the screen. "Mum?"

"Are you all right?" she asks.

"Now isn't a good time, Mum."

"They arrested Ezekiel, dragged him out of the Elder's Council and took him to 10 Pen for questioning."

"Mum, I'm so sorry."

"What do you know about it?"

"Nothing. You're telling me."

"It's because of that Daughter, isn't it? You still know where she is."

"Please don't bring her up, to anyone. I think you need to leave your house and warn the twins. I love you, Mum. Good bye." Daniel disconnects.

"I should go," I whisper. "This is my problem and I've dragged your family into it."

"No, it's our problem." He browses the Ander Smith site and reads the studio address aloud. "Do you really think he could help?"

"I do."

"Then we'll try to find him. He's in a suburb north of Vlas. If we can keep ahead of the Guard we should be able to make it on foot."

CHAPTER SEVENTEEN
Back Streets

A rack in the middle of the laundry room holds suits neatly pressed in individual plastic bags. Daniel grabs one, then an empty bag and shoves my wet clothes in it. He leads me from one hall to another. We reach the stairs. He pulls me down eleven flights. The red block letters on the door read, *Basement Level 2.*

Daniel turns the knob to an open room, dark, dry, and warm. There is a loud click. Blue fire lights beneath a boiler. We walk past shelves of labeled boxes, *6" pipes, 4" joints, bolts.* We stop at an oval metal door in the concrete wall. There is no knob or handle, only a wheel a foot in diameter.

Daniel spins it. "We're going into the sewer, just so you know."

I imagine a manure pit like the one behind the cow barn at Suzanne's, filled with human excrement instead of animal.

The door opens. The stench burns my eyes and nose. A brown river runs through the middle of a concrete tunnel. It could be worse. Daniel steps on a narrow ledge a few inches above the sludge.

I press my back to the side of the tunnel. My bare feet slither over the damp stone. "At least we aren't walking in it."

"Yet," says Daniel. "Our exit is on the other side of the tunnel."

"That is disgusting," I say. "How deep is it?"

"Mid-calf on me, and slippery. I fell once."

"Once?" I scrunch my face. "How many times have you been down here?"

Daniel tells me how, after he was first selected to be elder, he was moved to live with his brother in Vlas. Since he'd only been eight he hadn't had a lot of responsibilities beside school. He'd spent his unsupervised afternoons exploring first the building, then the city, by way of the sewers. "I kept hoping I'd find a monster, a snake, or an alligator or something."

"Did you?" I ask.

"Not even a newt."

The tunnel turns. The ledge widens. Our pace quickens. There's no time to talk. We continue for over an hour.

Daniel stops. "This is where we cross." He takes off his shoes, ties the laces and hangs them around his neck. "I'll carry you."

"I'd rather slip and fall on my own, thanks."

He sweeps me up in his arms.

"Daniel," I scream, and try to squirm free.

He holds me tighter. "I'm not going to drop you."

"But you might fall!"

He steps into the muck.

I stop fighting. I don't want to add to the difficulty of him crossing. I nearly gag as the thick, brown liquid rolls around his calves. He dips. I scream again.

He grins. "Just kidding."

On the other side of the tunnel he places me on a metal ladder. I hold the robe between my legs, grip the bars, and climb to a manhole cover. I push. The plate doesn't budge. Daniel reaches around me and shoves it aside.

There are shouts, music, and honking. On the street, heels, boots, and oxfords rush by. The wheel of a bicycle careens toward my face. It turns at the hole. The bicycle tips. The man riding it curses.

"Hurry," says Daniel.

I don't want to step onto a busy street dressed in nothing but Daniel's robe. I scramble to the pavement anyway.

Daniel rolls the manhole cover back in place. He brings me to the sidewalk. We walk past tobacco and pawn shops, and restaurants that smell like curry, cumin, and ginger. People flow by us like a stream. I'm jostled, but they don't look in my face, or say hello.

"I love this part of town," says Daniel. "People mind their own business."

We stop at a hotel crammed between a deli and dry cleaners.

"You back." A tiny, wrinkled woman greets Daniel in the lobby. "Not alone this time. Bring girl. Good."

"One hour," says Daniel.

The woman points to me. "She worth two hour."

Daniel shakes his head and holds up one finger. "One."

"What you have?" she asks.

"The suit."

The woman frowns. "You big and tall. What I do with suit?"

"It's worth a lot more than what I usually give you."

"Okay." She reaches for the bagged, pressed suit.

"No, the one I have on."

"Dirty?"

"I need the clean one."

"Half hour." She hands Daniel a tarnished skeleton key with ornate scrolls. "Room Fourteen."

The room is at the end of the hall near an emergency exit. Daniel shuts the door behind us. "Let me clean up first. I'll get Mrs. Marissa the suit then see if I can find something dry for you to wear."

"You know her by name?"

"I doubt it's her real name."

Daniel does as he said. When he comes back I'm clean and wrapped in a towel. I crack open the bathroom door and he hands me a slim-cut sweater dress. The yarn is a deep violet. There is a scoop neck and three-quarter sleeves. The hem falls to just below my knees.

I give it back to him. "It's very cute but I'm not sure I can do much in a dress. I think it would be best if I wore the jeans."

He pushes it back to me. "You can't. I traded your old clothes and robe for the dress."

"You didn't."

"I'm in a suit. We have to look like we belong together."

Naturally. My under things are still damp. I put the dress on over them. I comb out my hair with my fingers. I open the bathroom door.

Daniel stares. "Wow. You look really good."

I smile, and lean to him. He's going to kiss me.

But he doesn't.

Disappointment forms a lump in my throat. Daniel hasn't kissed me since the roof. I'm too much trouble. No boy in his right mind would want to get involved with me, and Daniel's probably finally figured that out. I swallow hard.

He drops a pair of tall, ivory-colored boots at my feet. "Put them on. Let's go."

Dress boots? Whatever. I slip my feet into them. At least they aren't high heels.

We leave our room with three minutes of our half hour to spare. Mrs. Marissa waves as we walk through the lobby.

Daniel yanks me away from the door. "Maybe we should go out the back."

"No." Mrs. Marissa hurries from behind the desk and blocks the hall. "No more time unless you have trade."

Daniel picks her up and sets her aside. "Sorry. Thank-you for your hospitality." He pushes the red bar on the emergency exit. An alarm blares. We run. Daniel ducks to avoid the laundry lines that crisscross the alley. Garbage cans, heaped with tins, paper and plastic, buzz with flies. I hold my nose. Daniel holds my hand. We don't stop.

"What happened?" I ask.

"Guards were coming out the manhole," says Daniel.

"How did they figure that out?"

"They have heat sensing guns."

We keep to the back alleys for hours, until the back alleys disappear. I recognize the warehouses I saw my first night in Vlas. We follow the rails north a few miles then head up the western ridge. Big houses sit on grassy lawns surrounded by tall trees.

Daniel stops. "We're here."

A tall brick fence surrounds the property. "How are we supposed to get in?" I ask.

"Climb?"

"In this dress?" I walk to the fence. "There has to be a door somewhere."

Daniel smirks. "Technically the gate is a door." I whack him on the shoulder. His smile only broadens.

"You think you're so smart, don't you?" I take out my controller and scan for attached devices. A local area network appears.

"What did you do?" asks Daniel.

"Nothing, yet." I look up. The gate creeps open.

CHAPTER EIGHTEEN
Ander Smith

Daniel takes a cautious step onto the drive. I follow. The pavement winds between pine trees and hardwood. We stop at a three-story house that would swallow half a dozen cottages the size of Mama's. "I can't believe he rails against the elite when he's one of them," I say. "He lives in a mansion."

Daniel smiles. "This house is hardly a mansion. It can't be more than three or four thousand square feet."

"Thousands of square feet?" Even Suzanne's house on the lake with its wrap-around porch and sprawling lawn isn't that big. "No one needs to live in something so—"

"What do you want?" Ander Smith's deep, gravelly voice interrupts us. He appears on the display by the door, his brow furrowed and a frown on his face. "Wait. Don't tell me. You found the missing Daughter and you're willing to share the reward, but first you need some upfront money to hire a big Vlas lawyer."

My legs tense. They want to run, but there is sarcasm in Ander Smith's voice. He isn't serious, but if I try to sneak out now, he might change his mind.

Daniel takes my arm. "We should go."

"Good idea," says Ander Smith, and the screen goes black.

Daniel pulls.

"No." I dart from Daniel to the door. "Mr. Smith, I saw your documentary on the aegis. I have to talk to you about it."

There's a loud buzz. A green light shines above the knob. The door opens. Ander Smith stands in the entry. He's as tall as Daniel, but wider. Even his hands are thick. "So you are the missing Daughter."

I freeze. He knows.

Daniel pulls me back and wraps his arm around me. "She is, and I want two-hundred and fifty thousand credits to help me hire a lawyer."

"Daniel." I twist and pull, but can't wrest myself from his embrace. "Don't encourage him."

"Trust me," he says.

Ander Smith laughs. "I have no interest in worthless credits from that corrupt so-called government." He grabs my arm and pulls me and Daniel in. "But only Gilchrist's daughter would show up on my doorstep asking about the aegis days before it's due to collapse."

I gasp. "Days?" He can't be right, but if he is, this is bad. I have to know more. "I thought we had until the summer solstice."

"That's when the solar storms will reach their peak, but my source doesn't think the substructure will last that long."

"What's going on?" asks Daniel.

"How much time do we have?" I ask.

"I was hoping you could tell me." Ander Smith pulls out a tiny black notebook and writes a few lines. "Does your father think he can save the aegis?"

"I don't know," I say. "Is that even possible?"

"Did you watch the documentary or not?"

"Most of it."

"What documentary?" asks Daniel.

Ander Smith shakes his head. "You didn't have a few hours to invest in something that means life or death for all of humanity?" His voice is so loud I tremble.

"I'm sorry," I whisper. "I was being held captive. I didn't have access to the network until this morning."

The fire fades from his eyes. "You do know how the aegis works, don't you?"

"Me?" I ask, panic rising in my chest. "I'm not an engineer. I'm a junior in high school."

"Didn't your father teach you anything?"

"How to scavenge," I say defensively. "I'm super good at finding high-value objects for resale."

"That's a waste." Ander Smith shakes his head. "For starters the boosters run off nuclear energy, but they're supplemented with solar power."

My shoulders relax. "Well, pretty much everyone knows that."

"And the biggest solar storms in over a hundred years are predicted to hit this summer. The aegis will drop as much excess energy as it can, but at some point the boosters will overload and explode. Then the aegis will fracture and crash, causing liquid plasma to vaporize everything beneath it."

My stomach turns. "Boom. Crash. Burn."

"Exactly." Ander Smith leans to me. "But what if the excess energy could be shunted into the grounds instead of the boosters?"

I hesitate. Last summer Mama and I added an electric wire around the garden fence after the goats broke in one too many times. We'd put out a solar panel, then driven a stake three feet into the dirt to prevent a fire in case the line ever got struck by lightning. "If it's such an easy fix why didn't they do it in the first place?"

"You have to imagine what it was like back then," says Ander Smith. "They were rushing to put it up before everyone died, and it was only supposed to be temporary."

"So they left it with a fatal flaw?" Somehow it sounds just like my parents.

"Not on purpose, but when Allarice banished everyone who refused alterations, she sent your father away with them."

"Even though he'd written the programming for the aegis, and was the only person left in the world who knew strophes?" I roll my eyes.

"He was her husband. She didn't want to be accused of favoritism, and she never intended to leave them out there. They were supposed to come back a few weeks later, scared into submission."

"But instead they all disappeared." Daniel looks at me. "They didn't die. You're one of the Lost."

"The who?" I ask.

"Of course they survived," says Ander Smith. "At least some of them. Hundreds of thousands of people don't just disappear, and if anyone could have hidden them and gotten them back safely into New Lithisle it was Gilchrist."

Daniel turns to Ander Smith. "Oh no. They're not in—"

I jab Daniel in the gut. He looks at me. I shake my head. I'm not entirely sure why no one in New Lithisle seems to know about Old Lithisle, but I'm not going to let Daniel blab it.

But Ander Smith has given me the answers I need. It doesn't sound like Gilchrist was planning on shutting the aegis down, only reprogramming it to withstand the solar storms. I'll have to double check his file to be sure, but my heart aches with relief. Daniel, Ruth and little baby LeAnne will live.

But I'll have to leave Daniel behind.

Like there was ever any other option.

"Who was your source on the aegis?" I ask. "I need to talk to him."

"He's on the documentary. I interview him at the three-quarter mark."

"I promise I will finish watching the film, but can you tell me his name?"

Ander Smith writes in his notebook, then tears off a page and hands it to me. "Reg Denney."

"How do I find him?"

"He changed his number and e-mail after I interviewed him, he got quite a negative reaction for going public with his concerns, but he works at the main aegis generator in Vlas. You should be able to catch him before or after one of his shifts."

"We have to go to the aegis generator?" I say.

"You shouldn't," says Ander Smith. "At least not tonight. The Guard is out looking for you everywhere."

"What do you know about that?" I ask.

"I'm a reporter. I've got my ear to the ground." Ander Smith gestures down the hall. "You're welcome to stay here. We've got plenty of guest rooms, and my wife fries up a mean omelet. Almost tastes like the real thing."

Daniel takes my hand. "Thank you for your gracious offer, but we'll be going now."

"Are you sure?" I ask.

"Yes." Daniel's voice is firm.

"I promise she'll be safe here," says Ander Smith.

"I'm sure." Daniel takes a step.

I stumble after him. "Wait." I turn back to Ander Smith. "What are you going to do?"

"My job is to inform the people. I know they don't believe me yet, but if we get a disturbance in the aegis before the final collapse, they may rise up and demand action."

"What type of action?" Something tells me I should let him know about the file, maybe even give him a copy, but I'm still not one-hundred percent sure what it is.

"There's the bunker under Mount Paul," says Ander Smith. "But of course it wouldn't fit everyone, and I've heard reports the elite have another plan, that Mount Paul is only a diversion." He shakes my hand. "Good luck."

"You too."

The door shuts behind us.

"What's the hurry?" I put a hand on my hip. "I think we should take him up on his offer. The night sky is almost up, and you haven't slept much."

"We have to get back to Vlas." Daniel takes quick, long steps down the drive. His fists are clenched and his face taut.

I run to keep up. "I know, but now?"

He doesn't answer.

"You don't believe Ander Smith about the aegis, do you?" I ask. "You still think he's crazy."

We reach the end of the drive. Daniel stops. "It has nothing to do with that." His chest heaves. "You're one of the Lost."

"Well," I say. "The way Ander Smith told the story wasn't exactly the way I heard it, and we don't call ourselves 'The Lost'." I use my dramatic voice, along with air quotes. "But I guess so."

"The Lost left New Lithisle because they refused genetic alterations. They believed it was a sin, an abomination."

"And?"

Daniel trembles. "I couldn't understand why the Prime Minister sent his guard after you. At first I thought maybe you were an imposter. I didn't care. I was almost glad, because then I knew I loved you whether you were Allarice's daughter or not. But this doesn't have anything to do with Allarice. The Prime Minister wants you because you're one of the Lost."

My heart stops. Daniel loves me. He said it. I tighten my grip on his hand. And something else about the Prime Minister and the Lost. "What did you say?"

"You're a threat to national security. Tens of millions of lives are at stake. I'm sorry, but this is bigger than we are. Just be honest with them. Tell them the truth about your father, and they shouldn't torture you."

"Torture me?"

Daniel's voice chokes. "You should turn yourself in to the Prime Minister's Guard."

CHAPTER NINETEEN
Poster Boy

I pull away from Daniel. "How can you think I'm a threat?"

"It's not you." Daniel reaches for me.

I step away.

"It's your father." Daniel's voice is earnest, full of concern. "And his contact. How do you know they aren't trying to cause a collapse, instead of prevent it?"

My face flushes. "Gilchrist isn't like that." I search my thoughts for evidence. "He's in jail facing treason because he wanted to save the aegis."

"So you admit at least some of the Lost want New Lithisle destroyed."

"No," I say. "They just don't want to interfere." Although, come to think of it, I don't know how much of a difference there is between wanting New Lithisle destroyed and letting it happen.

"I'm sorry," I say. "I made mistakes, but I don't want anything bad to happen to anyone, especially not you."

"I know." Daniel lifts his hand to my cheek. "But the information you have could mean the difference between life and death for everyone in New Lithisle."

"It's more than information." I take my controller and show him Gilchrist's file. "My father wrote a patch to fix the aegis. I think he was trying to get it to Grey Cat to be installed."

"Are you sure it's a fix?" asks Daniel.

I hesitate. "I haven't had time to go through the whole file, but—"

Daniel sighs. "You don't know."

"I'm almost sure. If I had a few hours and someone like Reg Denney to help I could figure it out."

"There's too much at stake. We need to go to the Guard. They have experts."

I throw my hands in the air. "There are no strophes experts left, besides my father. If you brought his file to the Guard they wouldn't know what to do with it. Ander Smith trusts Reg Denney. I think we should go to him."

Daniel doesn't answer. His gaze shifts to the thin, wispy clouds that pass overhead again and again. "There's a list of national employees on the network. If Ander Smith is right and there is a Reg Denney who works at the main aegis generator, I'm willing to try to find him first."

"Okay," I say.

Daniel turns on my controller. He runs a search. We scan through the alphabet until we find the ds.

Denney, Reginald, Aegis Main Generator, Environmental Services.

"What's Environmental Services?" I ask.

"He's a janitor," says Daniel. "Ander Smith's aegis expert cleans toilets and washes floors."

I stare at the list. "There has to be a mistake."

Daniel scrolls through a few more pages. "I'm afraid not." He tilts the controller to me. The display reads *Reg Denney, February Employee of the Month.* A thin man dressed in chocolate brown coveralls stands by a yellow rolling bucket, his hand on a mop.

"What now?" asks Daniel.

"I don't know," I say. "But just because Reg Denny works in environmental services doesn't mean he doesn't know what's going on. He could have access to classified documents at night, when no one is around."

"That seems doubtful."

"I still think he's our best option." I take the controller, flip back to Ander Smith's website and cue the aegis documentary to where I left off. "We need to at least watch this and see what Reg Denney has to say."

"All right." Daniel taps the screen. We watch as we walk.

On the clip, Reg Denney is dressed in a plaid flannel shirt. He has scruffy facial hair, grey, wiry eyebrows, and looks to be about Gilchrist's age. He explains much of what Ander Smith already told us, but with more detail. The aegis was put up in haste to enforce the emergency quarantine. Final coding was never finished, because the lead coder disappeared. Reg doesn't name him, but of course he's talking about Gilchrist. No one can enable the aegis to withstand the increased energy of the coming solar storms or install a shutoff, because the coding was written in strophes, a lost programming language. Numerous attempts to crack the code have failed.

The documentary ends with a plea for the people of New Lithisle to take action. I don't think that's going to happen. The copyright on the documentary is four years old.

"So what do you think?" I ask.

Daniel shrugs.

"We're going to find Reg Denney, right?" I nod my head and smile with exaggerated enthusiasm.

"I guess he sounded reasonable enough."

"Great." I stand on my tiptoes and hop a little to kiss his cheek.

Daniel doesn't even bend down to make kissing him easier.

I bit my lip, confused, but don't say anything. Now isn't the time to push him. We walk in silence for an hour. He doesn't hold my hand. He doesn't look at me. I walk closer to him. He moves away.

My gut turns. "You're bringing me to the Guard anyway, aren't you?"

"What?" Daniel looks at me with surprise. "No."

"But you're upset, about something."

Daniel takes a deep breath. He taps at my controller, then hands it back to me. On screen is a picture similar to the one I saw in his railcar. "That's your mom, right?"

"And my brothers."

"Brothers?" I knew about Ezekiel, but apparently there are more.

"The twins." Daniel scrolls down the screen. "Four of us in all."

Whenever I think of twins I picture the blond babies with chubby red cheeks I babysat every Monday for two years, while Mama washed their diapers and burp rags, but Daniel's brothers are dressed in long gowns with tasseled caps and flowing academic hoods. The clips must be from their graduation.

Daniel stands at least eight inches taller than any of his brothers. His hair is lighter, and his chest broader. They all have the same green eyes, but there is little else to indicate they are from the same family.

"So there it is," says Daniel.

I don't want to admit there's anything strange about the picture. "Your family seems nice."

Daniel takes the controller away. "But don't you see? It's obvious. I don't just have alterations. I'm the poster boy for them."

He moves to a new screen and shows me a list. *Hair, ML-216, Muscle*

Development, CH-414, Height, G-101. There are a least two dozen features listed.

Fin-head's words ring in my mind, *when alterations go right they make you a star.* Or, in Daniel's case, an elder.

I shove the controller back in his hand. "You didn't have to show me."

"Yes, I did. You need to know what I am."

I pull him to a stop, and take his hands in mine. The aegis moon reflects off the broken glass of the warehouse and lights his beautiful face.

"You're not a what." My voice trembles. "You're a who."

"I'm not so sure," says Daniel. "When my father found out Mum was expecting again, he mortgaged the house to do this to me. Every time they stuck a needle in her belly, I could have died, but he kept paying to have it done. And she let him." He laughs, short and soft. "Is that human? Sometimes I think the Lost had a point."

My chest aches. I wrap my arms around him. "You are the sweetest, kindest boy I know. You're not less-than-anything."

Daniel runs his hand through my hair. "I don't mean to complain. I really am grateful for the things I have, but I'd rather have nothing than lose you."

"I'm not going anywhere without you."

"No," says Daniel. "Not in New Lithisle. But when this is over you're going home, aren't you?"

I stiffen. Of course he's right.

Daniel pulls away. "It's okay. I deserve it. I wasn't supposed to have a girlfriend anyway."

I take his hand. "I'm glad you didn't listen." New Lithisle would be lost if it weren't for him, not that I'm willing to admit I was so selfish the only person I had planned on saving at first was me. "We're together for a reason. You have to believe that."

Daniel brings me close. "That's how I feel, like loving you is the best and most important thing I'll do my whole life."

My heart races. He said it again. He loves me. I lift my face to his. He leans to me. We kiss.

For a minute there's nothing in this world but him.

"So there's hope for us?" Daniel lips move against mine as he speaks.

There isn't. I smile, so I don't have to answer.

Daniel smiles back. "I knew it. You wouldn't kiss me the way you do if there weren't."

Apparently I would. I rest my head against his chest, so I don't have to look into his eyes. I shouldn't lead him on like this, but I don't know what else to do. I can't maneuver Vlas, the Guard, or any of this, on my own. And I do care for him.

At last we break from our embrace, and head toward downtown. Daniel smiles, holds my hand and doesn't let go.

CHAPTER TWENTY
Fire & Ice

Paper lanterns, red, yellow, and green, shine above us in the alley. I think I recognize some of the shops. I certainly remember the horrid smell.

"Are we going back to Mrs. Marissa's?"

"No," says Daniel. "In an emergency I'll stop there, but fortunately there are nicer places that can keep secrets."

"Nicer? How do you expect to pay?"

"I didn't give Mrs. Marissa everything." He flashes his cuff links.

"They're gold?"

"I never leave home without multiple forms of currency."

The alley clears. We're beyond the ghettos. We move to the main street. Couples, arm in arm, wander in and out of restaurants and nightclubs. For the first time I'm glad Daniel picked a dress for me. No one on the Vlas night scene gives us a second glance.

We stop in front of a stone hotel with tall, arched windows, a doorman, and bellboys.

"I can't take you through the lobby," says Daniel. "They've got dozens of recording eyes. I'll have to bring you around the side once I have our rooms."

"What am I supposed to do while you're gone?" I whine, but then bite my lip. Being with Daniel has made me such a baby. I've never been afraid to be by myself before. I'm used to it. I shrug, like I'm looking forward to a few minutes by myself. "I'll wait here. Take your time."

Daniel kisses me on the cheek. "I'll miss you too."

I smile.

Voices and footsteps come my way. I lean my nose to the glass and act way too interested in the necklaces, bracelets, and earrings on display. The edge of a coat brushes my leg. I press against the building.

There is a rap on the glass, from the inside. "Get away from the window," a woman with bright red lips shouts. I see her mouth move, but I can barely hear her speak. I step back.

"Watch where you're going, you clumsy—" A girl, maybe a few years older than me, looks in my face. Her mouth drops open.

I run. I don't know where, across the street, over cobblestone, into a bush. Short thorns scratch my legs and arms.

"I'm sure it was her." The girl must have followed me, because her voice is only a few feet away. "She's here in the park, somewhere."

"You must have been seeing things," says a young man. "No Daughter is going to be on the streets of Vlas by herself."

"It was one of them," she says, but her heels click as she walks away.

That was close. I stay in the bushes and wait until goosebumps appear on my arms, and I shiver.

"Amy?" Daniel calls.

I stumble out of the bush and wave. "Over here."

He runs to me. "Don't disappear like that."

I'm too tired to argue. "Sorry."

He leads me back across the street and into a nightclub. The music pounds in my ears. The lights flash. Couples gyrate on the dance floor. I stare.

"Keep going," says Daniel. He puts his arm around me and guides me through the crowd. We pass the bar, and men's and women's bathrooms. An exit leads to an empty hall inside the hotel.

"You're going to have to take the lift," says Daniel. "Our rooms are on the sixth floor."

"There have got to be stairs."

"Off the lobby, and you can't go there."

"What about an emergency staircase?"

"There's a rickety exterior fire escape."

"Sounds good."

"Just try the lift. I'll be right there. I promise nothing bad will happen."

"Where's the fire escape?"

Daniel brings me to the back of the building. The fire escape is a series of ladders and platforms. I reach for the first rung. I remember my dress. "You first," I say.

Daniel's cheeks flush red. "I wouldn't have looked."

The hotel entrance on the sixth floor is a window. We crawl through, and go to my room.

I gasp. Windows look over the park. There is an entry, sitting room and office. The bed has eight pillows. "What am I supposed to do with eight pillows?" I ask.

Daniel laughs. "Have a good night." But I can't tear my gaze from his. He leans to me. We kiss.

He pulls away. "I really should go," he says.

"Where will you be?"

"My suite is across the hall."

"So far?" I grip his arm.

"You'll be safe, I promise." He kisses me again. "I'll see you in the morning." The door to the sitting room shuts. A second door beyond the first opens and closes, as well.

I stand in the quiet. The stillness makes the hairs on the back of my neck stand up. Across the hall has never seemed so far away, but it is late, or early, depending on how you look at it, long past midnight. I need to get to sleep. I peel off the boots, slip out of the dress, grab two pillows and a blanket, and crawl under the bed. Daniel's arms felt safer, but this will have to do. I take out my controller, and piece together code from Gilchrist's file, until I can't keep my eyes open any longer.

Cars honk from the street below. I open my eyes, try to sit and bump my head. Duh. I'm under the bed. I wriggle out. A folded robe, tied with a pink ribbon, sits on the nightstand. I put it on. It's like the one Daniel had, only smaller, soft and scented like rose petals. I go to the window. The sun dips behind the Vlas skyline. Lights sparkle from the buildings.

I'd slept all day.

Daniel.

I hurry to the sitting room. He's at the table, his eyes fixed on his controller.

"Hey sleepy," says Daniel. "You had me worried. The maid couldn't find you. At first."

"Sorry," I say. "Did I miss anything?"

"Ezekiel was released after questioning, but they're still looking for us. They didn't bring in anyone else."

"What did they ask him?"

"About you, and where you'd been for sixteen years."

"Nothing about the aegis."

"No."

"Well, that's good," I say. "About your family. Right?"

"It is." Daniel pushes a loaf of heavy white bread toward me. "The room service here is great. Try the spinach artichoke dip."

I cut a thick slice and eat.

"I had the hotel stylist send you up some clothes, too." He points to a rack loaded with complete outfits, from casual, to business, to night.

"What am I supposed to do with all of those?"

Daniel grins. "Pick what you like, and send the rest back."

"Oh." I stuff down the bread and go to the clothes. A short, strapless dress in forget-me-not blue sparkles. The waist is wide and beaded. Strips of fabric flow over the skirt, short in front, but long in the back, like the tail of the bird. I hold it to Daniel. "I'd look great running to the aegis generator in this."

"You would," he says. "Put it on."

Something about his firm tone, like it's an order, makes me want to do it. I hang the dress back up. "We don't have time."

"Sure we do."

"What about Reg Denney? Shouldn't we be trying to get in touch with him?"

"I checked. He doesn't get off until midnight. We might as well relax a little, while we wait."

"Relax?"

Daniel's face flushes. "And maybe some other things."

My heart skips a beat. "Maybe."

Daniel jumps to his feet. His knee hits the table. It tilts. He steadies it. "I'll meet you on the balcony in ten minutes."

"Okay."

He smiles, his eyes wide.

I take the dress, and four-inch stilettos, to the bedroom. I shower, then comb my hair with my fingers. There is no blush or powder. I pinch my cheeks and smile.

The edges of my mouth sag.

I'm using him. When we kissed the first few times, I hadn't known what was going to happen, with Daniel or the aegis. Now I do. Some boys wouldn't mind if I kissed them and left. Daniel would.

I stall at the door. If I were a decent person, I'd tell him the truth. I'm leaving, maybe as soon as tomorrow, if things work out with Reg Denney. He can decide what he wants to do from there.

I take a deep breath and peek from the room. Daniel stands on the balcony in a black tuxedo. A soft piano melody floats from the courtyard below. He holds a red rose.

My heart swells. I don't want to be without him. Ever.

I shut the door. I can't do this.

There's a quiet knock.

I open it.

Daniel smiles. "Are you all right?"

I nod.

"May I have this dance?"

I should tell him we need to talk.

I give him my hand instead.

Daniel takes me in his arms. My heart flutters. He leads me to the balcony where we glide in slow circles over the inlaid stone. His sweet breath falls on my cheek. I lift my face to his, and ache with anticipation.

Daniel leans to me. His lips touch my ear. "Ezekiel was the one who sent me to meet you in Petrich."

I trip over my feet. "What?"

"He thought Elder Binyamin and Nasira were being short-sighted to only look at the reward money. He wanted a way to gain influence with you. When I left that morning, he said, 'Be yourself. Girls always fall in love with you.'"

I pull away. "Your brother set me up?"

"No," says Daniel. "Yes, but not all of it. I don't think Ezekiel expected me to fall in love with you."

I laugh like my head doesn't pound, and my heart doesn't break. "Who said anything about love?"

Daniel kisses my bare shoulder.

I tremble.

"Me, just now." Daniel draws me to him. "I love you Amy, and I wanted you to hear the truth from me. We're together now. My loyalties lie with you."

Longing floods me.

Daniel presses his lips to mine.

I'm lost in his embrace.

Mama says love can be a fiery volcano, or a steady glacier, but both move mountains. I'm not sure if what I feel is either.

"What if this can't last?" I whisper. My attempt at the truth is pitiful, but it's the best I can do.

Daniel kisses me again. "Don't worry. The way I feel about you isn't ever going to change."

CHAPTER TWENTY-ONE
Reg Denney

The notes from the piano fade. The beat from the nightclub pulses the air. Daniel holds me on the balcony. We watch the city sleep, and stir when it dreams.

In school we learned time and space are an illusion, that God lives in every moment and each moment lasts forever. Daniel is right. The way we feel about each other will never change, but our perfect place in time is almost over. If we find Reg Denney, and things work out as hoped, I'll leave for Petrich and home. I'll never see Daniel again.

But he'll be safe. That's what matters.

Daniel runs his hands down my shoulders. "You've got goosebumps. We should go where it's warm."

"We need to leave for the aegis generator. Isn't it about time?"

Daniel nods.

Inside I change into a navy fleece and jeans. I meet Daniel in the sitting room. He wears a long-sleeved white polo, khakis, and loafers.

"That's not exactly stakeout wear," I say. "You sort of glow." At least from the waist up.

"It's better to blend in than hide. You should probably wear something a little more out-on-the-town." He sifts through the clothes on the rack and pulls out black slacks and a blue silk shirt. "Wear it with the black pumps and pearls. You'll look great."

"You're quite the fashion expert."

"Well, I've had a stylist since I was eight. I caught on. You will too."

I hope not. "The blouse is beautiful, but I think I'm going to stick with comfy." I slip on a pair of canvas sneakers. I'm not walking to Old Lithisle in heels.

Daniel tries to talk me into taking the elevator again. We climb down the fire escape. We enter the park across from the hotel. Trees arch over the path. Dots of light float through the air. They glow, then fade.

I run and close my fingers around one. My skin pinches. I shake my hand.

"What are you doing?" asks Daniel.

"The firefly bit me," I say. "One has never bitten me before."

"Those aren't fireflies. They're from the aegis generator." He points. Beyond the park a beam of fire, like a molten tornado, swirls from the center of a concrete building and stretches to the aegis. The storm of fire cracks like thunder. Sparks fly.

Boom. Crash. Burn.

I dive to the ground and throw my arms over my head.

"The aegis is just dropping excess energy." Daniel takes my hand and pulls me to my feet. "They're harmless, so long as you don't go chasing them."

For now, but how much excess energy can the aegis drop?

We reach a chain-link fence topped with curls of razor wire. The barrier stands between us and a parking lot. There are spaces for a hundred cars. Less than a dozen are filled.

There are a few more minutes before Reg's shift ends. Daniel sits at the base of a tree and leans against the trunk. I sit next to him. There is another crack. More dots of light float, then fade. I press close to Daniel.

A door opens. A woman walks out. Her heels click on the sidewalk. She's followed by a group of men. I strain to see if Reg Denney is one of them.

"Is that him?" Daniel points to a man opening a car at the edge of the parking lot.

"I don't think so." I search the other men for plaid, as flannel is what Reg Denney wore during his interview with Ander Smith. He's probably in the coveralls tonight. "I'm not sure." I run to the fence anyway. "Mr. Denney, are you there? I need to talk to you."

Daniel pulls me back. "There are recording eyes all over that parking lot."

The men look our direction. They talk among themselves, then move on. I didn't think any of them was Reg Denney.

Daniel and I sit. A car's lights flick on. I shield my eyes. The engine roars. The wheels screech as it pulls away.

"Did someone else come out?" Daniel asks.

"I couldn't see." I scan the parking lot. "There's no one there now."

We watch the door. It doesn't open. Daniel puts his arm around me. I rest my head on his shoulder. Fifteen minutes pass, half an hour, forty-five minutes. My eyes close.

A hand clasps over my mouth.

I jerk awake.

"Shhh," Daniel whispers in my ear. He slides his hand from my face and points to the parking lot. A man in a plaid shirt stands at the back of a rusted green hatchback. He lifts a computer and places it on a wheeled cart.

"That's him!" I jump. Daniel pulls me to the ground. "Stay down."

"What is he doing?" I whisper.

Reg opens the door and rolls the cart inside the building.

"Something he doesn't want anyone to know about," says Daniel. "He shot out three recording eyes, came back with the car, and started to unload equipment."

I rise on one knee.

Daniel pulls me down. "He's got a gun. Now isn't the time or place to interrupt him."

Reg comes back out. He pushes the back of the hatchback down. It clicks shut. He climbs in the front seat, revs the engine, and drives away.

I tear myself from Daniel's grip. My feet pound over grass, then concrete. Taillights blink at a traffic light. The green hatchback turns right. I slide around the corner. The hatchback, blocks away, looks as small as a toy car. It turns left, and the street is empty.

"What part of he's got a gun didn't you understand?" Daniel jogs up from behind, breathing hard. "How am I supposed to keep you safe when you run off like that?"

"I have to talk to him." I anxiously scan the street for a car, a taxi, a bicycle, anything, but I don't know where Reg Denney went. Finding a ride to chase him isn't going to help now.

"I got the license off his car. We can find his home address."

"Oh." I feel so stupid. "Thanks."

Daniel sets the navigation on the network. We follow a yellow dot that bounces across the controller's display. The path leads back to the aegis generator, across the park to houses with porches and fenced backyards.

The green hatchback is parked in the drive of a tiny bungalow. The house is dark, and quiet. We crouch behind bushes. Daniel takes my hand. "Stay close."

He leads me to the drive. The car smells of burnt oil. The hood is still warm. The porch steps creak as we climb.

I peek in the window. Boxes, books, and magazines clutter the front room.

Daniel taps lightly on the door.

No light switches on. No footsteps approach.

"I don't think he's here." The hope that had buoyed me deflates.

"Where did he go?"

"He probably wasn't done at the aegis generator, but didn't want his car sitting in the lot all night. We should go back."

"I think it would be safer to wait here."

I look around the side of the house. A hammock hangs between two trees in the backyard. I imagine swinging in Daniel's warm arms. "All right."

Daniel wraps his fingers around the top of the fence. His right arm twitches, then drops to his side. He looks at me, his eyes wide. "Run." He topples to the ground.

I spin on my toes and sprint. I look over my shoulder. Daniel doesn't move. I stop. The light from the street shines on the mailbox. In the distance a horn honks. I hurry back, and roll him to his side. A thin grey dart dangles from his neck. I gasp.

"He'll be fine," says a woman. She stands at the end of the drive, dressed in thick-heeled boots and a long, black overcoat, her chin-length silver hair swept to the side. "We were worried he would fight back. We didn't want him to get hurt." A limousine pulls up behind her. "Put him in the car, and get me his controller."

Three men emerge from the shadows. They could be from the Guard, they have guns and are in uniform, but the Guard wore brown. These men are dressed in navy.

Two of them carry Daniel to the back of the limousine. The third retrieves Daniel's controller and hands it to the woman. She places it in front of a tire. "Drive."

The engine turns. There is the crunch of metal and plastic.

She lifts her hand. The car stops.

Daniel's controller is a clump of debris. There's only one copy of Gilchrist's file left, in my pocket.

"I'm sorry, I had to do it." Her voice is mother-like, steady and reassuring. "His brother was using it to track you."

I step backward, my heart pounding wildly.

"Please, don't run," she says. "I'm Grey Cat."

CHAPTER TWENTY-TWO
Grey Cat

The woman walks toward me, slow and controlled, the way I move when a mama goat has a new kid, and I don't want to spook her.

My legs tense. They want to run. I would, if Daniel weren't unconscious in the car.

"I'm the Deputy of Internal Security," she says. "Your father and I have been communicating for years."

She knows more than I put in the ad. "How can I be sure you're Grey Cat?"

She takes her controller, sets it on the drive, and kicks it toward me. The plastic case scrapes across the concrete. "Look."

I step forward. On the screen is a correspondence file. It's labeled *Gilchrist Ogilvie*. I open the first entry, addressed to *greycat40@vlas. net*, dated sixteen years ago. The year the aegis was completed, and I was born.

Dear Farren, it begins.

"You knew him before the pandemic?"

"Your mother and I were good friends."

"Which one?" I ask. Only Mama counts, as far as I'm concerned.

"Both," she says, a sly smile creeping across her face. "Didn't you know? Hannah and Allarice were tight."

Mama, and Allarice, knew each other? They were friends? I want to chuck the deputy's controller at her smirking face, but instead I scroll to Gilchrist's last entry. He writes the patch for the aegis is finished, but he's having problems uploading the large file.

I knew it.

"Come to the car," she says gravely, looking up and down the street. "You're not safe here. There are others who want you, and they have different methods and motives."

The Prime Minister's Guard. At least the deputy came with tranquilizer darts instead of bullets. I nod, and follow.

Daniel lies on the back seat. I sit on the floor by him, his face inches from mine. I breathe his breath, slow and even.

"You look more like your mother than your sisters." She strokes my hair. "They've all gone blond, the way she did, at the end."

I pull away. "They're not my sisters."

"Of course," she says. "You've never met them."

The limousine rolls toward the tall buildings at city center.

Daniel's head flops. Blood drips from where the dart hung in his neck. I wipe it away. More blood drips. I wipe again.

"You seem quite attached." The deputy raises an eyebrow. "To your pet."

I stiffen. A pet? But it could be a term of endearment. I shouldn't overreact. "He's been very helpful."

The deputy smiles again. "I'm sure he has." She laughs. "And quite a handsome helper at that."

My cheeks flush. I'm not sure if it's anger, or embarrassment.

"I'm sorry. I didn't mean to make you uncomfortable." She clears her throat. "Why don't you tell me how you got into New Lithisle?"

I put my hand to my chest. The magamp is still safe. "Gilchrist pushed me through."

"I see." The deputy lifts her gaze from the faint lump under my shirt.

She saw it. I pull my knees to my chest, and wrap my arms around them.

The deputy holds out her hand. "Give it to me."

I freeze.

"Not the magamp, the file your father was trying to send me."

I don't know which is worse. "Now?"

"There's no reason to delay."

I exhale, and pull my controller from my pocket. My hand shakes. She pulls it from my grasp.

My stomach drops. "Let me send you a copy."

"No." She taps and scrolls. "It's best I have the original."

"Gilchrist has the original." I reach for the controller. My fingers glide through air.

She slips my controller into her pocket. "The file is my responsibility now. You did an excellent job getting it to me, but your work is done. It's time for you to go home."

My heart stops. "Home?"

"You were never supposed to be in this far. I'm taking you to the wall as soon as we're done here."

That was the plan, to leave once the file was taken care of, but I was going to have a few more days with Daniel. I want to say good bye. "What about Daniel?"

"His brother gave us your location in exchange for his immediate, safe return."

"Immediate?"

"He belongs here. He's not a stray puppy you can bring home and neuter."

Heat rises in my neck. Daniel, a dog. I shift my back to the deputy, but I know Daniel and I can't be together. A quick, clean break would be best. This way he'll blame it on the deputy, and not me.

The limousine turns and dips into an underground parking garage. *New Lithisle Intelligence Agency* is painted in big block letters on the concrete. We stop in front of a bank of elevators.

The deputy slides over the seat. "This is our stop. You can say good bye." She opens the door and puts her foot to the pavement. "You have until he wakes." The door slams. The deputy takes a smoke from a slim, silver case, puts it to her lips, then lights it.

I lean my forehead to Daniel's.

His eyelids flicker.

My heart aches. "Don't wake," I whisper, willing the moment to last.

His eyes open anyway. "I thought I told you to run."

"She's Gilchrist's contact."

Daniel props himself on his elbow, his eyes to the window. "The Prime Minister's Deputy of Internal Security?"

"I gave her my father's file. She's going to take care of it."

"Thank God." Daniel kisses me, soft, and too quick. "Now we can concentrate on you. I think we should go back to the Barracuda. We need the time."

"We can't. The deputy is sending you to your brother, and me home."

"Home?" Daniel looks around the cab then whispers. "Like way-out-there home?"

"Yes."

"Why would she send you away? They've been looking for you for years."

There's a tap on the window. The deputy's lips move, *Say goodbye.*

Daniel grips my hand. "Come back into New Lithisle, and go to the Barracuda. I'll find you there."

"I can't."

"You'll figure out a way. I'll come as soon as I can."

I have to tell him the truth. Now. "You don't understand."

"No," says Daniel. "God brought us together. The deputy can't keep us apart."

But the decision isn't hers, it's mine.

The deputy, flanked by soldiers, opens the door. "Time for him to leave," she says.

Daniel's lips brush against my ear. "Promise you'll come back in."

I throw my arms around him, and hold him tight. "I'm sorry, Daniel. I'll never forget you."

The deputy pulls me away. I'm in the garage. The door slams, and my reflection passes as the limousine pulls away.

My heart feels like it's been torn from my chest, even though I know I should be glad. Things have turned out better than I could have ever hoped. Gilchrist's contact found me. She has the file he wanted her to have, and Daniel will be safe.

Tears run down my cheeks anyway.

CHAPTER TWENTY-THREE
Falling

The limousine turns onto the street, and Daniel is gone. A sudden chill fills the garage. I'm a pebble tossed by the lake, carried in the current, sinking. *Daniel will be safe*, I remind myself. *That's what matters.*

The deputy walks to the elevators. The doors slide open. "Hurry. We don't have all night."

The car is no bigger than the chicken coop, dark and stale. The deputy steps inside. The floor shudders.

"Are there stairs?" I ask.

"I'm not going to walk four flights," she says.

I don't move.

The deputy rolls her eyes. "Get her."

Soldiers grab my arms. My feet swing. They drop me to the elevator floor.

I'm falling. I curl in a ball. I'm going to die.

"The melodrama is unnecessary," says the deputy. "Surely you've ridden in one before."

I don't answer, but I have. The first scavenging trip I'd taken with Gilchrist had been to an abandoned city on the southern great lake. Our first, and last, stop had been to the old genetic research center. Broken glass, chunks of concrete, and pieces of furniture had littered the skyscraper's lobby. Gilchrist had pried the elevator doors open with a length of rebar.

"Are you sure this is safe?" I'd asked.

"The cables are thicker than my arm," said Gilchrist. "They're fine." He popped a panel, pulled out a few wires, twisted the ends, and stuck them into his controller. A grid of numbered buttons lit up. "Hang on."

The elevator groaned and shook. I held tight to the metal bar at my side. The car rose. My heart raced. I couldn't breathe.

"Relax," said Gilchrist. "I've done this a million times."

I loosened my grip. An arrow above the door pointed to *2, 5, 16, 22.* I let go of the metal bar.

The car wailed, then jerked. My feet flew in the air. My head slammed into the wall. Gilchrist lay across from me, his eyes closed, blood in his hair. His controller dangled above me. I pushed myself to the wall and stretched. My fingers couldn't reach.

The car dropped again.

I'd been sure we were going to die.

"We're here," says the deputy.

I look up. The deputy holds the door open. I crawl, and don't stand until the carpet is rough beneath my hands.

The deputy takes quick steps down a long hall. I stumble, then run to keep up. We stop at a plain white door. She places her hand on a flat screen. Lights flash. The door opens. Inside is an office suite, rooms with desks, tables, and chairs. The soldiers take positions outside the door, but the deputy and I go in.

She pulls a chair from a conference table, and motions for me to sit. "My contact from Old Lithisle will be in touch with us shortly. He has a few questions, then you'll be able to go to bed."

My heart leaps. "Is it Gilchrist? Is he still in jail?"

"How do you know about that?"

I shut my mouth. Suzanne's father told me the night I saw him in the wilds, but I'm not going to tell her.

The deputy sighs. "He hasn't been brought to trial yet, if that's what you mean, but your father isn't my only contact in Old Lithisle."

Relief floods me. Gilchrist is all right, for now. "Committee Member Harris will be signaling, then?"

"Why do you suggest him?" The deputy's tone is sharp.

A chill runs down my spine. "He's been my handler my whole life." My answer is generic, and true. It shouldn't implicate him in...what? The deputy is Gilchrist's contact. She's on our side.

A screen on the wall glows blue. "Amy, Amy," says Committee Member Trumble, slow and heavy. The display blinks, then fills with his round, ruddy face. "You've always been such a good girl, but now I'm not sure we can trust you."

The blood drains from my face. Committee Member Trumble? The truth of the situation sinks in. Gilchrist's New Lithisle contact is nothing more than a Committee plant.

"What did I do?" I should be brave, stand up to him, but instead I default to my usual defense. Play innocent. Say what he wants to hear. Big, wide baby-goat eyes.

"You committed treason," says Committee Member Trumble. "Along with your father."

My palms sweat. "I was only trying to get home."

Committee Member Trumble's eyes narrow. "Do you really expect me to believe that?"

I cringe. Not really. "I'm sorry. I, I ..." *I what?* Didn't mean to get caught? Because that about sums it up.

"Don't be so hard on her," says the deputy. "She couldn't have known what was in the file."

But she must know. *What was Gilchrist planning?* Asking might confirm to them I'm a sympathizer. There would be no tip-toeing my way back to welcome in Old Lithisle. I have to try.

"So what was in the file?" I ask, as nonchalantly as possible. "From the coding I guessed it had something to do with the aegis, but I couldn't figure out if Gilchrist was trying to shut it down, save it, or speed the collapse along."

"Interesting." The deputy tilts her head. "He wrote a patch to keep the aegis from collapsing."

Ander Smith was right.

"And that's treason?" I grip the edge of the table so tight my knuckles blanch. "Just asking. No strong opinion here." I hold my breath, and hope they don't see through my act.

"He was trying to meddle in the realm of the Almighty." Committee Member Trumble rests the tips of his fingers together. "God is judge, not man."

"Judge?" I say. "I'm not sure I understand. God takes no account of goats and dogs. He only judges people, with souls."

Committee Member Trumble smiles, but his right eye twitches. "Maybe my choice of words wasn't the best."

But he said exactly what he meant.

"Then they can live," I say. "So long as they stay in the aegis. Blood will never mingle."

"We tried that," says the deputy. "That's why I stayed behind sixteen years ago, to oversee that exact arrangement. We wanted to let them live out their natural lives."

"But they have refused the sterilization procedures," says Committee Member Trumble. "They've been breeding like rodents."

"And a new petition to explore the Wilds lands on my desk every week," says the deputy. "I can't control it anymore."

Technically, I agree with her, but heat rises in my neck. "So this has been a zoo? And you're the keeper?" I practically spit the bitter words from my mouth.

"That's enough from you," says Committee Member Trumble. "Apologize, young lady, or I'll charge you with sedition."

"So now it's illegal to ask questions?" My voice is a little louder than I intended it to be.

"When it's you asking them!" He slams his fist on his desk. "You are your mother's daughter, aren't you?"

"Enough." The deputy holds up her hand. "Stop before either of you says anything else you'll regret."

"She's already said too much," says Committee Member Trumble. "On their side, when they were the ones who sent us outside the aegis to die."

But Ander Smith and Daniel said Allarice never intended for them to die. Her plan had been to bring them back in, humbled and compliant. Did Committee Member Trumble know that? She was trying to force them to get alterations, but his wanting the aegis to collapse takes on a whole new meaning. He may be seeking purity of the human race, but there's something else he wants just as much. Revenge.

The deputy reaches into her pocket. My controller is only an arm's length away. I glance over my shoulder. The soldiers wait in the hall. Committee Member Trumble can't do anything but watch from the screen. In a minute I could send the file to Ander Smith.

I hesitate. I'll never be able to go home again.

I don't care.

I dive across the table, and grab the deputy's arm.

My body flips. My head cracks on the floor. The room whirls. The deputy's boot is on my neck.

"That's it," Committee Member Trumble bellows. "She's made her choice. Lock her up."

"She's a child," says the deputy. "And you can't kill both her and her father. There will be no one left who knows strophes."

"We'll live without it." He points his shaking finger at me. "I warned them from the day you were born you would be trouble, Seventh Daughter of Allarice. You are as proud and arrogant as your mother, and because of it you will share her fate."

His words explode in my gut like shrapnel. "No. I'm not anything like her."

"You have been weighed in the balance and found wanting," he says. "You will die with the animals you love so much."

"Please think about—" says the deputy.

"Do it!" he screams.

There is a long silence.

She sighs. "All right."

"Pray for forgiveness, Amy," says Committee Member Trumble. "Perhaps in death, God will have mercy on your soul."

"You're the one who will need forgiveness," I yell, but the screen flashes to blue, then fades to black.

He's gone.

The deputy lifts her foot.

I gasp. "They're going to kill Gilchrist?"

"They haven't tried him yet." She steps back, her tone threatening. "But things aren't looking so good, for either of you."

The floor has dropped from beneath me again, but this time I'm not in an elevator with emergency brakes. There will be no gentle stop. Gilchrist and I are going to die, and so is everyone in New Lithisle.

CHAPTER TWENTY-FOUR
Purged

Cold air blows from the vent. I shiver on the floor.

God, forgive me.

How could I have not seen New Lithisle's humanity sooner? Tasted it in Daniel's kiss, heard it in Ruth's laughter, felt it in little baby LeAnne's soft, smooth arms. Would I have worked harder to figure out what Gilchrist's file was? Gotten it installed? The aegis would be fixed, and Daniel safe.

The deputy stands at the door, her hand on the knob. "If you want to sleep on the floor, I suppose I can have the soldiers watch you here, but there is a bedroom down the hall."

"I thought you were going to lock me up."

"Do you want me to bring you to the cells in the basement?"

"No."

"Then come."

The deputy leads the soldiers and me down another hall, past a dozen doors to a second suite. This one has a kitchen, sofa and chairs. She brings me to a bedroom. "The soldiers will be stationed in the great room. You would have been under their care regardless, for your safety, but I want you to know I have no intention of locking you up, or leaving you to die."

"But Committee Member Trumble—"

"He's angry, but the day will come when he will be very glad I didn't dispose of you."

Strophes.

"I'm not a programmer." I narrow my eyes. "Or an engineer." And for them, I never will be.

"You could be. Don't think we haven't kept an eye on your math and science scores." She pulls the covers down on the bed and plumps the pillows. "And don't let anyone use your mother to insult you. She didn't intend to create monsters. She only wanted to save lives."

"You don't have to defend her."

"Apparently I do." The deputy walks to the door. "Good night. I'll come for you in the morning."

I turn off the lights and crawl in bed.

You'll share your mother's fate, Committee Member Trumble said, but I'll never end up like her.

"I won't," I whisper to myself, but I fall asleep and dream I'm in the bathroom of a grand mansion. Somehow I know it belongs to the Prime Minister, but when I look in the mirror, I'm not me. I'm Allarice. A gun is clasped tight in my hand.

I scream.

I've heard the story of how Allarice killed herself a dozen times, but no matter how I try, I can't control her movements, my movements, as she presses the muzzle of the gun to her gut.

There is a loud explosion, then silence. Awful silence. I slump. Bright red blood pools beneath me on the white marble floor.

I force myself awake.

My shirt is soaked with sweat. My heart pounds.

Committee Member Trumble had preached from the pulpit that Allarice couldn't handle the guilt, but Gilchrist hadn't blamed her. He told me he thought she'd never been able to reconcile what she'd always been taught with what she'd come to believe.

She only wanted to save lives, the deputy had said.

I roll to my side. Allarice shouldn't have mixed animal and people genes, but she did. Nothing can change the past, but the people of New Lithisle have souls, and letting them die now would be as bad as killing them.

Light seeps around the long dark curtains that flow from ceiling to floor. Blue numbers glow on the clock, 7:37 AM.

There's a loud knock. The door swings open.

"The doctor will be here any minute," says the deputy. "Clean up."

"You didn't say anything about a doctor last night."

"I've spoken with Committee Member Trumble. He has relented, as I knew he would. But he's demanding a health clearance. Now hurry."

They must be worried I'll bring back a deadly disease. I go to the bath, brush my hair and splash water on my face.

"He's here," the deputy calls.

A small man stands at the kitchen table. He is smooth skinned and dark-haired with bushy black eyebrows. He smiles and bows. His stethoscope dangles over his long, white jacket. "Please sit."

He listens to my heart and lungs. He looks in my eyes and ears. He presses on my stomach. "She appears to be in excellent health."

"Then give her the shot."

I jump from the chair. "I don't need any shots."

The doctor freezes over his open bag. His eyes turn to the deputy.

She pushes me down. "You have to get it if you want to go home." She tilts her head to the doctor. "Don't stand there. Give it to her."

He takes out a needle and vial.

"What is it?" I ask.

"A hormone to start your monthly cycle," he says.

"My cycles are fine." I pull, but the deputy's grip tightens.

A needle sinks into my arm. The doctor injects yellow fluid. The spot where the shot went in burns. I rub until the pain stops.

The deputy lets go. "I'm sorry, but this sort of thing is best done sooner rather than later."

"What sort of thing?" I ask, but as soon as I say it, I know. Heat rises in my neck. There's no way I could be with child, Daniel and I didn't do anything, but they are such hypocrites. They won't let Suzanne, me, or any of the girls attend university. They tell us it's our duty to replenish the devastated population, be fruitful and multiply, but my child wouldn't be good enough for them if Daniel were the father.

The deputy turns to the doctor. "Thank you. You may go."

He smiles again, clutches his bag, then hurries out.

"As helpful as your little boyfriend may have been, he's one of the most contaminated specimens in New Lithisle."

"Daniel isn't a specimen."

"Call him what you want. We couldn't take the chance of any of his genetic material making it beyond the wall."

I want to yell at her, but my stomach cramps. I double over. I run to the bath. Blood drips down my legs. I open the vanity. The shelves are empty.

The deputy is at the door. "You need sanitary supplies. I should have thought of that. I'll have some sent up." She taps on her controller and walks away.

I wrap a towel around my hips and lie in the tub. The cramps grow stronger. There is more blood. I hold my gut and cry.

Soles squeak on the floor. The deputy is back.

"Am I ever going to be able to have children?" I ask.

She hands me a bag. "Of course. You were given a very low dose, but you will be uncomfortable for a few days."

I'm not uncomfortable. I'm in misery.

I open the bag. There is a bottle of pills, PJs, underwear, and pads.

"Take two of the pills now and again in four hours," says the deputy. "They'll help with the pain. Change when you're up to it, and I'll get your things washed."

The pills look like the white caplets Mama gives me when I have a fever. I take them, then crawl back in the tub and pray for the pain to end. I huddle under another towel and close my eyes.

I inhale Daniel's scent. His mouth covers mine. I open my eyes. I'm home, in my loft, snuggled beneath my comforter. "You found me?" I say. "Way out here?"

He strokes my cheek. "I told you I would." He kisses me again. "I'm an excellent tracker."

"You must be." I smile and run my hands through his hair. My fingertips graze a strap of leather around his neck. "What's this?"

"My collar," says Daniel. "The deputy told me I had to keep it on if I wanted to come home with you." He lifts his head and shows me the engraved brass tag. *My name is Daniel. I belong to Amy.*

He scratches behind his ear. "I have a rabies tag too. I told her I was up to date on my immunizations, but she made me get another shot anyway." He crawls to the foot of the bed, curls on his side and rests his chin on his hands. "Good night, my love."

"What are you doing?"

"I can spend the night here, can't I?"

"I suppose, but that's where Posey usually sleeps."

"Who's she?"

"My cat."

"Cat?" Daniel growls. Posey leaps on the bed. Daniel jumps at her.

They tear to the floor and scamper down the ladder.

I wake. I can't breathe. Daniel doesn't act like that. Not really, but is he part dog? He could be. He showed me his long list of alterations, and the deputy called him one of the most polluted specimens in all of New Lithisle.

Daniel isn't a specimen.

He's not.

But he's not like me either.

I hold my gut, stand and turn on the shower. Cool water runs over my face and drips from my hair down my chest and back. Blood, tears and water pool at my feet.

CHAPTER TWENTY-FIVE
The Elite

I sit on the edge of the bed. My head spins. I grab the corner post and pull myself to my feet. I totter to the bath. The little white pills the deputy gave me weren't the same as the ones Mama's given me back home. I've hardly been able to move for hours. At least the deputy was right about the pain. I'm numb.

I leave the bath. Light streams across the floor. I squint. The deputy stands at the great room door. My clothes, clean and folded, are in her hands. "Dress. We'll be leaving shortly."

I step toward the deputy. I sway, and sink to the floor.

"I let you rest all day. The others are already in Petrich. We need to be there by night."

"Others?"

The deputy tosses the clothes to me. They scatter. "Be ready in ten minutes."

Stupid pills. We're leaving for Petrich, and I spent the day asleep instead of finding my controller, and getting back to Daniel.

I put on my bra, secure the magamp and slip on my shirt. I try to stand. I wobble. I lie on the floor, pull off the PJ bottoms, and wriggle into the jeans. That will have to do.

There's a knock. The door swings open. A curly tussle of red hair frames a child's face. She's not alone. The girl behind her is a little taller and fuller. Her hair is dark. Smudges of dye stain her hairline.

"Gramma told us to help you get ready," says the older girl.

"I'm fine," I say.

"You're not packed." She picks up the PJs and goes to the bath.

The redhead climbs on the bed and bounces. "I'm Sadie. My sister is Mira."

"Who's your Gramma?"

"The Prime Minister's Deputy of Internal Security."

Of course. "I'm Amy," I say.

"We know who you are." Mira carries the white bag from the bath.

Sadie stops bouncing. "Gramma said you're from Old Lithisle, that you've been through the wall before. Is that true?"

"Gramma doesn't lie," says Mira.

"I am," I say. "Why do you ask?"

"Don't answer." Mira shoves her sister.

Sadie falls on the pillows. "Gramma said people live out there, that it's not really poisonous."

"I told Gramma she couldn't trust you," says Mira.

"But I'm the adorable one." Sadie rests her hands on her hips and taps her toe.

My controller.

"I have tons of clips from home," I say, smiling wide. "I could show you."

Sadie leaps off the bed. "I want to see clips!"

I reach into my pocket. I dig and poke. "Oh no. I forgot. Your Gramma borrowed my controller. I'm so sorry. Maybe some other time."

"I could ask Gramma for it," says Sadie.

"Please don't bother her," I say. "She's so busy." I pause. "But it is mine. If you just found it, you could bring it back to me."

Mira takes Sadie by the wrist. "You are so gullible. Gramma didn't borrow her controller, she took it."

Little brat. "Her taking it from me doesn't change the fact it's mine."

"What's yours?" The deputy pushes the door open.

"She was trying to trick Sadie into getting her controller back," says Mira.

"She couldn't have fooled me," says Sadie. "I was only being nice. You told us she needed to like us."

"Girls, you may go."

"Aren't you going to yell at her?" asks Mira.

"Mira."

Sadie smirks and runs to the great room. Mira sulks after her.

"I know you have a tender heart," says the deputy. "I'm counting on it, but there is no perfect solution to this problem."

"Perfect shouldn't be the enemy of good," I say.

"I know Daniel and the others look human. They act human. It can be very confusing, but they aren't."

I press my lips together.

"It's not like I want everyone in New Lithisle to die." The deputy turns her face and discretely wipes away a stray tear. "For sixteen years I tried to end this humanely, but I've come to accept what's going to happen is the most merciful thing that can."

"Genocide is merciful?"

"They're not an intended species. Their deaths can't even be considered extinction."

"Prove to me they aren't human."

"You know what the Writings say."

I do. Diverse kinds are not to mingle, but we're not even supposed to wear a garment of mixed fibers. I'm not as convinced as I was in religion class. My polyester-cotton hoodie isn't evil. I don't understand why the Committee focused on part of the writ, but not the rest of it. "Daniel isn't an abomination," I say, holding my chin high.

"Maybe not, but he doesn't have a soul." Her tone harshens. "Unlike you."

"What is that supposed to mean?"

"When Daniel dies he won't be judged, he'll be at peace, as if he never was, but if you insist on interfering, God's plans will still be accomplished, but you will die and spend eternity in the pit of fire." She holds her hand to me. "I am trying to save you, Amy. I don't want you to end up like your mother."

I see red in the corner of my eye. White towels, stained with blood, lie on the bathroom floor, the way they must have the night Allarice took her life. My gut cramps. I won't end up like her. I take the deputy's hand.

She pulls me to my feet. "Come to the car."

Mira and Sadie join us in the great room. A woman leans against Mira. She has the same long, slim figure as the deputy, and red hair like Sadie. She must be the girls' mother. Her dry, cracked lips hang open. Mira leads her toward the door. The woman can barely shuffle.

The deputy lets a soldier walk with me down the stairs.

Sadie comes with us. "Do you like me?" Her words echo down the bare stairwell.

"Sure."

"Do you like Mira?"

"I don't dislike your sister."

She puts her hand in mine and smiles. "Good."

The aegis moon is in the sky when we reach Petrich. I stand at the window overlooking the city. From our series of suites I see the mission. I look to the ridge, and the road to the Barracuda. Will Daniel still come, even though I told him I wouldn't meet him?

"The constellations are beautiful," says the deputy. "Aren't they?"

Not especially. One is particularly distasteful. "When will I get my controller back?"

"I thought you'd decided against heroics."

"I had hundreds of clips on it, of deer, bear, wolves, even a cougar. It took me years to get them all. I want them back." I'm careful to not mention the boar. I don't want to sound too liberal.

"Your controller is evidence."

"You mean Gilchrist's file is evidence."

That must mean she still has it.

"You won't be getting it back." She pulls the curtains shut. "Go to bed. We go through the wall tomorrow."

"We?"

"Those of us left in New Lithisle without alterations."

My gut churns. Ander Smith was right, again. Mount Paul was a distraction, and anyone who runs for safety to its bunkers will end up dead.

CHAPTER TWENTY-SIX

Evacuation

The great room is loud with voices, like the deputy held a party and forgot to invite me. I open my bedroom door a crack. Seventy, maybe eighty men, women, and children mill about the room. Except for the occasional child who laughs, their faces are taut and grim. They're dressed in canvas pants, long skirts and overcoats. They clutch bags and suitcases.

The elite are ready to leave.

I sat up most of the night waiting for a chance to look for my controller, but the suite had gone from quiet with a few soldiers, to this. I'll never get it back.

No.

I can't think that way. I'll find it. I have to.

Pain shoots through my gut. I double over. A glass of water sits on the nightstand beside two pills. The deputy had taken them from the bottle and left them there last night, had told me I wouldn't be able to handle the journey home without them.

That's why I didn't take them. Without the pills I care.

The smell of cilantro and cumin wafts into the room. Sadie slips in after it. She carries a fat burrito on a bright blue plate. "Are you hungry?"

"Very." My stomach hurts, but I haven't eaten since the bread with Daniel. Was it really only a day and a half ago? I bite off a mouthful of burrito and chew. "When are we leaving?"

Sadie sits close to me on the bed. "They've started, but Gramma says you have to stay here until everyone else is gone."

"Good." I don't want to meet any of the others anyway.

I finish the burrito. Sadie takes the plate to the kitchen. A few minutes later she returns, Mira in tow.

Mira looks anxiously over her shoulder. "It's time to go." She gestures for me to follow.

The suite outside the bedroom is empty. There isn't a single soldier in sight.

"Where's the deputy?" I ask.

"She's downstairs," says Mira.

I lean to the window. A bus waits by the curb. Bags and suitcases are being loaded into the storage bins. There are no soldiers.

Sadie takes my hand. "We'll go down the stairs with you."

Mira, Sadie, and I make our way down the hall, to the stairwell, then the first floor. No one follows. No one watches.

I don't have my controller, or Gilchrist's file, but I can leave. I might not get another chance. At least Daniel and I could escape with the magamp. If I end up in an Old Lithisle jail cell, I won't be able to help anyone.

I hold my gut. "I forgot to take my pills. Why don't you two go ahead?"

"Don't leave us." Sadie squeezes my hand tight.

"The door is locked anyway," says Mira.

"I should go to the bath before we leave." I point to a door with a sign that reads *Women's*. "Go ahead without me."

Sadie's eyes well. "Are you trying to dump us too?"

Shoot, she can be as cute as a baby goat.

"No." I stoop to Sadie's height. "I'm fine. I can hold it."

I shouldn't give up on finding my controller so easily, anyway.

The deputy meets us at the door. "Quickly."

I walk by her side. She shoves Sadie and Mira behind us. We pass the deputy's limousine, and stop at the back of the bus. The deputy looks left, than right. She pushes Sadie and Mira forward. They scramble over bags into the back of the storage bin.

Mira's hair is dyed. What color is it, really?

She's altered. Sadie must be too, and the deputy is using me to sneak them out of New Lithisle.

My jaw drops. "You have got to be kidding."

"I lost their paperwork. I didn't want to make a scene."

"You're lying."

The deputy's air of confidence falls away. "You're the only one who can get them through. Help me, and I'll help you."

"Promise you'll get me my controller back." I lower my voice and narrow my eyes.

"After the trial. I will."

"Now." I hold out my hand.

"Committee Member Trumble didn't trust me with the file any more than he trusted you. I haven't seen it since yesterday."

"Who has it?"

The bus rocks, like the driver has taken off the brake. "We don't have time to argue," says the deputy.

"You should have told me what was going on."

Panic fills the deputy's eyes. "Please. I've already made arrangements to have the girls taken care of. They'll never pass on any animal genes, and you and your magamp are my only hope of getting them through the wall."

Taken care of. Spayed, like kittens. That's what she'd said about Daniel. *He's not a puppy you can bring home and neuter.*

"I'll do it," I say, "But not for you. For them." I don't want Sadie and Mira to die, or be separated from their family.

I follow the girls into the belly of the bus. The deputy shuts the gate. A sliver of light shines from the floor. Diesel fumes rise to my nose.

A small hand wraps around mine in the dark.

I pull Sadie to me and hold her tight. The engine roars and the wheels grind as we pull away.

By the time the bus stops, Sadie isn't the only one pressed against me. Even with the three of us huddled together, we shiver.

"How are we supposed to get out?" I ask.

"Gramma didn't say."

I feel for a latch.

"We should wait," says Mira.

"Do you want someone besides your Gramma to find us?" I ask.

There is no answer.

I find a handle. I pull. The gate pops. We're in the Borderlands, by the Barracuda village, on the circle drive outside the welcome center.

"Follow me," I say. I hold the gate up. Mira and Sadie slink out. I grab Sadie's hand and run. Broken glass clinks beneath our feet. I dash around corners. We reach the break room. I peek out the window. A line of terrariders idles on the path to the aegis.

"We'll wait here," I say. "If anyone comes we'll hide in the basement."

I see a spot of brown plush under the kitchen table. The toy has white tusks and tufts of fur on the tips of its ears. I crawl and bring it to Sadie.

I grunt like a wild boar. "Isn't he cute?"

Sadie wipes tears from her eyes. "No."

"No?" I cuddle him then put him in Sadie's arms. "He's adorable."

Mira bats him away. "He's unclean."

Pig people calling a pig unclean. I've heard everything. "He's polyester." I pick him up and tie him to my belt. Maybe little baby LeAnne will like him.

"You are like your mother." Mira sticks her nose in the air, like she's smelled something foul.

Me. Maybe I am like my mother. Maybe that's not all bad. "You can be glad for it," I say. "If I weren't a sympathizer, I'd leave you here to die."

Mira scowls, but doesn't answer.

One by one the terrariders are loaded. One by one they take off into the woods. There are none left.

Mira, Sadie and I go back to the bus. No one is left. I reach into the deputy's limousine, and pull bottles of water from the mini-fridge.

"Let's go," I say.

"Where?" asks Sadie.

"We're going to have to walk."

"Is that what Gramma told you to do?" asks Mira.

"She didn't tell me anything, so you're just going to have to listen to me."

We walk on the paved path until it becomes dirt. We enter the pine and continue for at least a mile. Sadie whimpers. I put her on my back. We keep walking.

The hum of a terrarider sounds ahead of us. The rumble of the engine grows louder. I pull Mira into the trees.

"It's Gramma," she says. "She's come for us."

"What if it isn't?" I ask.

Mira yanks her hand from my grasp. She runs onto the trail.

The terrariders stops.

"Where is your sister?" asks the deputy.

"Here." I come to the trail. Sadie wriggles off my back. She runs into her grandmother's arms.

"Where did you go?" The deputy's eyes flash with anger.

"You didn't tell me what to do. I made sure no one found us."

"You should have waited."

"I told her to," says Mira.

"Not that it matters now," says the deputy. "Climb on."

I don't move.

"We're already behind," says the deputy. "Hurry."

"I'll bring your granddaughters through the wall, if you give me my controller back."

The deputy shakes her head. "I already told you I don't have it."

"Who does?"

"I'm saving my daughter and granddaughters. It's the best I can do." Her voice softens. "There was never any guarantee the file would work."

"Gilchrist thought it would."

"And he's never been wrong?" She raises an eyebrow.

I hesitate. She's right about that. "What's the plan?"

"They're evacuating us by helicopter. Take the girls in south of the crossing. Wait in the woods until everyone is boarded. Bring them onto helicopter six. I'll take care of them from there."

"How am I supposed to get both of them through the wall?"

"You've done it before, with the boy."

"He passed out," I say. "And I pass out coming in."

The deputy takes out her controller. "Then the magamp's not adjusted properly." She taps. "There. So long as they are both in physical contact with your bare skin, you should all get through safely."

"What did you just do?"

"Remotely log into your magamp."

"Since when have you been doing that?"

"I had to make sure it was charged and ready to go." The deputy sits in the driver's seat. The girls wrap their arms around her.

I sit on the back and grip the roll bar. The terrarider bounces through the pine. We pass the junction. Long before the trees gnarl the deputy stops. "I'll meet you on the other side."

Sadie and Mira don't move.

The deputy pulls from their embrace. "Girls, it's time."

Mira climbs down. Sadie stays put. She looks at me with expectant eyes.

"Hop on," I say. She launches off the terrarider and onto my back.

"I'll get you back to her," I say.

"I know," says Sadie.

The terrarider turns the corner. We move south, off the trail. I'm not sure how far I have to go to avoid detection, but I don't remember the clearing by the aegis being very big.

We hear the evacuation before we see it. Helicopter blades pound the air. We emerge beyond the trees. I don't see the elite, or anyone from Old Lithisle. I trust they can't see us.

The aegis shimmers and cracks.

Mira swears, a string of words Mama would have washed my mouth out for. "I'm not going through that," she says.

"You have to." Sadie lets go of me and pulls at her sister. "Mommie and Gramma are waiting on the other side."

"This is how they're going to get rid of us." Mira tilts her head to me. "Grampa wanted her dead too."

"I'm not going to let anyone get rid of you." I check the magamp. The charge light glows green. "I know it looks scary, but I promise. I can get you through."

I hope I haven't just told them a lie.

We link hands and run through the wall.

CHAPTER TWENTY-SEVEN
Disposable

Running through the wall feels like being bitten by two or three deadly vipers instead of a thousand. It's a huge improvement.

There's no guarantee the file would work, the deputy had said.

Gilchrist couldn't even adjust the magamp properly, but I'm expecting his patch to fix the aegis?

No. Positive thinking only. I'll find out who has the file, and follow him all the way to Old Lithisle to get it, if I have to.

We stumble into the dirt on the far side.

Mira smiles.

Sadie bounces.

"You did good," I say.

I take Mira and Sadie to the base of the ridge. We walk on damp clay under an outcropping of rocks. Water drips from moss onto my hair and shoulders.

I pull them to a stop. "There they are."

Gilchrist's orange tent is untouched. A helicopter's engine grows loud. The helicopter tilts, then lifts above the trees and, over the ridge.

We dart from tree to tree. There are four helicopters left. They're black with long numbers painted in white on the tail. Two start with the number six.

"Which helicopter is the one you're supposed to get on?" I ask.

Sadie points. "There's Mommie."

The deputy holds the girls' mother's arm as she leads her to one of the helicopters.

"That must be it," I say.

"Are you sure?" asks Mira.

"It starts with a number six."

I take a step.

Committee Member Trumble comes from behind the helicopter.

My heart pounds against my chest. I hold the girls back.

He offers his hand to the girls' mother, and helps her onto the helicopter. He and the deputy walk away.

"Now."

We sprint across the ground. I toss Sadie into the helicopter. Mira climbs in on her own.

"Stop." The barrel of a rifle points at me. "Who are you?"

I push it aside. "Amy Ogilvie."

"Gilchrist's daughter?" The solider, not much older than me, lifts the front of his helmet.

"I'm a key witness for the prosecution."

"How do we know you aren't one of the other daughters? An imposter?" He frowns, and shoves me out the door. "I'm taking you to Committee Member Trumble."

I glance at Mira and Sadie. They're on either side of their mother. They'll be all right.

The soldier grips my wrist and yanks me across the field. Committee Member Trumble stands beside the deputy.

"This one was trying to sneak on," says the soldier.

"I had to go to the bath," I say. "I forgot which helicopter was mine. I thought I was getting on the right one."

"Leave her with me." Committee Member Trumble comes to my side. "I didn't see you come through the gate."

"What gate?"

He points to a portal between two black pylons, gigantic magamps in the base of the wall.

"I'm sorry. I thought I'd take a minute in the woods, but then I saw a helicopter leave, and I thought I might get left behind."

Committee Member Trumble's gaze is firm on me. He knows I'm lying. I want to run.

"Farren, put her in helicopter three. She'll ride with me."

I glance at the number on the helicopter behind him. It starts with a seven but the last number in the sequence is three. I look where I left the girls. The number ends with a five. The last helicopter in the line starts and ends with a six.

Oh, no. I lean to the deputy's ear. "I think I put the girls in the wrong helicopter."

"What?"

"They're in with their mother."

The deputy takes my wrist and pulls me to helicopter three. "There's nothing that can be done now, but be ready to act."

"And do what?"

"Provide them safe passage to Old Lithisle, no matter what."

Except I may not be going to Old Lithisle any time soon. "Who has my controller?"

"Committee Member Trumble."

Of course. There's no way I'll be able to pick it off him. I'm going to have to go all the way home, hope Suzanne's father can get me to Gilchrist or his controller, and pray the aegis doesn't collapse before I get back.

The deputy leaves. A second helicopter lifts into the air. A soldier shuts the door of the helicopter with the girls in it. The blades begin to spin.

I relax, and pull the seatbelt across my lap. I'm not sure how the deputy plans to keep her granddaughters away from the Committee once they're in Old Lithisle, but at least they'll get there.

The helicopter hums and vibrates. I close my eyes. I imagine running down the worn dirt path to Mama's cottage, the geese honking and flapping to get out of the way, and Mama's arms warm and tight around me. Will I even be able to see her? If the aegis is saved, and the Committee traces it back to me, I'll never be able to run down that pathway again.

The deputy grips my arm. "Go after them," she urges, her voice filled with muted terror.

Two soldiers drag Sadie and Mira across the dirt. Sadie's face is red and wet with tears. Her mouth is open in a scream. Over the beat of the blades above me I hear one faint, desperate word. "Mommie."

The soldiers thrust the girls through the portal. Committee Member Trumble shouts. Soldiers yank the black pylons from the wall. The aegis flows into the hole.

A blur of color sweeps by, a long jean skirt, yellow shirt, and red hair. The girls' mother.

I leap from the helicopter. My ankle twists. Pain shoots through my leg. I stumble, then run.

The woman reaches the wall. She doesn't slow.

"Stop!" I cry.

She turns to me, but my words come too late. Our eyes meet. Her hair lifts, dances around her face, and becomes a wisp of smoke. The haze envelopes her, and she's gone.

I can't move.

The deputy screams. My heart races. I can't see Mira or Sadie. Did they watch their mother die?

"Foolish girl," says Committee Member Trumble. "Get back in your helicopter."

I should. Going back to Old Lithisle is my best chance of getting Gilchrist's file.

But I was the one who put the girls in the wrong helicopter.

I killed their mother.

I step toward the wall.

"Don't you dare," says Committee Member Trumble.

My pace quickens.

"Freeze."

I run.

A loud shot echoes through the air. I look over my shoulder. The deputy lies in the dirt between me and Committee Member Trumble.

There are more shots. I jump into the wall. Bullets fade into vapor around me. I slam into the ground on the other side. My head spins, but I'm awake. I stagger to my feet.

"Get the gate back up." Committee Member Trumble waves his arm at the soldiers. "Stop her!"

"Mira, Sadie," I call.

Mira peers at me from behind the wheel of a terrarider.

Outside the aegis soldiers carry the pylons from a helicopter.

I hop on my good foot to the terrarider, then climb aboard. "Girls, get on."

I press the ignition button.

Silence.

Mira lifts Sadie onto seat behind me, then pulls herself onto the rear rack. "You need a key."

Why would they take the stupid keys? They aren't ever coming back. I reach under the dash and look for wires. Gilchrist taught me how to jack cars. Terrariders can't be that different.

The pylons are in place. Soldiers, guns aimed, wait at the wall for them to activate.

I don't see Committee Member Trumble, or the deputy.

The portal flickers.

I finish twisting wires and press the ignition. The engine turns.

"Hang on," I say.

Sadie wraps her arms around my waist. I hope Mira is holding on to something. The wheels spin. Dust flies. We tear out of the clearing. I pull the accelerator tight to the handle. We swerve through the hardwoods, past the junction and into the pines. Beyond the welcome center we veer onto the Barracuda path. I park in the woods, break off a branch and smooth our tracks from the pavement.

A terrarider pulls out from behind the welcome center. I fall to my knees and crawl through the tall grass, Sadie at my side, Mira close behind. The terrarider circles the brick building then pulls onto the road. I'm almost to the woods. The terrarider screeches to a stop. We lie flat. Footsteps approach. I hold my breath.

A boot presses my shoulder. "What are you doing here?"

CHAPTER TWENTY-EIGHT
Second Chance

I roll to my back.

Fin-head stands over me.

"I was coming to you." I sit, and motion to the girls, still flat on their bellies in the grass. "Please help us hide. There are soldiers behind us."

Fin-head shakes his head. "They turned around miles ago, but they weren't soldiers from New Lithisle." He pauses, and tilts his head. "Who were they?"

I'm not sure if he's just curious or thinks I'm up to something, but I can't tell him what's really going on. "Please, not now. The girls need someplace quiet and safe to rest."

He gets back on his terrarider. "Elder Daniel's been waiting for you. Ruth will be glad to see you too."

"Daniel's here?" For the first time in days, hope sparks in my chest. Even though I told him I wasn't going to be here, he came.

"Since yesterday." Fin-head revs his four-stroke and heads toward the village.

The girls stand by the terrarider.

"Get back on."

Mira crosses her arms. "He's a fish person. I'm not going anywhere with him."

"He's a good man," I say. "He and his family will take care of us."

Mira doesn't budge.

Her mother just died. Her grandmother could be dead, and she's still the brattiest child on the planet.

I open my mouth to say something like, *And what do you think you are?* But I close it. I don't know how I'd react if something happened to Mama. I shouldn't judge. I pull Mira onto the terrarider by her collar then drive to the Barracuda village.

Ruth greets us at the door. LeAnne is in a sling cuddled against her mother's chest. "She's asleep." Ruth pulls down a corner of the blanket so I can see her face.

Still no scales.

Why do I keep checking?

Ruth nods to the girls. "Elder Daniel told us he was expecting you, but he didn't say you'd be bringing guests."

"He didn't know." I carry Sadie on my hip. She clings to me like a baby raccoon. Mira sulks at my side.

"Amy." Daniel comes from the hall. "You're all right."

My heart skips a beat. He's as human as I am. For a second I can't think of anything but being in his arms. I go to him, Sadie still attached. "I need to talk to you, alone."

Sadie grips me tighter. "No."

Daniel puts his hand to my elbow. "I need to talk to you, too."

Ruth steps between us. "I'm sure there's nothing you two can't say in front of all of us."

Daniel hesitates. "Actually there is."

"This is your boyfriend, isn't he?" says Mira. "We're all going to die, and all you can think about is kissing."

My face flushes hot. "He's not my boyfriend."

"Of course I am," says Daniel.

"No one's going to die," says Ruth.

The room falls silent.

Sadie tugs on my shirt. "Mommie is dead, isn't she?"

I see Sadie's mother again in my mind, her eyes fixed on me, and the swirl of smoke she vanished into.

Mira collapses on the floor. There is a loud cry, then sobs shake her body.

Sadie dangles her legs to the floor, then lets go. She runs to her sister, rests her head on Mira's back, and strokes her hair.

My eyes well. I shake.

"What happened?" asks Ruth.

I put the girls on the wrong helicopter. We would be on our way to Old Lithisle now if I hadn't been such an idiot. I drop to my knees above Mira and Sadie. "I'm so sorry."

Daniel comes to my side. He puts his arms around me. "You were tricked, weren't you?"

I fall into him, and cry. "Yes."

"Can someone tell me what's going on?" Fin-head crosses his arms.

"Her father told her the aegis was going to be vulnerable to collapse this summer because of a solar storm. He gave her a computer program that would supposedly correct the problem, but it wasn't a fix, it was a virus. As soon as they installed the program, the aegis began to collapse."

I push Daniel away. "What?" I shake my head. "No. The deputy tricked me. She never installed Gilchrist's program."

"But the aegis is collapsing." Daniel points an accusing finger toward the ceiling and the heavens beyond. "The timing seems like a little more than a coincidence."

Ruth opens the window and tilts her head to the sky. "Everything looks fine to me."

"Energy is dropping from the aegis in Vlas," says Daniel.

"But hasn't it always done that?" Fin-head scratches his bald head.

"Tiny little drops near the generator, but now they're this size." Daniel presses his hand into a fist. "They're falling in the suburbs and beyond. Everyone's been ordered to stay inside."

"Ander Smith said the collapse could happen sooner than the summer solstice," I say. "It's begun."

"Are you sure your father's file didn't start this?"

"There's no way." I admit I don't know Gilchrist well, beyond the scavenging trips we've taken, but he's always been kind and thoughtful, even to animals, if a little distracted. Although his contact seemed content enough to let everyone with alterations die, except for her own grandchildren. "I don't think."

"Is there a way to reverse it?" asks Daniel.

Mira screams. "You are all so stupid. Grampa is the one who wants us dead. He's planned it for years."

"Who's your Grampa?" asks Fin-head.

Mira sobs.

Sadie lifts her face. "Grampa Trumble."

I remember the deputy's ring, plain gold that she swiveled nervously around her finger. It is the same style as the one I've seen worn by Committee Member Trumble, which, come to think of it, was odd, as no one ever mention him having a wife or family.

"Farren Trumble," says Daniel. "The deputy's name is Farren Trumble."

My stomach burns. Committee Member Trumble had his own granddaughters shoved back into the doomed aegis, then shot his wife, even if it was by accident. She took the bullet he meant for me, so I could save her girls.

A third terrarider parks in front of the house. John opens the door and looks to Fin-head. "They're gone. We brought the rest of the terrariders here. Do you still want to try to make it to the auction tonight?"

Fin-head turns to me. "Who were they, and what were they doing with helicopters in the Wilds?"

I hesitate, but it's time for the truth. I explain the elite, the evacuation, and Old Lithisle.

"Well," says Fin-head. "Do you think it's too late to try to install your father's file?"

"I don't have it anymore. The deputy took it and gave it to Committee Member Trumble."

"What are our options?" asks Daniel.

"I want to hear what's coming out of 10 Pen," says Ruth. "Is the Prime Minister's office actually saying the aegis is collapsing, or did they just tell people to stay inside?"

"Stay inside," admits Daniel. "But who are you going to believe, the people who saw the problems coming all along, or the people who said nothing?"

"So the aegis may not actually collapse." Ruth wears a stiff smile. "We shouldn't overreact."

"Let the workman be found at his labors." Fin-head sighs. "I guess we go to Petrich with the terrariders. We need the credits."

"You need the terrariders," I say. "Evacuate to the Wilds."

Ruth gasps. "Leave New Lithisle?"

Fin-head doesn't smile or frown. "We're Barracuda. Trust me, no one is going to put in a gateway for us."

"You have to know I didn't find your sweatshirt in a thrift shop," I say. "I can get you out."

Daniel whispers in my ear. "Amy, it's not safe. They'll want to bring all the Barracuda through. There are dozens of them."

"Then I'll bring through dozens." I turn back to Fin-head. "Your house in the valley is in decent shape. The apple trees were blooming and the wild boar have kept the trees from overtaking the fields. You could plant and harvest by next winter."

    Fin-head's eyes well. He takes Ruth's hand.

    "You want to go, don't you, Daddy?"

    "Only if you do."

    "John?" Ruth turns to her husband,

    "You know I would follow your father anywhere."

    Ruth holds baby LeAnne closer. "All right. We'll evacuate."

CHAPTER TWENTY-NINE

Disturbance

The line of terrariders hums through the woods. The Barracuda carry the few things they can. Most of their meager belongings, including the cases of food they bought with Daniel's payments, sit in their houses. *Our parting gift to the Coyote,* Fin-head had said.

I sit with Mira and Sadie behind Daniel. The terrarider doesn't bob or weave. The last driver passes us.

I tap Daniel's shoulder. "I have the magamp. No one can get through without me. We should pick up the pace." I sound like Gilchrist.

"Thirty miles per hour is the off-road speed limit," he says.

Not in the middle of nowhere. I sit back. Next time I'm driving.

Sadie pats my hand. "Are you going to save everyone?"

I look ahead at the loaded terrariders. "We might have to take a break to charge up the magamp, but yes, I think we'll get everyone through."

"Even Daddy?"

"Daddy?"

"He's in Vlas. N6379 Wells Road. Gramma wouldn't let him come with us because he had too many alterations, but you're saving fish people. You'll save anyone."

My heart sinks. I might be able to get a few dozen Barracuda to safety, but Sadie wanted to know if I was going to save everyone, with a capital E. "I tell you what, I'll get you and your sister settled with Ruth, then I'll go to Vlas and find your daddy. He'll be priority number one, okay?"

Sadie smiles.

Daniel frowns. As soon as we reach the aegis clearing, he pulls me aside. "You can't come back in. The solar storms could get worse."

"I told Sadie I would."

"I'm not going to let you risk your life."

"I'm going back to Ander Smith anyway." I stand with my shoulders back, as tall as I can. "We may be able to organize an evacuation."

"There are millions of people in New Lithisle. You aren't going to be able to get them all into the Wilds with one little magamp."

"We can try."

"I will. I have resources you don't, a network of Believers, my family. You still have the Prime Minister's guard on your tail. You could end up in prison."

We reach the wall.

Fin-head runs to us. "Who goes through first?"

There is silence. Anxious faces turn to one another.

"I can, but I don't need to," says Daniel. "I'm going back to Vlas when you're all through."

"I will." Ruth steps forward. "LeAnne and I."

"Don't be ridiculous," says Fin-head. "I'll do it."

"All right." I take his hand. Flesh is webbed between his fingers. I look away. "Ready?"

"Tell me when."

"Run!"

In a minute Fin-head and I are through the wall.

He's still as a statue, his eyes fixed on the sky. Then he bursts into song. "The spacious firmament on high, and all the blue, ethereal sky." He laughs, loud and hard.

"Are you okay?" Ruth calls through the wall.

"Very," he yells back. "I've not been this good in a long time."

Ruth and LeAnne are the next to come through, then John and the girls. After the first dozen people I stumble to the ground inside the aegis. "I need to rest a few minutes."

Daniel stoops and kisses me. "I can do it for a while."

"Only if you promise to give me the magamp back when you're done." I'm only half-joking.

He crosses his heart. "I promise."

By the time the last Barracuda is safe in the Wilds, hours have passed. The first of them reach the crest of the ridge. Joyous exclamations echo through the woods as the sun paints the western horizon. They haven't seen a sunset in over a decade. The children never have.

Daniel stands near Gilchrist's tent.

"Come on." I take his hand and tug. "Ruth and the girls are getting ahead of us."

"I need to get back to Vlas."

"I know," I say. "But I told the girls I'd get them settled in. We can leave in the morning."

"There's not time. I've already been away almost two days, and we talked about this. You're not coming."

"Daniel."

"You don't know what it's like in Vlas, and what about the Guard? They're not after me. We'll both be safer if you stay." Daniel takes my hands, fear and longing on his face. He's right.

I don't care. "I'm not giving you the magamp."

Daniel pulls me close and kisses me. "I already have it. I brought the last family through, remember?"

I push him away, exasperated and angry at myself. "You promised you'd give it back."

"I did give it back, numerous times, but it was lack of planning on your part that kept you from ending up with it."

I open my mouth to complain, but he leans and kisses me harder.

"What's going on?" Fin-head strides toward us from the base of the trail.

Daniel jumps. "Nothing."

"I'm not talking about you two." He points to the aegis.

The wall shimmers, then dots of light float and vanish.

Daniel gasps. "Energy is dropping." He lets go of me and moves to the edge of the aegis. "Way out here."

I stare. This can't be good for Vlas.

Daniel leaps.

"Don't you dare!" I reach, but he's already through the wall.

He taps at his controller's display. "I can't signal Ezekiel. The network is down."

"The storm must be causing too much interference," shouts Fin-head.

Daniel nods in agreement. "There's no other choice. I've got to get to Vlas before it's too late!"

I stand as close as I can to the aegis without getting zapped, and yell into the heaving electrical field. "I'm going with you!"

There is another spray of light. Daniel shields his face with his arm.

The display passes.

"I love you," he mouths as he climbs on a terrarider. "I'll be back in three or four days." He holds up three, then four fingers.

"Come back out here and get me!"

"I'm trying to protect you."

I stomp the ground. "I don't need anyone to take care of me."

Swirls of orange and red cloud the aegis.

The wall clears.

Daniel is gone.

I stuff a scream down my throat. *How could he?*

Fin-head puts his hand on my shoulder. "Worrying isn't going to do any good. Come with me up the ridge. It'll be best to keep your mind off Daniel."

But I'm not worried. I'm angry. I step away. "No. I'll wait here."

"For days?"

I cross my arms, and clench my jaw.

Fin-head sits.

We wait.

And wait.

I sigh. Fin-head's got a point. I can't stay here for days. I pull my hair back, wipe my eyes and stand.

Pink sparkles in the dirt. I pick it up. "Ruth dropped her controller."

"No, that's yours. We thought you might be heading back into New Lithisle, so she had me run it to you."

My chest tightens. "My controller is old, black, and scratched, and the deputy took it from me."

"Ruth had me buy you a new one the day LeAnne was born, when we were in Petrich. She was going to give it to you after she asked you to be LeAnne's godmother but, well, you know how that turned out."

I press the power button. My start up tune plays. The screen blinks. My wallpaper is on display. My icons line up. "How did my stuff get on here?"

"Daniel had your old controller with him. John transferred the files on the ride home."

I search the drive. Gilchrist's file is there.

My head spins.

"Daniel!" I scream. "I found Gilchrist's file! I have the aegis patch. Daniel!"

"What?" The blood drains from Fin-head's face.

"The aegis patch was a file on my controller."

Fin-head stares. "Elder Daniel! She's got the file. Come back!"

Our cries are met with silence.

CHAPTER THIRTY
Controller

Daniel is long gone.

If he'd stayed we'd be on our way to Vlas. There'd be a chance we could save New Lithisle. Instead, hope seems as far off as the stars that dot the sky.

Fin-head puts his controller in his pocket. "I couldn't get a signal either, but I'm sure we'll be able to get a message to Elder Daniel somehow. Coyote come by this way all the time. We'll stay as long as we have to."

"Coyote?" Great. Our last hope is people with tails.

Fin-head shrugs, and sits.

I do the same, and watch the sparks inside the aegis fly. I imagine them the size of Daniel's fist. How big are they now? Can anyone in Vlas still be alive?

A tall, slim figure passes through the terrariders. I leap to my feet. "There's someone on the inside."

"Who goes there?" calls Fin-head.

The aegis clears.

"Daniel!" I jump up and down. "I have Gilchrist's file! I have Gilchrist's file!"

Daniel comes to the wall. "I'm so glad you're still here. I was worried you wouldn't be. I didn't want it to end the way it did."

"We have her father's patch," says Fin-head.

"What?"

Fin-head and I talk at once. I hold the pink, sparkly controller to the wall.

Daniel runs through. He takes me in his arms. "Put it on my controller. I can bring it to Reg Denney."

My grip tightens around the controller. "**We** can bring it."

"I didn't come back to take you with me."

"I have to come." I jab Daniel in the chest. "What if you can't find Reg

Denney? What if he doesn't know how to install the file? Gilchrist taught me a little bit of strophes, enough to hack into any program he wrote. I might be the only person who can do it."

There is a loud click.

Fin-head holds a semi-automatic pistol to Daniel's chest. "Her argument sounds pretty convincing to me. You take both of us in."

"What are you doing?" I stare at the gun, unable to move.

"You wouldn't shoot me." Daniel's voice shakes.

"I'd rather not. You have money and connections. We're probably going to need all three of us to get this done." He waves the barrel. "Bring us through."

Daniel hesitates, then takes my hand and Fin-head's wrist.

We run.

Fin-head holsters his pistol.

I finally breathe.

He ducks aegis fireflies. "Get on the terrarider."

Daniel climbs into the driver's seat.

"No," says Fin-head. "Amy's going to drive."

"She's not careful." Daniel turns his focus to me. "Nothing personal, Amy, but we need to arrive in one piece."

"You drive like a Grandma, except Grandmas drive faster." Fin-head pulls his hoodie aside and shows his gun.

Daniel slides back on the seat.

I get on.

Fin-head takes a second terrarider. He screeches out of the clearing.

I pop the clutch. The front wheels lift off the ground.

Daniel grunts and wraps his arms tight around my waist.

Most of the trail is clear. The few times the lights drop we plow right through them. They burn, but it's better than slamming into a tree.

We pull around the welcome center.

The bus and limousine are gone.

Fin-head stops. "I was worried the Coyote had already gotten to them."

"What are we going to do?"

"Go to the village and see if the truck is still there. It's broke, so I doubt they took it, but it could take me a few hours to fix." Fin-head releases the brake on his terrarider and rolls forward. I pull in front of him. "Maybe we should take the terrariders to Petrich."

"There's not enough gas," says Fin-head. "We'd end up walking most of the way."

In the Barracuda village, Fin-head leads us to a pole barn with cracked windows and rusted siding. He pulls a ring of keys from his pocket, but the lock is already sawed off.

"That doesn't look good." He slides the plank door open.

The truck is parked over a work pit.

Fin-head turns the key in the ignition. "They drained the diesel."

"Don't you have more?" I ask.

"There's a five-hundred gallon tank outside, but if they siphoned a few gallons out of the truck, I doubt they left anything in that."

The tank stands next to the barn on tall metal legs. Fin-head squeezes the fuel nozzle. One drop forms and drips to the dirt.

"Daniel and I could look through the houses and see what cooking oil is left," I say.

"Good idea." Fin-head rolls up his sleeves and heads back into the barn. "You know where the hidden pantries are, don't you?"

"For the most part." I take off.

Daniel follows. "What are you going to do with the cooking oil?"

"Run it in the engine."

"You're telling me you can run cooking oil in the truck?"

"Yes." For being so smart, sometimes he doesn't know very much.

"Then what about the terrariders? We can fill them and take along extra and make it to Petrich."

I stare at him. "They have gas engines. The truck is a diesel."

"And that makes a difference?"

"Yeah." We reach Fin-head's house. The pantry shelves are bare. The Coyote have already been here, too. I push and pull the tall, solid wood shelving unit off the back wall. I slip behind it. There's a door. I step inside and hold out my controller for light. There are stacks of food cases.

"Here's some corn oil." I pass four gallons to Daniel. "Bring them to Fin-head."

"Fin-head?" Daniel frowns. "His name is Leroy."

My cheeks flush. "Sorry, Leroy. There may be some kerosene, too. I'll keep looking."

"I'll be right back," says Daniel.

I read the print on the cardboard boxes, *Tender Sweet Peas, Early*

Corn, Unbleached White Flour. I know Ruth kept kerosene lamps for when the generator went down, but I'm not sure if she stored any extra kerosene, or if she kept it with the food. *Thin Spaghetti, Julienne Potatoes, Garbanzo Beans.*

There is a shuffle in the pantry. "I'm not having any luck." I lift my controller and follow the stream of light back to the door. The pantry is empty. "Daniel?"

There are footsteps in the kitchen. I peer out. A boot slams the back of my knees. My legs crumple. A bushy tail swishes in my face.

CHAPTER THIRTY-ONE
Coyote

Sharp metal is cold against my neck. "Call for help, and I'll slice your throat."

I put my hands up in surrender. The knife pulls away, and I turn my head. He's only a pup, my age, if that. He wears baggy, patched clothes, and his hair is cut in short, ragged clumps.

"This way." He pulls his hand from my neck. Metal rings forged with long claws are pushed over each fingertip. I look for fur and fangs. His canines are pronounced. There are no other signs, but the tail, of course. He holds it in a nervous arc. "Move it."

The Coyote leads me out the back door. He sits me behind the outhouse. He pulls a brick-sized, two-way radio from his backpack, presses the button on the side, and speaks. "Big C, do you read me? Have you got your ears on? Answer!"

He lets go of the button. There is static.

"The network is down," I say.

"Only idiots use the network."

"I'm just saying—"

"Shh." He clamps my neck with his claws again.

"Amy?" Daniel calls from the house. "Where are you?"

There are footsteps then a gentle tap on the opposite side of the outhouse.

My gut tightens. I didn't think to make copies of Gilchrist's file. I have to get my controller to Daniel now, no matter what happens to me.

I kick the Coyote in the stomach. He stumbles. His claws slice into my neck. I gasp, but leap on top of him. I pin his hands to the ground. He flails beneath me. "Daniel! Coyote!"

The boy growls. Shivers run down my spine.

Daniel is at my side, his eyes wide "You're bleeding."

I grit my teeth, and try not to cry. "I'll be fine."

"Should I get Leroy?"

I shake my head. "Get his claws off."

Daniel reaches for the Coyote's hands. He pulls back. "I'll hold him down. You take off the claws."

He takes the Coyote's wrists.

"What about the rest of him?"

"You're already on top of him." Daniel brings the Coyote's arms closer to me. "Now you can reach."

I gingerly pull on the first ring. Flesh peels off with the metal.

The Coyote yaps and howls.

I gag. "I'm so sorry."

"Don't be," says Daniel, and he's right. I feel bad for the boy, but not enough to leave the claws on.

I bite my lip, and wriggle off the second claw, and the third.

The Coyote writhes.

I work as quickly as I can. Blood stains my hands. Ten claws lay in the dirt.

"Throw them down the privy," says Daniel.

I hold out my shirt, drop the claws onto the fabric, carry them to the dark hole, and listen as they plunk at the bottom.

Outside the Coyote sobs.

Daniel stands above him. "Now what?"

"We need to dress his wounds."

Daniel touches my neck. "You're still bleeding."

My head swirls. "I guess I could use a bandage, too."

Daniel and I lift the Coyote by the arms. His legs drag. We sit him in Ruth's rocker. There are still medical supplies in the nightstand by my old bed. Daniel wraps my neck, then I dress each Coyote finger. He doesn't look at us, and doesn't say a word. I finish, and his whimpering stops.

"Where are the others?" Daniel asks.

The Coyote doesn't answer.

"Let's bring him to Fin—" I pause. "Leroy. I can watch him there and you can collect more oil."

Daniel agrees. We lift the Coyote again. This time he shuffles between us.

Fin-head rolls from beneath the truck. "What have you got there?"

"They declawed me." The Coyote tries to pull away, but Daniel and I keep a firm grip.

"He attacked me in your house," I say. "He said he'd slice my throat."

Fin-head sits and wipes the grease off his hands. "Let me see."

I tilt my neck.

The Coyote holds out his hands.

Fin-head looks at the Coyote. "Elder Daniel and Amy aren't Barracuda. They don't know about the treaty."

"Big C won't care," says the Coyote. "He's going to kill me."

"Where are the claws?" asks Fin-head.

"I threw them down the outhouse."

Fin-head shakes his head. "I'm sorry, Scout. I don't have time to deal with this now, but the claws aren't going anywhere. I'll talk to your father as soon as we get back from Vlas."

"The claws were growing into his skin," I say. "He can be glad we took them off."

"He?" Fin-head raises an eyebrow. "Scout is the Coyote leader's daughter, and you should have asked me what to do with her. She wouldn't hurt anyone."

That's not what it felt like when she had her claws in me, but I guess under the dirt she could look like a girl. A half-starved girl, but a girl.

Fin-head lies on the creeper and slides back under the truck. "Take Scout down to the Leveque's and change into some clean clothes. You're both covered in blood."

"I won't violate Coyote code." Scout juts out her chin. "We don't take anything we don't need."

She needs it all right, and more, a Suzanne total make-over.

"Don't worry about that," says Fin-head. "I'm giving it to you."

"What about a tether for her?" I ask.

"Scout's not going anywhere."

Sure, he'll slap one on me, but the Coyote he'll let run loose.

Scout and I walk down the street. Daniel goes to look for more oil.

"Is he your boyfriend?" she asks.

"No," I say.

She stops. Her eyes follow him as he enters the Merrick's house. Her tail wags, ever so slightly.

Ick.

The door to the Leveque's is open. We go to the daughter's bedroom. Jenny, like the rest of the Barracuda, didn't have a lot, but what she had was clean and mended. I take a long-sleeved stretch top for myself, my jeans aren't too dirty, and pick brown leggings and a white shirt with large pink flowers for Scout.

She curls her lip. "Pink?"

"There's always the dress."

She takes the leggings and uses scissors to cut an opening for her tail. The top is fitted with a loose ruffle at the hips. She turns in front of the mirror, and a half-smile creeps over her face.

"What about your hair?" I ask.

"I'm a warrior. I can't have it dangling in a fight."

"Just because it's short doesn't mean it can't have style."

"Big C cuts it."

"With a dull knife?"

She frowns. "We don't have anything else."

"Come on." I pick up the scissors. "Let me even it out."

Scout sits. I trim the sides of her hair close, but leave layers on top. I pull sleek strands in front of her ears.

I hold a mirror to Scout's face.

She smiles again, but now it's bigger, and more confident.

She pushes the mirror down. "What's really going on with the Barracuda?"

"Are you a spy or something?"

"I'm a scout. Big C had me wait here to find out what happened. They've never abandoned their village like this before."

"So scout isn't your name, it's your job."

"It's both."

Too bad for her. "They left, and they aren't coming back."

"There's more to it than that."

There's no reason to lie. "The aegis is collapsing."

"You're trying to scare me."

"Look out the window." Drops of light float and fade. "That should scare you."

Scout's eyes narrow. She doesn't move, but her breath quickens.

"Don't worry," I say. "We're going to Vlas. I'm pretty sure we can fix it."

"But the Barracuda got out first." She faces me. "How did they?"

"That doesn't matter."

"If the Coyote are brought to safety, we'll allow you passage to Vlas."

"There's no time, and your walkie-talkie doesn't work. There isn't anyone you can tell."

"I don't have to waste my time with you." Scout dashes out the door.

I run after her, to the barn.

She stops in front of Fin-head and Daniel.

"Wow," says Daniel. "You look different." He smiles.

Scout's tail wags.

Bile rises in my throat.

"The truck isn't going to work," says Fin-head. "I need parts I don't have."

"I can help." Scout turns to Daniel. "I can bring you to the limousine."

CHAPTER THIRTY-TWO
Limousine

"Don't trust her," I say. "Scout threatened to keep us here unless the Coyote got out safely."

"I didn't threaten anyone."

I point an accusing finger at Scout "The threat was implied." I turn to Fin-head. "We need to combine the gas we have left, take one terrarider and get as close to Petrich as we can. We'll be long gone before the rest of the Coyote find out we left. Her radio doesn't work."

"What did you tell her?" asks Fin-head.

"That getting to Vlas is a matter of life or death." Scout steps so close to Daniel they almost touch. "I'll do whatever I can."

"What about the other Coyote?" Daniel puts his hand on her shoulder. "Will they cooperate? Time is of the essence."

Scout blushes. She pulls her wagging tail to her side, and holds it still. "They don't have to know. I can bring you into camp the back way."

"I'm not going," I say.

"Amy," says Daniel. "Even if we made it to Petrich on the terrariders, I doubt the trains are still running. The limousine is our best chance of getting to Vlas."

"If she's not lying." Besides, there have to be hundreds of cars in Petrich. There isn't one I couldn't borrow with a little hot wiring.

"I agree with Elder Daniel," says Fin-head. "Okay, Scout. Lead the way."

They take off to the street.

I wait.

They keep on.

"Wait." I hurry after them. "I want the magamp, and I have to transfer copies of the file to both of you."

"Good idea," says Fin-head, but they don't stop or slow down.

"I'm taking a terrarider to Petrich. If you get the limousine, great, pick me up on the way, but I don't think we should take a chance on the Coyote."

Daniel stops, alarm on his face. "We need to stay together."

"At least for now," says Fin-head.

I hold out my hand. "The magamp is mine."

Daniel hesitates, then pulls it from his pocket, and gives it to me. "Please be patient. Don't go running off on your own. Scout will get us the car."

Like he has any idea what she'll do. I lodge the magamp down my shirt.

We reach the terrariders. I sit in the driver's seat, transfer copies of Gilchrist's file to Daniel and Fin-head's controllers, then press the start button.

"You're coming with me Daniel, aren't you?" I don't mean it as a question.

"We're all going with Scout." Fin-head climbs on the second terrarider. "Elder Daniel, get on with me. Scout, you can ride with Amy."

"She's not riding with me." I narrow my eyes. "And you can't take both of the terrariders."

Scout shoves me. "Looks like we are."

I fall off the terrarider, not entirely from Scout's push. "Did you see that?"

"Maybe I should ride with Amy," says Daniel.

"No," says Fin-head. "I'll handle her. You go with Scout."

I open my mouth to tell Fin-head he can't make me do anything. He pats his side before I can get out a word. I see the lump of the holstered gun beneath his hoodie. I climb on behind him, and hold tight to the roll bar. Daniel puts his hands on Scout's waist.

My throat tightens.

Scout drives around the welcome center, then back toward the wall. At the junction, she turns north, toward the campsite by the stream I almost went to my first day in New Lithisle.

Thank goodness I didn't.

She pulls into a clump of young pine and arranges the branches to hide the machines. "We'll have to stay off the trail from now on."

I lag behind, in case we get ambushed.

Daniel walks by Scout. "I'm sorry about the claws," he says. "Can you tell me more about them?"

"Warriors earn them. They're never to come off. I got mine when I turned eighteen."

She's an older woman.

"Don't they hurt?" he asks.

She answers, but they've gotten too far ahead for me to hear.

I watch the woods and try to ignore Daniel and Scout. Ours aren't the only footprints. Clumps of fur are caught in the undergrowth. There are murmurs in the air. They grow louder. I dodge trees, and duck behind a broad trunk. Canvas tents, the color of mustard, are pitched in a worn clearing. A tiny stream runs a few feet from my hiding spot. The water is cloudy brown, and the banks eroded. A woman comes with a plastic jug. She holds it under the current until it's full. She has fur on her cheeks and neck. Her shaded-sable tail is matted and full of burrs.

A hand clamps over my mouth. "Idiot," Scout whispers in my ear. "Someone could have seen you." She half-drags me back to Daniel and Fin-head.

"You found her." Daniel's voice is filled with relief.

"But I'm not going to save her behind again. She's got to do what I tell her to."

"You will, won't you?" Daniel holds out a pleading hand.

I roll my eyes. "No one was going to see me."

Scout growls.

The hair on the back of my neck stands up.

We circle to the north, and cross the stream far above camp. I clear it in one easy leap. We're surrounded by trees. Scout motions us down. "This is where I go in alone. Wait."

"You're going to drive the limo here?" I ask.

"I'm going to get the key," she says.

I shake my head in disgust. "We don't need a key to get a car started. We wasted all this time, and risked coming close to the Coyote for nothing."

"Let's go back to the terrariders," says Fin-head.

Scout doesn't move.

"It's okay," says Daniel. "I would have done the same thing. Who drives cars without keys? Besides these two."

"They told me the car wouldn't start without the right key."

"Maybe they didn't want you to take it," I say.

"Where is the limousine?" asks Fin-head.

"At the scenic turnout," says Scout. "But I'm not going without the key."

"Of course you have to come with us," says Daniel. "We need you."

"We kind of don't." I glare at Scout.

"She can't go back without the claws," says Daniel. "Her father would take it as a sign she'd rejected the pack. He'd have her torn to pieces."

"She's coming with us," says Fin-head.

Scout's face brightens. "Then let me get the key."

"It's not worth the risk," I say.

Fin-head agrees. Scout huffs, but we retrace our steps over the stream and around camp. We cross onto the trail and make our way to the clump of pine.

Scout lifts a branch.

"Little traitor." A huge man, covered in fur and with metal claws half a foot long, jumps at her.

"They kidnapped me," she stammers.

He cuffs her in the head. She falls to the ground.

"Look at you, all gussied up. Are you a Coyote, or a debutante?" He kicks her in the stomach.

Scout grabs her gut and gasps.

There's a loud click. Fin-head holds his gun level. There is a loud bang and a puff of smoke. I watch in horror as the man collapses.

"Big C! Big C!" Scout crawls from under his motionless body. Blood stains her shirt. She struggles to roll him to his back. She runs her fingers down the edge of his sternum, folds one hand over the other, and presses down with her palms. Blood spurts from his chest with each compression.

I drag her off. "He's gone."

Scout shakes. She turns, and lunges at Fin-head. "You killed him."

"I did," he says. "And, frankly, I've wanted to do it for a while." He pushes her aside, then climbs on the terrarider. "Elder Daniel, with me. Amy, get her on with you."

"No," I say. "She's been traumatized."

"He would have killed her."

"So you shot him?" I raise my shoulders and hold out the palms of my hands.

Daniel shakes his head. "Do as he asks."

I sigh, and reach my arms under Scout's. She thrashes. I pull. She digs her feet in the dirt.

"I can't move her," I say. "What am I supposed to do?"

Daniel picks Scout up, one arm under her knees the other at her shoulders. She curls into his chest, and sobs. He carries her to the terrarider, and sits in the back. "I can't hold on," he says. "Drive slow."

I try. We bounce over a bump. Daniel holds Scout tighter. I drive slower.

We pass the welcome center, the trail to the Barracuda village, and continue on the road to Petrich. A blue sign with white letters reads, *Scenic Overlook.*

Fin-head stops his terrarider under the sign.

"Elder Daniel, stay with Scout. Amy, we walk from here."

"No." Daniel tries to sit Scout on the terrarider, but she clings to him. "Leave Amy here. I'll go with you."

"You're the feelings guy. She's the carjacker. That's not going to change in the next two minutes."

"You're expecting Amy to get the car?" asks Daniel.

I redo my ponytail, and flip it into a loose bun. "I'll be all right."

Daniel's chest falls. "I want to help."

"You are." I lean to kiss him.

Daniel takes my hand and kisses me harder.

Scout growls.

Daniel ignores her. "Be careful," he whispers. "I'm not sure who we can trust." He glances at Fin-head.

"I'm not sure we have a choice."

"We'll talk later." He squeezes my hand, then lets me go.

I follow Fin-head up the hill. Near its crest we crawl. We spy from behind tall ferns. The bus and limousine are parked by a small brick building with entrances labeled *Men's* and *Women's.* Three men with tails patrol the lot.

"Are they armed?" I ask.

"Guns are illegal."

But he has one.

"Buster," calls Fin-head. "Is that you?"

A Coyote with a thick black tail looks our way.

"Parley," says Fin-head.

They argue about where to meet. Fin-head and I come halfway down. Buster comes halfway up. The other two wait, one at each vehicle.

"I killed Big C." Fin-head speaks slowly, emphasizing each syllable. "We left his body along the trail near your camp."

Buster's shoulders tense. "That's quite an opener."

"My people are on the outside. You can move into our houses, have our supplies. We're done with New Lithisle. I just need the limousine."

"What?"

"I don't want any trouble. We've left almost everything for you. Give us the limousine. It's more than a fair trade."

Buster swears. "You're talking crazy. How do you expect me to believe any of that?"

Fin-head reaches beneath his hoodie. "I don't want to kill you, but I've got a sig, a round in the chamber, and thirteen shots left in the cartridge. I'll use them all, if I have to."

"You're bluffing."

Fin-head draws the gun, aims, and pulls the trigger. The front glass of the bus shatters.

The Coyote dive to the ground.

Fin-head runs down the hill. "Get the car started. I'll cover you."

I sprint after him, open the limousine door, and pull the panel from beneath the steering wheel. I find the wires from the ignition and twist them together. The engine starts, then stalls. I wiggle the wires. The engine starts then stalls again.

"There's a short," I say.

Fin-head rounds up the Coyote, sits them on the pavement then comes to the car. "A kill switch. Scout was right. We have to have the key."

CHAPTER THIRTY-THREE
Stuck

"What's a kill switch?" I ask.

"An electronic anti-theft device," says Fin-head. "The key has a radio chip embedded. If it's not transmitting to the receiver it causes a short."

"There has to be a way to override it."

"Crawl through every inch of the electrical system until you find the receiver." Fin-head turns to the Coyote. "Where's the key?"

"Big C has it."

"Had it," I say. "Is it worth going back to the body?"

"They've found him by this time."

"Then I guess we look for the receiver." I start at the ignition, and follow the wires backwards. I pop the hood for Fin-head, but he talks to the Coyote. One of them leaves and comes back with Daniel, Scout, and the terrariders. Scout stands with the Coyote, but her arms are crossed and her shoulders slumped. She keeps her eyes turned to the ground.

Daniel comes to me. "What are we going to do?"

"We'll get it started, eventually."

"No. About him." He glances at Fin-head. "He shot a man in cold blood. We've got to get away from him."

"He shouldn't have killed Scout's father," I agree. "But they had history." And Big C hit and kicked his own daughter.

Daniel furrows his brow. "What if he decides he has history with either of us?"

"Let's get to Petrich first," I say. "How's Scout?"

Daniel's tense shoulders relax. "She vented. I think it was good for her. Some transference too. She was more upset with me than Leroy, or her father."

"Why would she be angry with you?"

"She said you said I wasn't your boyfriend, and that I made her look like an idiot."

"She made a play for you after her father was killed?"

"No. Before that, but don't blame her. You know what Ezekiel says. Girls fall in love with me. They can't help it." There's not a hint of irony in his voice.

"I can't believe you said that."

"Ezekiel said it, not me."

"Your problem is you're too good-looking."

A faint smile lifts Daniel face. "You think I'm good-looking?"

"It's not an opinion. It's a fact, like the sky is blue, or the sun rises."

"I still like to hear it from you." He leans to me, like he's going to kiss me. "You're beautiful, and that's a fact." The engine turns.

"You did it." Daniel pulls away.

I wriggle from beneath the steering wheel. "I didn't."

The hood slams. "Let's go," says Fin-head. "Good luck, Buster. I'm sorry I won't have the privilege of working with you. You're a good man. I think you'll do right by your people. Come on, Scout."

"She's not going with you," says Buster.

Scout shoves past him. "There's nothing left for me with the Coyote." She gets in the back, with Daniel and me.

"You're not going to let her go, are you?" asks one of the other Coyote. Buster shrugs. "She's got to do what's best for her."

Fin-head gets in the driver's seat. The door shuts. "Better get some sleep while you can."

Scout lies on her seat and turns her back to us.

Daniel kisses me, tells me good night, then kneels at my side. He bows his head and whispers. Prayers for an apocalypse.

I lie next to him, and listen to his quiet repetitions as I fall asleep.

"Don't panic," says Daniel.

I sit. Sirens scream. Smoke surrounds the limousine. "What's going on?" I ask.

We pass through the haze. Firemen in long yellow jackets hose a building with streams of water. Lights fall from the aegis. They're not fireflies anymore. They're Molotov cocktails.

Petrich is on fire.

"Things aren't as bad as they look," says Daniel. "Historic downtown is on the flammable side, but the brick and steel buildings seem to be holding up."

"It's bad enough," says Fin-head. "We're out of gas, the stations are closed, and trains aren't running. We're heading to the mission to see if they can help."

"What if Elder Binyamin and Nasira are there?"

"This isn't their region," says Daniel.

"But he was in charge of the mission."

"They have missions all over New Lithisle."

"Elder Binyamin and Nasira?" I scrunch my nose. "Why?"

"Didn't they explain it to you?"

"Nasira only told me what to do."

"They've had a difficult time. Their daughter was taken last year. They were looking for her when they found you."

"Taken by whom?"

"Traffickers. The Believers down south don't follow the sterilization and identification mandates. Disobedience makes them vulnerable. Little ones are kidnapped and sold to eager couples, while the older ones…" His voice fades. He takes a deep breath. "Kalila was our age. She was very beautiful."

I remember how scared I felt when the strange men asked about me as I sat in the back of Fin-head's pick-up. "I'm sorry."

He takes my hand. "Tell Elder Binyamin and Nasira, when you see them again, and ask about Kalila. They like to talk about her, but it's not a subject most people bring up."

I nod. Not that I want to see them again, but if I do, I'm sure I'll look at Nasira with kinder eyes.

We pull in front of the steel and glass building. We wait for a break in the falling lights, then run. The foyer echoes with our footsteps. The chair behind the long, low desk is empty.

"Hello," Daniel calls. "Is anyone there?"

I jump over the desk and push the big black button.

There is a loud clank from down the hall.

"Who's there?" a man calls.

"Elder Daniel, from Vlas."

"We're in the basement."

We follow the voice.

The basement has support posts and temporary partitions. The thick scent of roses mingles with the rotten smell of mildew.

"Elder Daniel." One of the men hurries to Daniel, takes his hand and shakes it like it's a water pump. "Who do you have with you?" The man looks at Scout then me.

"Refuges from the Borderlands, Barracuda and Coyote," says Daniel. "Will you give them sanctuary? I promise a generous donation."

The man's gaze rests on Scout's tail. He grimaces. "They aren't our usual guests, but circumstances are unusual. How long will you be staying?"

"A few hours at the most. We're on our way to Vlas."

"How do you expect to get there?" asks the man.

Fin-head explains our situation. "Do you have any contacts who can get us gas? Even a few gallons would be helpful."

"It's a long shot, but I'll check." He disappears behind one of the partitions.

Daniel leans to my ear. "We made it to Petrich. We've got to do something about Leroy."

"I suppose," I say, but I'm not sure. "Do we really need to?"

"He killed in cold blood. Courts should decide criminal's fates, not vigilantes."

"But you said yourself there is no law in the Borderlands. I'm sure he'll behave differently here."

He frowns. "Do you really believe that?"

I don't, but the more I consider our circumstances the more I think we might need someone not afraid to use deadly force. I look away.

A second man comes from behind the partition. He's the one who came down the stairs that first night and refused to pay for me until Nasira told him to. "The network is down, but I was able to get a call out on the land lines. We've got someone on the way."

"We need to hurry, then," says Daniel. "Could you spare something for us to eat?"

"And sanitary supplies," I say. "Please."

"Sanitary supplies?" Daniel looks at me as if he's never heard of them before.

Maybe he hasn't.

I scratch my temple. "Never mind. Is there a bath?"

The man points down the side of the basement. "There, in the back."

I take a step.

Daniel holds me back. "Scout, go with her."

"I don't need a babysitter."

"And I don't want to be one," says Scout. "You take her to the ladies room, if you think she's going to get lonely."

"Please, just go together." Daniel lets go of my arm. "Watch out for each other."

I walk to the bath. Scout follows. There's only one commode, but there are pads on a shelf beside rolls of toilet paper. I take one and squish it between my fingers. I sigh. The pad is as thick as a baby's diaper. The stall door squeaks as I shut it.

"You've sure got Elder Daniel snookered." Scout's sharp voice slices the air like a knife. "But you can't fool me."

This is just what I want to hear while I'm sitting on the toilet. "Daniel and I are none of your business."

"He thinks you're together, and I can see why." She makes kissing noises.

"That is so mature." I kick the side of the stall. "Maybe if you hadn't thrown yourself at him, you wouldn't feel so humiliated."

Scout shouts. "You're just a-"

I flush the toilet and grin. "I'm sorry. I can't hear you."

I come out. She goes in and slams the stall door shut.

There are screams from the basement.

My heart stops.

"Get down!" a man shouts. "This is the Prime Minister's Guard."

CHAPTER THIRTY-FOUR
Guard

The bathroom is tile, white walls, and one stall. There is no cabinet to sneak in, no window to climb out. I pull at the stall door. "Let me in. I need to hide."

"You can't let them take me." The bravado in Scout's voice is gone. "They'll send me to the work camps."

"They're not after you." I tug at the door again. She holds tight. I jump, and grasp the top of the stall. I kick my foot up.

The bathroom door flies open. Footsteps rush toward me. Strong hands pull me down, then push my face to the floor. I'm surrounded by brown uniforms.

"You're making a mistake." Daniel shoves his way through the soldiers until he's at my side. "Let her go."

"I'm sorry, Elder Daniel." The man from the mission comes up behind him. "You must not have known, but she's a dangerous fugitive."

A soldier pulls my arms behind me and tightens a strap around my wrists. The thin, hard plastic digs into my skin. They drag me from the bath.

"Captain Zeller?" There is a soldier on a phone with a long curled cord that winds from behind a partition. "We've got the girl that came in with the young elder, but the ID scan is negative." He pauses. "No, there's nothing." He stops again and looks at me. "I'm not sure. She could be." There is more silence. He holds out the receiver. "Identify yourself."

"Don't," warns Daniel.

But I don't see a reason to lie, and being uncooperative isn't going to help. "Amy Ogilvie."

The soldier looks at me with a blank face.

I take a deep breath and quickly add Allarice's surname. "Amy Ogilvie Mendoza."

The soldier puts the phone to his ear. "Did you hear that?" He listens for a few seconds, then holds out the receiver again. "No. He wants your title. What's your title?"

The words stick in my throat. Using Allarice's surname should have been more than enough evidence of who I really am without actually saying it, but my title may be the only thing that will get us out of this mess. Maybe I should have admitted it a long time ago. "The Seventh Daughter of our Great Mother Allarice."

The lights overhead flicker. The soldiers and mission workers stare. I'm more of a curiosity then the girl with a tail, or the man with a fin on his head.

The soldier hands the phone back to the man from the mission. "She's the one," the soldier says. "Load her up."

The others hesitate.

"Now. He wants her up there ASAP."

"Not if I can help it." Fin-head throws himself at one of the soldiers and tackles him to the ground. The others grab his hands and cuff them.

They do the same to Daniel. He shakes his head, dazed. "But I didn't do anything."

His innocence doesn't matter.

They pull me to my feet and march me up the stairs. Fin-head and Daniel whisper behind me. Outside they lock us in the back of an armored van, a steel box with barred windows in the front and back.

I sit next to Daniel on the bench. "I'm sorry. I should have listened to you."

"I'm the one who needs to apologize. I can't believe the mission people called the Guard."

The van rolls.

A tiny figure runs from the mission.

Scout waves her arms over her head, and screams as she runs, but I have no idea what she's saying. The van turns, and she's out of sight.

"Will she be all right?" I ask.

"They'll take care of her," says Daniel.

The way they took care of me? I want to say, but I don't. Daniel would feel bad.

"So, Seventh Daughter?" says Fin-head. "Is that true?"

I bite my lip and shift my gaze to the back window. "Sort of."

"You either are or you aren't."

"I wasn't raised to be one."

"But legally, you are," says Daniel.

"So who got the fifteen million credits?" Fin-head frowns at Daniel. "Since I know it wasn't me. No wonder you could afford to be so generous with your support."

"Fifteen million?" I say. I might have been tempted to turn myself in for that much money.

"No one got the reward," says Daniel. "And none of it would have been mine. Ezekiel was going to get his lawyer's fee, but most of it was for Elder Binyamin and Nasira."

I'm angry, until I remember what Daniel said about their daughter. They probably wanted the money for the missions, to find their daughter.

What will Mama do if I never come home?

Fin-head tips forward, lands on the floor, then pushes to his knees. "Daniel, move your back to me."

"What?"

"Just do it."

Daniel shifts. Fin-head bites at his wrists. The plastic cuffs pop. Daniel is free.

"Now reach in my pocket," says Fin-head. "Slow. Don't move too much. The soldiers aren't watching now, but try to not look suspicious."

Daniel takes a knife and cuts Fin-head loose. They slip back into their seats. Daniel reaches behind me and cuts my cuffs.

Daniel wraps his hand around mine. "Now what?"

"Hold tight." Fin-head nods toward the window. The van pulls onto the highway going north. "We're on our way to Vlas."

Daniel kisses me. "Rest. You might not get another chance until this is over."

I snuggle close. I feel safe with him at my side. I close my eyes and fall asleep.

Daniel's warmth is gone. He and Fin-head are at the back door.

"What's going on?" I ask.

"Get ready to go," says Fin-head. "And cover your ears." He steadies his gun, and shoots the rear lock.

The sound rattles my skull.

The door opens. On either side of the road is tall pine.

I grip the seat. "This isn't Vlas."

"Mount Paul," says Daniel. "The Guard are trying to take you to the bunker."

"You mean there's more than one group of elite?" I say.

"Who knows, but this is the road to Mount Paul."

"How far are we from Vlas?" I ask.

"Seven or eight miles west, but it's rough terrain."

"Hang on," says Fin-head. He leans out the van and shoots again.

The van bounces, then veers to the right. I body slam into the wall. The lights from the van flash across the scenery in a three-sixty.

We come to a stop.

Daniel grabs my hand. "Now." He pulls me out the back and into the woods. There are more gunshots. Daniel runs faster.

I tug at his hand, trying to slow him down. "Fin-head. We can't leave him behind."

"He's got a job to do."

"With the gun? Shouldn't we try to talk to the Guard first? If they were taking me to the bunker, maybe they were trying to save me."

"It's too late for that now," says Daniel. "And we don't know for sure what they wanted."

We run east until my chest burns and my legs tremble.

Daniel stops. "We can rest."

I drop to the ground. My heart races and my head pounds.

Light floods the aegis sky. For a second it's as bright as day, then it's like a meteor shower and the northern lights rolled into one. There is a tint of orange in the east.

The sight would be beautiful, if it weren't heralding the deaths of millions of people.

A branch cracks.

I hold my breath.

"It's about time you two stopped." Fin-head steps from the brush, panting. He bends over, his hands on his knees. "I didn't think I was going to be able to catch up."

"You're all right," I say, relieved, but worried about the soldiers he left behind. "What happened?

Fin-head sits beside me. "They tried to follow, but I fired a few rounds, and that slowed them down." He pockets his empty cartridge, slaps in another, and holsters his gun.

I hope they were only slowed.

"We can walk then." Daniel offers me his hand. "Let's keep a nice, brisk pace until we reach the railroad tracks, and see where we are."

"I just got here," says Fin-head, but he stands and walks after us. There is a list to his gait.

"Did you get hurt?" I ask.

"A long time ago, but it likes to remind me once in a while."

Daniel doesn't slow.

The eastern sky grows brighter.

"Is it almost dawn?" I ask.

"No," says Daniel.

I breathe deep. The taste of smoke fills my mouth. I run up the ridge. I skid to a halt. A wall of fire races up the gorge toward us.

CHAPTER THIRTY-FIVE
Fire

Daniel pulls my hand. I slide down the embankment. Heat flushes my face. Sparks ignite the pine needles at my feet.

Fear locks me in place. "We're going the wrong way."

"Trust me." Daniel leans down and kisses the top of my head.

I grip his hand tighter. We turn onto a hard dirt path. I look back, but the smoke is so thick I see only forms and shadows.

"Watch your step," says Daniel.

The next I take is into water.

"There's a waterfall this way." Daniel wades ahead of me. "We'll be fine if we hide behind the spray."

The water reaches my knees. I follow the sound of the cascade. The water is up to my chest. I swim.

"Help!" cries Fin-head.

Daniel dives into the water beside me. I keep on without him. The waterfall dunks me in the plunge pool. I bob up on the inside. The air is cool and fresh. I crawl up the granite. Back home water carves deep caves in the sandstone, but here the waterfall is big and the overhang small.

I wait. The water tumbles in front of me and splashes my face.

"Daniel!"

The water, wind, and fire rumble, but there is no answer.

I shiver.

What if Committee Member Trumble and the deputy are right? What if I am a foolish, meddling girl? I'll die without saving the aegis, and eternity will be like this moment, cold and hot all at once, alone, but in fear for those beyond my reach.

There is a loud crack, and a burning trunk crashes into the river below the falls.

Please, God, save them.

The water breaks. Daniel and Fin-head emerge. They choke and gasp. Daniel stays low while Fin-head climbs the rock. When Fin-head is safe Daniel comes up. He sits at my side.

"What happened?" I ask.

Daniel looks to Fin-head.

"I can't swim," says Fin-head.

My head snaps back. "But you're a Barracuda."

"I know." Finhead's shoulders slump. "Irony at its best."

We sit together on the rock for at least half an hour. My teeth chatter.

"The fire must be past." Daniel slides off and into the water. "Amy, come with me." I jump in after him. Bubbles brush my skin and buoy me to the surface. I swim to shore and stand in the light of the glowing embers. The forest is scorched. Pockets of fire still burn. The rest smolders.

Daniel sinks to the ground beside me. "I didn't think I was going to make it. Leroy held me beneath the water, and I couldn't breathe."

"He tried to drown you?"

"No, Amy. He can't swim, and he got shot back there. He didn't want us to worry, but he's lost a lot of blood."

"What should we do?"

"He'll come with us but-." Daniel's focus shifts from me to the blackened trees. "But once we get him someplace safe, we'll have to leave him."

"Is there any place safe?"

"The train station." He turns. "Don't tell Leroy, but it's to the tracks then the station, okay?" He wades back into the water.

In a minute he and Fin-head are back in the pool. Fin-head flails. Daniel speaks low, steady words. Fin-head relaxes, then floats. Daniel pulls him to shore.

"I should look at your wound," I say.

Fin-head shoots an exasperated look at Daniel. "Can't keep a secret, can you?" But he lets me cut through his pants. The injury is only a graze, red and raw, but not deep. I tear off my sleeve and make a dressing.

When I'm done, we pick our way over the burnt ground. I can't remember when I last ate. The burrito? Even thirty-five hundred calorie bars sound good.

We cross the valley, dodging the lights when they fall. By the time we reach the far ridge it is day, but no aegis sun rises. The sky billows like a sheet on the line, umber instead of blue.

At last we reach the suburb where Ander Smith lived. We detour down his drive, but the curved road leads through burnt trees to a charred skeleton of a house.

I step back from the smoldering ruins. "I hope he made it out."

"I'm sure he had a plan," says Daniel. "He knew what was coming. Either way he's not going to be able to help us."

We retrace our path. The air fills with electricity. The hair on my arms stands. I look up. More lights are coming but this time they're not raindrops or bucketfuls. They pour like a stream. My eyes search for a dark spot on the ground. I drop, cover my head with my hands, and pull my knees under my chest. Pain bites at my back and sides, but I must have found a good spot. Daniel and Fin-head cry and moan. I cover my ears. I can't bear to hear.

One, one-thousand, two, one-thousand, three, one-thousand.

The light passes.

"What was that?" I ask.

Daniel pushes to his feet. "W-w-we have to hurry. They're only going to get w-w-worse the closer we get."

I help Fin-head stand. He leans on me. His weight grows heavier as we walk. We reach the main road. Fin-head stumbles with each step.

I stop. A brick house, parts of the first floor blackened, but the second story intact, stands at the end of a drive.

"We're still miles to the generator," I say. "We need to rest and get something to eat." I point to the house. "We could try to find something there."

"We can't break into random houses." Daniel frowns. "We're not far from the tunnel. We'll be fine."

"We don't know what will be at the train station." My face flushes hot. "There could be thousands of people. Tens of thousands. It's a straight shot to the generator over the road with no interference."

"Except from the collapsing aegis," says Daniel. "The underground system will be safest. That's how we'll go."

"The aegis is a known entity," I say. "People are unpredictable. I'd rather face a fireball than another squad of soldiers. Or fortune hunters."

"Fifteen million is inspiring." I feel Fin-head's gaze on me. "Even at the end of the world."

"Amy," says Daniel. "We already talked about this."

"What do you think?" I ask Fin-head.

"I'm slowing you down," he says. "But you'll need me. I think if I had a little water and some pain pills I could keep up."

I change direction. "To the house, then."

Daniel doesn't move.

Fin-head and I keep walking.

Daniel sighs and follows us.

The door is locked. Fin-head takes out his gun and shoots the bolt. The door jerks, then inches open.

"Hello?" I call.

My voice resonates in the two-story foyer then fades.

The inside of the house smells like smoke, but is undamaged. Fin-head lies on a sofa in the living room. I enter a large bedroom. Drawers are open, contents spilling to the floor. A huge suitcase, half-full, is on the unmade bed.

Daniel's posture stiffens. "They left in a hurry."

I rummage through the walk-in closet while Daniel chides me about taking things that aren't mine. Like, with the aegis collapsing, anyone but him cares. I find jeans and a short-sleeved tee. I layer it with a hoodie.

I come from the closet. Daniel stands in front of a wall adorned with pictures in matching black frames.

"Hey." I point. "Isn't that you?" A freckle-faced youngster with braces smiles, but I'm pretty sure it's him. He was even cute back then.

Daniel's face brightens. "They must be Believers." He taps the photo. "I think that was my thirteen-year-old portrait. They need to update."

"So you know the people who own this house?"

"Oh no." Daniel shakes his head. "I couldn't possibly know all of the Believers in my region personally. There are over a hundred thousand of them."

"Then why do they have a picture of you on their wall?"

"I'm their elder," he says, as if it's obvious.

Creepy.

We find our way to the kitchen. The pantry and refrigerator are full.

I've never seen so much food in one house. I bring Fin-head a tall glass of purple grape juice and two pain pills. I pour some for myself. The juice is fresh and sweet, even though grape harvest was months ago. Paradise couldn't taste better.

Daniel eats leftover mashed potatoes and gravy from the fridge. I take out a huge bowl of pasta salad, put it on plates and bring some to Fin-head. I explore the house while I eat. It's as fine as Suzanne's but different. Modern. Suzanne's house has servant's quarters. Here there are gadgets, washing and drying machines, an electric vacuum, and a dishwasher.

"I think I'm good to go," calls Fin-head.

I take my last bite of salad and set the plate on a narrow table in the hall. "Let me put something better on your wound first." I find antibiotic ointment, stick-free pads, and gauze in a bath upstairs. I bring them to Fin-head.

When I'm done he stands. "That feels better." He looks around. "Where's Daniel?"

"In the kitchen," Daniel answers.

He's at the island writing on a thick pad of paper. "I'm leaving them payment and a thank-you note." He takes the thin, silver ring off his pinky.

"That might pay for the food, but it's hardly going to cover the damage to the door and foyer," says Fin-head. "They have enough money. Keep the ring."

"It's platinum." Daniel tapes the ring to the paper, to be sure the homeowners find it when they return, he explains.

Fin-head shakes his head.

We wait at the door until a light storm passes. Fin-head's limp is almost gone. There is fresh energy in my step. We leave the suburb. Soon we're at the railroad tracks.

"To the tunnel," says Daniel.

"To the aegis generator." I set my jaw and press my hands into fists.

My skin tingles. The hair on my arms stands.

Not again.

I look up, but it's not a cluster of fire, or even a stream. A burning mountain hurtles toward us, roaring like a hundred trains. The air flashes bright and hot.

Down the rails the tunnel is in sight, but even if we could run, and

213

Fin-head can't, we'd never make it.

Daniel shoves me to the ground. He jumps on top of me. Fin-head leaps on Daniel. The thought is sweet, but they aren't going to be able to protect me. We're all going to end up like the deputy's daughter.

A wisp of smoke, and then nothing.

CHAPTER THIRTY-SIX
Underground

We're going to die.

Except I have one thing the deputy's daughter didn't. The magamp.

I reach for Daniel. "Take my hand," I yell but I can't even hear myself. I touch flesh with one hand, then the other.

God, let me have both of them.

Pain jolts my body. Every muscle contracts. I scream and scream.

Then the pain is gone.

Daniel and Fin-head are heavy on top of me. Daniel exhales.

My heart leaps. "You're alive," I gasp. "The magamp worked. The shield protected us."

Fin-head stirs.

Daniel pushes him off. "We've got to get to the tunnel before that happens again."

"No." I take hold of Daniel's shoulders. "Don't you see? With the magamp we can go straight to the aegis generator. We'll be there in less than an hour."

Fin-head slowly rises to his knees. "I'm with the young elder. The risk is too great, and there might even be an underground entrance to the generator complex."

"What about people?" I cross my arms. "I can't expose myself to everyone who might be at the train station." Fin-head pulls my hood over my head, then does the same with his. "We'll keep quiet and move quickly."

Daniel tilts his head toward Fin-head. *Remember our plan,* he mouths.

I do. Another reason to not go to the tunnels, but they take off and I follow them down the tracks anyway.

The air inside the tunnel is hot, thick, and dry. We follow the light of Daniel's controller through the haze.

Daniel keeps a firm grip on my hand. He holds me back as Fin-head walks ahead. "Stay close to me," he says. "When we reach the station, we'll leave him behind."

"He's doing much better," I say. "I think he should come."

"My concern isn't his leg, and you know it. He's too hot with the gun. I'm worried to be in a tight situation with him."

I don't want anyone else to die so we can save lives, but I'm not sure how we're going to get to the aegis generator, especially if Reg Denney isn't there. "We may need Fin-head's special skill set."

"He held a gun to my chest. He's too unpredictable."

I wasn't the one Fin-head threatened. No wonder Daniel sees things differently. "All right."

We're a few hundred yards in the tunnel before we see the first of the evacuees, a small group of men and women dressed in business suits, dirty and tattered. They watch us, but don't say a word.

The further we walk the more people we see.

"Have you been on the outside?" A man steps from the side of the tunnel. "Has it stopped?"

"No." Daniel deepens his voice and speaks with an uncharacteristic cadence. "The storm is worse. You're best off in here, at least for another day."

The man lifts a light and comes closer. "Don't I know you?"

"That doesn't seem likely, does it?" Daniel hurries away.

The man walks back into the shadows.

"That was close." Daniel pulls his collar around his neck and lowers his head. "He was one of my deacons."

By the time we see the tiled arch at the station entrance the tunnel is so crowded we're stepping over people.

Fin-head pulls Daniel and me to an oval steel door in the concrete. He toggles the bar on the door until it loosens. He cracks it open a fraction of an inch. The stench of sewer reaches my nose.

"Come on," says Fin-head.

"I have business to take care of in the station first," says Daniel.

"What business is more important than getting to the aegis generator?"

"Getting past the guards stationed there," says Daniel.

"I've thought about that." Fin-head pats the hoodie over the gun.

"There's a safer way," says Daniel.

"I'm listening," says Fin-head.

"Bribe them."

Fin-head's focus shifts to Daniel's fingers. "I don't see any more rings, and the network's down. You can't transfer credits."

"There's a roll of silver rounds in my rail car." Daniel points across the station.

Fin-head is quiet for a moment. "You go. Amy and I will take the sewer to the other side and meet you there."

"Amy comes with me."

My gut twists. Daniel's making his play to get rid of Fin-head.

"No." Fin-head furrows his brow.

"We'll stick to the station walls," says Daniel. "I'll keep her safe."

"Safe is in the sewers."

"Amy," says Daniel. "What do you want to do?"

I look at him. I look at Fin-head.

Daniel squeezes my hand.

My heart skips a beat.

Fin-head frowns. "Well, someone's got to make it to the generator. I'll see you on the other side in half an hour, if you make it." He enters the sewer and disappears into darkness.

I take a step after him.

Daniel pulls me back.

"What happens when we're not there?" I ask.

"Don't worry," he says. "This will work."

I follow Daniel into the light of the station. Soldiers dressed in blue, not the brown of the Prime Minister's Guard, patrol the thick crowds. There's no clear walkway, but Daniel takes long, even strides. We don't stick to the walls. We head straight for the train platform.

"Elder Daniel?" a man asks.

Daniel turns his face from the speaker and walks faster.

We reach the platform. Daniel takes the stairs two steps at a time. I leap to keep up. We pass between two trains. A wide staircase leads to street level.

A flash of light fills the empty corridor. I shield my eyes.

Daniel stops, takes both of my hands, and looks down at me earnestly. "The streets are too dangerous. Please stay here." His voice cracks. "I need to know you're safe."

I pull my hands from his, and lift my chin. "I'm coming, and if you leave me behind I'll go on my own." Or find Fin-head, but I'm not going to mention that.

Daniel hesitates, his eyes full of uncertainty. "We're only going one block for starters, to my apartment building." He sighs, undecided, as if the choice is his.

Another burst of light fills the street. The air trembles.

Daniel pulls me from the station entrance. "Please, Amy. Leroy's not here. He can't make you do anything you don't want."

"He didn't." I turn and take brisk steps toward the entrance.

Daniel grabs my arm. "I know I shouldn't have left you at the wall. I came back because I realized I was treating you the way they always treat me, telling me what I can and can't do, but you still have a choice. Stay in the station and be safe."

"I left safety behind a long time ago." The first time we kissed, when I knew I couldn't leave him to die. "Two are better than one. We'll do this together."

Daniel smiles faintly, resigned. "Okay. Let's go."

We climb the stairs. The square is surrounded by tall buildings. The ground level windows are smashed. At first I think somehow the aegis did it, but then I look through the broken glass. Shelves are knocked over, displays upset. Looters thought they could take advantage of the collapsing aegis.

Daniel pulls me aside. My foot grazes a leathery corpse. Hollow eyes stare at me. The mouth is open in what must have been an agonizing scream. Clutched in his charred arms is a metal box. A computer? A gaming console? It doesn't matter now. Either way it wasn't worth it.

"Come on," Daniel pulls my arm.

The air glows bright and hot. We run. A cascade of fire impacts the street behind us. A million sparks explode. They toss me to the pavement. Daniel's hand tears from my grip.

I scream.

He clasps my hand. "It's all right. I'm here."

Daniel pulls me to my feet. My knees and palms are scraped and bloody. I limp toward the park besides Daniel's building. The trees around us, only a few weeks ago so tall and green, are now black and broken.

We dash into the parking garage moments before another mountain of fire crashes to the ground. Daniel brings me to the elevators. He presses the button with the up arrow.

"Shouldn't we take the stairs?" I say.

"I wasn't lying about bribing the guards at the generator," says Daniel. "Or that we had silver in the coach, but we've got bullion in the apartment too. We have to get it and we don't have time to run up and down twelve flights of stairs."

"What if the electricity goes out? I can't believe the elevator is still working as it is. We could get stuck."

The door to the elevator opens.

Daniel doesn't move.

The door shuts.

"This way," he says. We go to the stairs, but he heads down. He opens the basement door. "Wait here."

I can't breathe. He's leaving me. "We shouldn't separate."

"I'll be back in a few minutes."

"But..." My voice fades. But what? I'm the one who won't step in an elevator. I take a deep breath. "I'm coming with you."

"No. You're safer down here." He leans his forehead to mine. "Please stay." Our noses touch. His lips find mine. He kisses me, soft and slow. Time and space drift apart. Warmth spreads from my heart.

I love Daniel.

I pull away and look in his eyes. Mama was right. Love can move mountains, and together, Daniel and I will send the ones of fire back into the sky where stars belong.

I can't keep the smiles from my face. "Go." I nudge him toward the elevators. "I'll be waiting."

CHAPTER THIRTY-SEVEN
Collapse

The elevator doors shut. The pulleys wail as the car lifts. I lie on the concrete and close my eyes. For the first time since we met I let myself imagine a future for Daniel and me. There is a long, white gown with a beaded train, a bouquet of violets, or maybe purple irises, and a three-tiered vanilla and chocolate marble cake. Not that I'm planning on getting married anytime soon, or even to Daniel, but Suzanne has had her wedding planned since she was twelve. I'm way behind.

The elevator car trembles in the shaft. I leap to my feet. I'm ready. When the door slides open I'll tell Daniel I love him. He'll smile, and kiss me again.

I totter, but it's not me. The floor quivers. The walls quake. I stumble to my knees. A shard of metal strikes my arm. Blood oozes. A slab of concrete smashes through the ceiling. I dive out of the way. More concrete and metal fall. I crawl over the debris to the oval steel door. I tug at the round handle. The wheel jerks, then turns. I pull it open and fall inside. Cracks like lightening flash across what's left of the basement ceiling. A blast of wind roars. I'm thrown against the sewer wall. My ears whistle. My vision blurs. Everything fades to black.

I wake. I'm covered in grey dust and fragments of metal and concrete. There is a gaping hole where the basement used to be. The angry aegis ripples.

"Daniel!" I clatter over piles of wreckage. Chunks of building lay on the street and in the park. "Daniel!"

I drag myself through the rubble and frantically peer under beams and slabs. A bright glimmer shines. I crawl and lift a silver round from the dirt. Daniel went to get bullion. I dig. There are more rounds. I scratch and paw. My fingers bleed. There is only concrete.

The air sparks around me. My hair stands on end. I hear the rumble of a thousand freight trains.

"Daniel!"

The mass of energy hits me. I writhe and contort.

Even if Daniel had survived the building collapse, there's no way he could make it through this without a magamp.

The shocks stop. I crumple to the ground. Sobs shake my body.

Why, God? Why Daniel? I could have let the rest of them die, but he was the one I wanted to save.

Was that the problem? Was my sacrifice really selfishness?

I've learned my lesson, God. I have. Please, please bring Daniel back.

There is no answer.

There never is. My skin tingles. I look up. Flames hurtle toward me.

If I got rid of the magamp I might end up looking like beef jerky or garden dirt, but I doubt I'd feel the pain too long. One intense moment.

What did Daniel feel?

I reach down my shirt. I clasp the silver in one hand and the magamp in the other. The roar of the aegis quiets to a mournful howl. Committee Member Trumble was right. I am going to end up like my mother. We both thought we could outsmart God. I guess we were both wrong.

I loosen my grip. The magamp rolls from my fingers. I close my eyes and search the universe for one of the perfect moments Daniel and I shared.

My eyes flash open.

Love. That's what Daniel felt. In his last seconds he would have thought of me, prayed I'd make it to the aegis generator in time so I, his mother, and brothers would live. And isn't love what God is supposed to be? If he weren't he wouldn't be worth worshipping, or obeying.

I snatch the magamp from the dirt. Fire and pain rage through me. I push through the agony and stand. Daniel would have wanted me to keep on. I limp to the oval steel door, and the safety of the sewer. I let my eyes adjust to the dim light, and look for directional markings. There isn't time to mourn.

My heart doesn't care.

Daniel is gone.

I clutch my gut and cry.

CHAPTER THIRTY-EIGHT
Sewer Rats

Sparks burst into the tunnel. I jump out of the way, and scoot further along the ledge inside the sewer. I wipe the tears from my eyes, and try to get my bearings. The walls run north and south. The aegis generator lies to the east. I hesitate. Navigating above ground would be easier, but Daniel and Fin-head were right. The magamp might be able to protect me from the aegis, but it's not going to help if there is more falling concrete. I walk the direction Daniel and I took the day we escaped the Guard down the laundry chute. There are junctions ahead. I'll find my way somehow.

The brown river in the middle of the tunnel has dried to a trickle. I slosh through an inch of sludge. I stop at the first intersection. *South 54th Street.* But I was going north, wasn't I? East would be to the right. Or is it to the left?

An hour passes. I turn again and again. The street names all start to sound the same. Am I going in circles? They say that's what blindfolded people do.

I search for beams of light from the street. I find a manhole, climb the metal bars embedded in the concrete, put my back to the cover, and push with my legs.

The iron disc doesn't budge.

None of them have. Too heavy and clogged with sand and grit. If I had passed beneath the aegis generator, I wouldn't have even known it.

I pound on the iron and scream. There is no one to hear.

I pause and listen. The rumbles from above have become a never ending barrage. Fin-head hasn't made it to the aegis generator either, if he's still alive. Or Gilchrist's file didn't work.

God, let it not be that.

I slide down the rusted bars and sit at the tunnel's edge. I've tried to escape to the streets half-a-dozen times. I can't find my way back to where Daniel's building stood and I haven't found another oval door.

I pull out my controller, find the clip of Daniel I took outside the aegis, and tap play.

He sleeps.

That's it. No smile, no laugh, no sweet and sincere, I love you. My love sleeps.

Tears well.

I shouldn't have picked up the magamp. I'm living longer only to feel my defeat more intensely. If I had died, Daniel and I might be together now, somewhere.

An overhead pipe clangs. I jump. Footsteps echo, then stop.

"Leroy?" I call.

The footsteps start again, quicker and louder.

I run toward them. I turn the corner.

A man stands in the tunnel. Light shines from a grate below. His mouth and eyes are hidden in shadows, but his chin, nose and brow protrude. Long whiskers quiver.

"Who are you?" His voice is thin and high.

"I'm sorry," I say, in a strong bold tone I hope hides my fear. "I thought you were one of the Barracuda. We were traveling together and got separated."

"We're a long way from their territory." The man steps closer. He has large, rounded ears, a snout, and over-sized incisors.

A Rat.

I shriek, then cover my mouth to hold it in.

His long, hair-less tail flicks.

"I, I was looking for the aegis generator," I stammer. "Would you know where it is?"

"Now," says the Rat.

There is a chorus of squeaks from the darkness. Rat people swarm.

I spin and run. Their footsteps close in. I slide around the corner. I skid into the wall. Rat hands catch me. Tails wrap around my arms.

"The aegis is collapsing," I say. "We're all going to die, unless I get there."

They don't say anything. They tie my wrists and feet, hoist me like a log at the sawmill, and carry me.

I stifle a whimper and force myself to speak in what I hope is a clear, commanding voice. "Where are you taking me?"

They squeak.

Is that all they can do? But the first Rat spoke.

They carry me for what feels like forever. The tunnel gets hotter and hotter. Sweat runs down my forehead, and stings my eyes.

They bring me to a bright underground chamber that's three steps above the sewer, dry, with a vaulted ceiling, and cluttered with rusted machinery. They toss me to the floor. The brick scrapes my cheek. A door opens and shuts. Shoes click towards me. The Rats who brought me part for the newcomer. The shoes are black and so shiny I can see my face in them. The pants are grey pin-stripe. I can't see higher.

"Who are you?" he asks.

I tell him.

He wants to know more.

I answer all of his questions.

He steps back. He wears a suit with a floppy red bowtie. The whiskers on his snout twitch. "Bring him in," he says.

There is scampering, the creaking of doors, and footsteps. I see a baggy grey hoodie with *Leroy* embroidered in red on the front.

Fin-head.

My chin trembles. My chest heaves. I sob. "Daniel's dead."

Fin-head bites my hands free so quick the Rats gape.

I throw my arms around him. "He went to his apartment while I waited in the basement and the next thing I knew the whole building was gone. And so was he."

"There, there." Fin-head rests his chin on my head. "Are you sure? Did you see a body?"

"The building was in pieces." Daniel would be too. I cry harder.

"Untie me," demands Fin-head. "You've heard our stories. You know we aren't lying."

The Rat with the bowtie takes a knife and cuts the rope from Fin-head's hands and both our feet. He points to a ladder that leads to a door half-way up the wall. "The generator is there."

"I need my gun back."

"No. I've done enough." The rat twirls one of his whiskers with a long, ratty finger.

"If we don't get the file installed everyone is going to die. That includes you."

"What happens up there is none of our concern." He smiles. "It might even be good for us. Rats are survivors. We could expand without competition, except from the Cockroaches, but I think we could learn to share with them."

There are Cockroaches?

God, should this place be destroyed?

"You're not a rodent any more than I'm a fish," says Fin-head. "A few rat genes aren't going to spare you."

From the looks of it, they have more than a few rat genes.

The Rat sneers. "Good luck with saving them." He gestures to the surface. "Those hypocrites are going to get what they deserve." He turns and walks.

Fin-head lets out an exasperated sigh. "Can you at least tell me what security is like?"

"I have no idea. Our territory is down here." The Rats file out. The last tail curls around the door. I shudder.

Fin-head puts his hand on my shoulder. "Are you going to be okay?"

"No," I say. "But I'll get the job done." For Daniel's sake.

"Don't give up hope. He might have made it. Stranger things have happened."

But I was there. "He's dead." I hold back tears, and clench my jaw, go to the metal ladder and climb.

Fin-head holds me back. "I'm not going without my gun."

"I have a few rounds of silver." I reach in my pocket and show them to him.

"Good. We can bribe a Rat." He walks to the door.

I grip the ladder.

"Are you coming?"

I climb down. "Yes." I don't think he needs his gun, but I'm not going to let myself be separated again.

Two Rats stand guard in the tunnel.

"Give me a silver round," says Fin-head.

"I don't have rounds to spare," I say.

"One, Amy."

I reluctantly pull a round from my pocket and hand it to him.

He skips it down the tunnel like a pebble across the lake. The silver clinks, tings, and sparkles. The Rats' ears perk. They scramble after it. Fin-head follows them, darting from support beam to support beam. He presses against the concrete and fades into the shadows. I run after him.

A Rat picks up the round. "It's new, uncirculated."

"We have to save it."

"We're supposed to be watching the Barracuda and the girl."

"After we put it away. They won't get far if they try anything."

The Rats scurry. We follow. They enter a room off the tunnel. We go beyond and wait. In a moment they leave and head back to the chamber.

Fin-head and I go into the room. There are heaps of bright, shiny things, hubcaps, copper pots, cutlery.

"They're pack rats?" I say.

"Compulsive hoarding is the proper medical term. The Rat Project did something strange to their brains." Fin-head stoops, picks up his gun from a collection and holsters it.

"I thought guns were illegal."

"Don't ask me where they got so many of them."

I find my coin. There are hundreds of others. I fill my fists.

Fin-head gives me a disapproving look.

I put back all but the one from Daniel's.

"You can take two extra," says Fin-head.

"Two?"

"You'll see."

We walk along the edge of the tunnel. We hide behind the beam by the chamber. The Rats talk as if the aegis sky were still blue and filled with peaceful clouds.

Fin-head tosses a coin down the tunnel.

The Rats put their noses in the air.

Fin-head tosses the second coin.

They skitter after it.

Fin-head and I dash into the chamber.

The slide of a shotgun racks.

I lift my hands in the air and turn.

The Rat with the bowtie has the barrel aimed at us. "You weren't trying to leave with something of mine, were you?"

"We didn't take anything of yours." Fin-head puts heavy emphasis on the *yours*.

A hand and the brass butt of a dragoon pistol rises above the Rat's head and slams down with a thud. His knees buckle. He falls to the ground.

A Rat I don't recognize stands behind him. He drops the pistol and it clatters on the floor.

"Stephen?" says Fin-head. "I remember you. You were at the Genetic Studies Institute, weren't you? Your wife had cancer."

He squeaks.

"Is she doing all right?"

He nods and smiles.

"My daughter had her heart surgery," says Fin-head. "She made me a grandpa a few weeks ago. They're both healthy and happy."

The Rat clasps Fin-head's hands. He squeaks, fast and high.

He can't talk.

But what did Fin-head mean about Ruth?

The Rat squeaks a good-bye then waves Fin-head toward the ladder. We climb. Flakes of rust stick to the abrasions on my palms. The wounds smart.

Fin-head reaches the door. "Are you ready?"

I don't answer. This is it, ready or not.

Fin-head turns the lever and pushes.

CHAPTER THIRTY-NINE
Aegis Generator

The door opens. The room is quiet, except for a gentle, mechanical hum.

"All clear," says Fin-head.

I swing from the rung to the grey floor. We hide behind an enormous water tank. Heavy cast iron pipes, bright with blue paint, arch from the tank to a dozen long holding ponds. The needle in the wide-faced gauge next to us dances in the red zone.

I scoot away from the tank.

"Where to?" Fin-head takes his gun from the holster and loads a round in the chamber.

"There has to be some sort of computer control room, right?"

"You don't know where to go?"

"No."

"This complex covers five acres."

"Are you serious?" Bauer's corn field is five acres. When Suzanne and I want to get lost we run deep in the stalks. The boys can never find us, until we want to be found.

Fin-head moves to the door. "We'll have to find someone who knows."

The narrow hall is empty. Fin-head kicks in the first door we come to. His gun is up and ready to shoot. There are more pipes, but no people.

We move to a second door, and a third. By the fourth Fin-head's gun is holstered. He calls, "Hello?"

There is no answer.

The hall corners four times. We're back where we started.

"Are we sure this is the aegis generator?" I ask. "Rats brought us here."

"They didn't have a reason to lie."

"I'm going to check." An exit sign shines above the door at the end of the hall. I run.

"I wouldn't do that," says Fin-head.

I push the bar. Wind snaps the door from my hands and slams it into an exterior wall. A hot, fiery gust blasts me down the hall. The sparks clear. The swirling generator beam sinks beneath the weight of the aegis. The wind screams, as if in pain, then the beam pushes up again.

Fin-head grabs my wrist, drags me across the floor and around the corner.

My lungs burn. I sputter and cough.

"We're going to have to make it over there," says Fin-head.

"Where?"

"To the center building with the beam. The control room has to be there."

"There is nothing but fire out there." My gut tightens and my heart pounds.

"We could look for an underground route, but I think the Rats brought us as close as they could."

I walk to the corner and peer. Daggers of light pierce the scorching air. "I guess it's not too far." I try to sound optimistic.

"Come." Fin-head walks to a bathroom and holds the door open. He swivels a faucet handle. Nothing comes out. He enters a stall, takes off his hoodie and dunks it in the toilet bowl.

Gross.

He wrings it out then puts it back on. "Give it a try."

I take off my sweatshirt and do the same. The wet soothes my seared skin. I don't care if the water is from a toilet. I wish I could bathe in it.

Fin-head takes my wrist.

I pull away. "We both need to hold on. I can't have you getting away from me by mistake." I put my hand in his.

"I wouldn't let go by mistake."

"The magamp can handle both of us."

Fin-head shakes his head. "This close? What if it can't? I don't have to make it to the generator. You do."

My body shakes. "We need each other, remember?" It's what Fin-head said when we left the Wilds, but now Daniel's gone. I sob.

"You have to do it." Fin-head lifts my chin and wipes a tear from my cheek. "For him."

More tears flow. "You could be safe with your family. You didn't have to come."

"Sure I did."

"Why?"

He shrugs. "The right thing to do is always the right thing to do."

He makes it sound so simple.

"Thanks, Leroy," I say. Not Fin-head. Leroy. Leroy Greene, father, grandfather, wise leader, thoughtful friend.

I hold tight. We sprint down the hall.

Light blinds me. Where is the door? The one we came from, the one we're going to. I'd be happy with either. We're going to die, lost, in this stupid courtyard.

Steam scalds my skin.

I scream.

The water in the sweatshirt is cooking me.

I pull at the fabric.

"Keep going," yells Leroy.

Go where?

He pulls me.

I stumble into a hot brick wall. Great. Steamed, then baked.

A steel door hits my face. We take a few more steps. The wind slams the door shut behind us. I open my eyes. We're in a long, empty, dark hall. An alarm blares.

I crumple to the floor.

Leroy takes off his sweatshirt. "Sorry about the steam. Bad idea, but we've got to get cold water on our skin before blisters form."

I struggle to my feet. I pull off my sweatshirt. My skin is red and blotchy. I follow Leroy down the hall. We turn the corner.

A pair of soldiers dressed in blue point their rifles at us. "You shouldn't be here. All civilians were evacuated to the train station." The guard who speaks can't be much older than I am. He shakes.

"She's not any civilian," says Leroy. "She's one of the Twelve Daughters of our Great Mother Allarice. She's here on a mission."

I glare at him. My being a daughter is my secret to share, not his, and what is he thinking? The Prime Minister's Guard hauled me away when they heard I was a Daughter.

The guards look at me with wide, open eyes. They lower their guns.

Leroy pulls out his. "Put your weapons down. Hands in the air."

The guns clatter to the floor.

Leroy snatches the handcuffs from the first guard's belt. He sits them down, back to back, and chains them together.

"How many of you are there?" Leroy asks.

They tremble but don't say a word.

Leroy shoves the muzzle of his gun to a guard's temple. "Answer me!"

"Sixteen, sir. One unit, that's all. Everyone else was evacuated."

"Patrolling in groups of two?"

"Yes, sir."

"Are there any scientists or engineers left working on the generator?"

"No, sir."

"Where's the control room?" asks Leroy.

"I don't know."

Leroy holsters his gun. He fishes in the guard's pocket and pulls out a controller. He tosses it to me. "Break in and find a map. There's got to be one."

I tap and scroll while Leroy drags the guards to a stairwell. He slides their rifles out of reach and shuts the door.

"Any luck?" He looks over my shoulder.

"He was logged on," I say. A map of the generator flashes on screen. "This way."

My skin prickles. I should get to some water but we're so close. I'm not going to stop now.

The halls are a maze. I follow the bouncing dot on the display. We reach a door labeled *Control Room - Authorized Personnel Only.*

I turn the knob. "It's locked."

Leroy takes out his gun.

I push it away. "One of the patrols could hear us." I run to a room across the hall. I pull open desk drawers. I find a tiny screwdriver and a paperclip. I bring them back and poke at the lock. It turns.

"A professional pick lock, too," says Leroy. "Maybe you are worth fifteen million."

I scrunch my nose. "That's not funny."

He smiles. "I thought it was." He pushes the door and it slides over the short, grey carpet. "Let me go first. If they've got a stationary guard anywhere, it'd be here."

"Okay."

Leroy steps inside. A gunshot rings.

My heart stops.

There's a second shot. Leroy slumps to the ground.

"Leroy!" I dash to his side. He looks at me and tries to smile. Blood trickles from the corner of his mouth. His eyes roll back.

"I've been waiting for you," says Committee Member Trumble.

CHAPTER FORTY
Soulless

"I'm sorry." Committee Member Trumble stands over me. "I didn't want to kill him. He drew, and I didn't know what else to do." He puts his hand on my shoulder.

I pull away.

"I only wanted to offer you a chance to come home, before it's too late." His voice is calm, familiar. Reassuring.

My heart aches. Home. "Is that even possible?"

"I wouldn't be here if it weren't."

I hesitate.

"We have to leave now," says Committee Member Trumble. "There's no time to delay."

I don't move.

"The collapse has started and nothing you can do will stop it."

"No," I say. "I have to try."

Committee Member Trumble frowns. "What about your mother? You'll die, and she'll be left alone. How can you do that to her?"

Mama. She has already endured years of hardship because of me. If I die, she'll face a lifetime of solitude too. But when others told her to get rid of me, because I was Allarice's daughter, she chose to bring me into this world. By example, if not words, she taught me the same thing Leroy's mother must have taught him. To do the right thing.

Leroy's gun shines in his open palm. I dive and roll. Committee Member Trumble's barrel points at my head. Mine points at his.

He laughs.

My chest sinks.

"You wouldn't shoot me." He holsters his gun and sneers. "Killing isn't who you are."

Like valuing life, all life, is a bad thing. I stand straighter, even though my arms shake and my stomach roils. "Don't think I can't."

"Oh, I know you can, technically. I've seen you on the shooting range. You can hit any target." He smiles. "But you won't. You're a bleeding heart, just like your mother was. You couldn't even kill a chicken. Do you remember that, Amy? What was that little hen's name? Penny?"

I lower the gun.

The year Mama had sent me to kindergarten other parents in town had complained. They weren't supposed to know Allarice was my biological mother, but I guess the older I got, the more I looked like her.

Committee Member Trumble had been sent to decide if I should be left with Mama, or moved to what they called a "safe house." Mama called it a prison.

Mama had told me to fetch a hen for our special dinner with Committee Member Trumble. She'd stood at the kitchen sink, her hand on the red pump while water poured out. "Don't just stand there, Amy. I need it now. Go to the coop and bring me a nice fat hen, one that hasn't been laying as many eggs lately."

I'd dragged my feet. One of my daily chores was to collect the eggs every morning, and I knew who was laying, and who wasn't. Penny. She was old, and I was lucky if I found one egg in her nesting box a week, but she had a soft, happy cluck, and followed at my heels through the barnyard. I opened the door to the coop, slipped inside, and tried to decide who would die.

There was Belle Noire, the shiny black hen, then there were Rhoda, Ruby and Reba. They were red and plump like Penny. I looked from hen to hen, and couldn't find a good reason to eat any of them.

Mama called from the house. "If you don't bring me a hen, I'm coming out there to get one myself."

I grabbed Penny and Belle Noire and ran to the goat shed. Mama wouldn't find them there. Then I thought of Rhoda, Ruby and Reba. I ran back, stuffed them under my arms and brought them to the goat shed, too. I made three more trips, until the chicken coop had no chickens, and the goat shed was full of them.

"Amy," Mama cried. "Come here."

I didn't. I sat in the corner of the goat shed for what felt like forever, my knees tucked to my chest, Penny under one arm and Belle Noire under the other.

Hours must have passed.

"I don't know where she went," I finally heard Mama say. "She was here a minute ago. I sent her to the chicken coop."

"I think I saw her," said a man. Footsteps approached the shed, the latch lifted, then light shown across the floor. Committee Member Trumble stepped in.

"You've got an awful lot of chickens in here, young lady. What do you plan on doing with them all?"

"She's supposed to be bringing in one for the stew," said Mama.

I held Penny and Belle Noire tighter.

"You naughty little girl." Committee Member Trumble's voice was bright and cheerful, but he wagged his finger at me, and frowned.

"I love Penny," I whispered.

Committee Member Trumble ripped Penny from my grasp. "God gave us clean animals to eat. You should be grateful you aren't starving."

I ran after him, but at the chopping stomp, Mama caught up with me. She held me back, her arm around me. The ax descended, and Penny's head rolled to the ground. Committee Member Trumble held her convulsing body. He made me pluck her feathers, and shook his head with disappointment all supper as I'd gagged on the stew and cried.

"You're the one who's soulless." I raise the gun for Penny, Daniel, Leroy, and everyone else in New Lithisle. I pull the trigger.

Committee Member Trumble sways. His right arm hangs limp at his side. He falls to his knees. "Not that good of a shot after all, are you?"

I put Leroy's gun in the back of my pants, snatch Committee Member Trumble's gun from his holster, then hurl it down the hall. "If I wanted you dead, you would be."

"That program of your fathers isn't going to work." Committee Member Trumble tries to stand, but crashes to the floor. "Go ahead. Try to install it. You'll die for a lost cause, and spend eternity in the pit."

"Any eternity is too good for you," I say. "You'll die, and become nothing. No one but God will remember you, and all the horrible things you did."

"You blaspheme." The strength in Committee Member Trumble's voice fades. "I only wanted to keep this grave sin from staining your soul. Repent, before it's too late." His eyes close. His chest continues to rise and fall, but there's no use arguing with him.

I close Leroy's eyes. I fold his hands over his chest. *God, remember him.*

Ruth. How am I going to tell her?

I take a deep breath, hold back the tears, and run toward the roar of the generator. The beam towers above me, a geyser of fire that reaches beyond the ceiling to the sky. My heart trembles. I can't breathe.

I scan the round room, poured from concrete, with the beam in the middle. I run the circumference. There are no desks, no computers. I take out the soldier's controller and search for more details. The guidance system tells me I'm in the control room. There is no other.

The concrete cracks beneath my feet. I jump. The rift widens. Steam pours out. I run. A crevice opens in front of me. I skid to a stop. I grab the wall and feel for footholds in the smooth concrete. There are none. I slip.

My head pounds. I'm too late. I'm at the aegis generator, in the control room, and it's crumbling around me.

Is it too late to repent?

No. I'm not sorry, at least not for what Committee Member Trumble thinks I should be.

Glass shatters. Pieces fall around me. A rope dangles.

"Tie it around your waist!" a man yells.

Plaid.

Reg Denney.

CHAPTER FORTY-ONE
Boom Crash Burn

My legs scrape against the concrete as Reg Denney pulls me up.
He swears. "What are you doing? Trying to get yourself killed? I've got enough on my plate without rescuing damsels in distress."

I climb over the windowsill and tumble to the floor. "I'm here to help. Ander Smith—'

"That nutcase?" Reg Denney drops the rope and sits at a computer. "I hate him, was demoted because of that silly movie of his. I used to be lead engineer, might have had this all fixed long ago, but then I was demoted. Wouldn't have a job at all if it weren't for the union."

"I don't really know Ander Smith," I say. "I saw his documentary, but it's my father who sent me." I take my controller from my pocket. "Gilchrist Ogilvie. He used to—"

Reg Denney spins around. The fire from the generator beam blazes in his eyes. "I know who that double-crossing, good-for-nothing deserter is." He looks at my controller than turns away. "I don't want any help from him."

"He didn't desert you. He's been working on a patch for years."

"He didn't let me know about it."

"Maybe he tried," I say. "Communication wasn't easy. He's been outside the aegis."

"On the outside?" Reg Denney swears again, and waves his arm like a conductor. "Probably spent his time dancing beneath rainbows with kittens and puppies while I slaved in this hole, trying to fix his mess."

He hits enter. "There. That should do it, and I didn't need anyone's help."

The windows rattle. The floor shakes.

The aegis bellows.

Boom.

I cover my ears. Every cell in my body vibrates.

Reg Denney holds out his hand. "Give it to me."

I hand him my controller.

He taps and taps. He swears. "Pigs! Stupid clips of pigs! Where's your father's file?"

I take the controller back, open Gilchrist's file, and hand it to him. Reg Denney pops out the memory card. He puts it in the computer on his desk. He pecks at his keyboard.

The floor around the generator beam shimmers. It disappears in fire. Cracks shoot across the dome. Chunks of concrete fall.

Crash.

Reg Denney swears again.

"Run the program from the memory card," I say. "We don't have time to copy the file to your system first."

"I can't stop it now." He drums the desk with his fingers.

I reach over his hand. I hit *Escape.* The transfer stops.

Reg Denney pushes me. "What the—" And he breaks into another stream of curses.

"Shut up." I push back. "Let me finish." I type in strophes for *run program* and hit enter.

The generator beam dips, and rumbles toward us. I leap under the desk. I'm squashed against Reg Denney. I grab his wrist. Fire fills the office.

Burn.

Pain racks my body. I scream.

God, please.

The light fades. A cool breeze caresses my skin. I stand on the cliffs above the lake. Blue water stretches to the horizon. Waves crash on the rocks below. Footsteps approach from behind. Daniel wraps his arms around my waist.

I jump. "You scared me."

He kisses my neck. "I didn't mean to."

"How did you get here?" I ask.

He turns me to face him. "I've been waiting for you."

He leans to kiss me, but I hold him away. I have to tell him I love him before another second passes.

He fades.

"Daniel?" I reach for him.

He vanishes into light.

Even in eternity I can't tell him what he means to me.

Was Committee Member Trumble right after all?

No. My mind is playing tricks on me. I'm not dead. But if I am going to die, I'd rather stand before God's judgment seat accused of mercy than indifference.

CHAPTER FORTY-TWO
Awake

I cough and cough. A rough hand pushes a thick plastic mask over my nose and mouth. I shove it away.

"We're giving you oxygen," a woman says. "Keep the mask on. Breathe."

I open my eyes. The aegis control room is charred black. Paramedics lift Reg Denney to a stretcher.

"Your uncle will be all right," says the woman.

"My uncle?"

"Don't talk," she says. "Breathe."

I sit. "The Barracuda in the other room. He was with me."

The woman eases me to the floor. "I'm sorry. He didn't make it."

But I knew that.

Didn't I?

"I need his body," I say.

She smooths my hair back. "We'll make a note of it."

There is a pinch in my left hand. Another paramedic tapes a needle in place. Fluid drips from a clear plastic bag down a tube and into my vein. The infusion is as cold as ice.

"The aegis?" I ask.

"The solar storm is over. There shouldn't be anymore."

So that's what they're telling everyone.

"Daniel Brennan? Have you heard anything about Elder Daniel Brennan?"

"I'm sorry, honey. I don't know him, but if he was at the depot he's fine. Everyone who stayed underground is fine."

The second paramedic pulls a needle from the tube that runs into my arm. She drops a syringe in a red, plastic container. "I gave you a little medicine to help you relax. You need to rest."

"No." I try to sit again, but my arms go limp. I need to find Daniel. I have to bring Leroy's body back to Ruth, and tell her what

happened. I need to....
My thoughts dull.

I wake in a light blue hospital room. Nurses smother my upper body in the silvery burn cream. I fall asleep, but they wake me up to apply the medication again and again. I'm so full of drugs I don't feel the pain. Fluids drip into me day and night. I ask for my things. They give me a white plastic bag with *Patient Belongings* printed in blue on both sides. The silver rounds are still in my pant pocket. The magamp is wrapped in my bra.

They call me Penelope Denney. "Uncle Reg" must have woken in the control room before me. There is a fake ID transmitting from my controller. He visits me once and swears me to secrecy. The people of New Lithisle are to never learn what really happened, how close they came to destruction. I have no reason to tell anyone. Gilchrist's program worked. That's all that matters.

I scan the news for word of Daniel. He is listed among the missing, then one day I wake and he is presumed dead. The Believer channel fills with nothing but clips of him. I turn it off.

After one week I'm discharged. A nurse has pity on me and brings me clothes that aren't torn, bloody, and burnt. Jeans, a tee, and a hoodie. Perfect.

I go to the morgue to collect Leroy's body. I sign Penelope Denney a dozen times. They bring me an urn ten inches high and six inches wide.

"You cremated him?" I say.

"We cremate everyone." She places a box on the counter. "Here are his things."

I step outside the hospital. I haven't seen the aegis since the near-collapse. The azure sky and wispy clouds are gone. Beyond the shimmering, transparent surface there is open sky. On the western horizon dark storm clouds form.

I sit on a bench beneath a burnt, leafless tree and open Leroy's box. I find his blood soaked hoodie with *Leroy* embroidered in red, the holster, a hunting knife with a birds-eye maple handle, and his controller. I had the gun. They must have confiscated it.

The trains are running at the station. I trade five silver rounds for passage south, a backpack, sleeping bag, tent, and food. In Petrich I walk over the tracks, across empty lots, and through abandoned streets to the mission. The lobby and halls are crowded with people, but I manage to find Scout.

She hugs me. "I wanted to come with you. I tried. I'm sorry."

"I'm glad you didn't. You'd be dead too."

I tell her I'm going back to the Borderlands. I offer to bring her to the Coyote.

"I'm staying here," she says. "Elder Binyamin and Nasira have been so kind. I want to help."

I can't picture Nasira being anything but cranky, but Scout seems happy. "They're here?"

"Not right now. Nasira pawned her necklace to buy supplies. A lot of people lost everything. They're having a hard time providing the basics to everyone in need."

Daniel said Elder Binyamin and Nasira were good people. Just not to me. I guess the fifteen million on my head was enough to throw them off. I leave the last silver round in the collection box at the desk. The silver belonged to the Believers, anyway.

The Coyote are active in the Borderlands. I don't see them, but I hear their yip-yapping howls. There are a dozen fresh burial mounds in the field by the old Barracuda village. They didn't have an underground train station to hide in when the aegis started to collapse.

The light on the magamp shines green. I run through the wall, and hike up the hill. The valley is filled with life. Fences are mended. Fields are tilled. The windows on the houses are open and laundry hangs on lines.

Ruth runs from the porch of the little white farm house. She takes me in her arms. I don't have to say anything.

I'm alone.

She sobs, and her tears soak my shirt.

The next week Leroy is buried in the cemetery of a brick church with a tall white steeple. He's laid beneath a headstone that bears his name, and the name of his wife.

That night Ruth and I sit by the fire. She rocks LeAnne in her cradle. "Daddy lived a good life," she says. "The only thing left he wanted was to be buried beside the woman he loved. Thank you, Amy, for bringing us home."

"He'd be alive if it weren't for me."

"How can you even think that? We'd all be dead without you."

Tears well, then overflow. With Daniel and Leroy gone, I feel like a failure.

Ruth puts her arms around me. "That night, when he left to find you, he knew he might not come back."

"Is that what he told you?"

"He said he thought you were going back to try to fix the aegis. He didn't know if you could, but if you needed his help, he was willing to die trying. That's the way he was." She smiles. "I was fourteen when my legs started to swell. I couldn't even walk without getting short of breath. The doctor told Daddy I needed a valve in my heart replaced. 'She's going to die without the surgery,' he said, 'And by the way, that will be one hundred and fifty-thousand credits.' Yeah, right. If we'd been on the outside it would have been one thing. Daddy could have mortgaged the farm, the business, something, but we were refuges. We had nothing."

"So he signed up for the Barracuda experiment."

"Allarice was dead. The genetic experiments had turned disastrous. Once people had handed over huge sums of money to be altered, but by that time they couldn't pay people enough to be turned into freaks."

Unless it was a matter of life and death. Dear Leroy.

"Daddy was never a handsome man, or proud, but when he saw himself for the first time, after they were through with him, he cried."

"Your father was a good man."

"I know," says Ruth.

I run temperatures at night. Ruth insists I stay with the Barracuda until I'm fully healed, not that I know where I'd go if I were well. I can't contact Mama or Suzanne. Even if I thought it would go safe for them, my new controller, like Daniel's, has no way to connect to satellites.

Sadie and Mira ask about their father. I tell them everyone was evacuated to the train station, so I couldn't find him at home, but I'm sure he's okay.

For their sake, I hope he is.

"You're going to go back and get him, aren't you?" Sadie tugs at my shirt.

"We'll see," I say. The only thing I want is to go home, hear Mama's sweet voice, feel Golden Star's warm fur, see Posey curled at the foot of my bed, but I'm a traitor. Did they hang Gilchrist? By this time the Committee must know the aegis isn't going to collapse. They would probably hang me, too.

A month passes in the Wilds. One morning, when the first rays of morning cross my pillow, I realize they are from the summer solstice sun. The time has come to move on. I load my backpack and head downstairs.

"Where do you think you're going?" asks Ruth.

Sadie bounces. "To find Daddy, aren't you?"

I pick her up and swing her in a circle. "Yes." There's no future for me back home, or with the Barracuda. New Lithisle is the only place I know of where I can finish school, and there is the matter of the 15 million credit reward. I can't bear the thought of wasting that much money when it could be useful.

Ruth catches Sadie and me. "You don't have to leave, you know. You're welcome to stay here."

"Yes, she does." Mira crosses her arm and taps her foot. "It's about time."

"Mira's right." I give Ruth and the girls a hug. "I'll be back, but I'm not sure when. I have a few things to do."

I help Ruth clean up after breakfast, say my goodbyes, then walk across the valley. The hot sun beats down on the green fields filled with crops. I wipe the sweat from my face, and climb the ridge. The aegis pulses, or maybe it breathes, the chest of a slumbering giant, rising and falling with each breath. Strange. The aegis didn't do that before.

I head down the hill. Through the leaves I see spots of orange. Gilchrist's tent. I walk toward it, but there is a rustle in the woods. Something big is on the move, maybe a deer or a bear. I pull out my controller, and set my recording eye.

The movement stops.

I lower my controller. An animal would keep on. "Hello?" I ask. "Is anyone there?" Only the wind whispers. "It's me, Amy."

The branches shift. The deputy steps out. "Where are the girls?"
I gasp. "I thought you got shot."

"Sadie and Mira." The deputy drops the armful of sticks she was
carrying, and runs to me. "What happened to them?"

"They're fine. They're in the valley with my friend." I nod in the
general direction of the farm house.

"You left them in the Wilds, with fish people?"

My jaw tightens. "I said, they're fine."

"Gil! Your daughter! Get up."

My heart stops. "Gilchrist? He's alive?" I run to the clearing. The deputy
follows. The tent flap lifts.

"Pumpkin!" Gilchrist drops his mug, coffee flying, and runs towards
me.

I spring into his arms. He squeezes me tight. "We were so worried. I
can't tell you how happy we are to find you."

I spend the morning with Gilchrist and the deputy. Gilchrist plays
with my controller while the deputy updates me on Old Lithisle. When
the refuges landed, the sympathizers had enough evidence to convince
the court Committee Member Trumble had violated Old Lithisle's laissez-
faire policy toward New Lithisle. He was banished, while Gilchrist was
set free.

"No one's had contact with him in weeks," says the deputy.

"He was at the aegis generator the day it almost collapsed," I say.

"What happened to him?" she asks.

I shake my head. "I don't know." No one at the hospital ever mentioned
him.

I tap Gilchrist on the shoulder. "So why are you loose? Didn't you
interfere in New Lithisle too?"

"Funny thing." Gilchrist rubs his chin. "They had your old controller
and this file I supposedly wrote, but it was in strophes. No one could
figure out exactly what it was." He laughs.

Gilchrist signals Mama for me. We talk for an hour. Golden Star perks
his ears, wags his tail, and licks the screen when I tell him he's a good
dog. Posey yawns, and goes back to sleep. Baby goats run and jump in
the yard. For the first time since Daniel died, my heart isn't empty.

"The battery is getting low," says Gilchrist. "Time to say good bye."

"So soon?" says Mama. "But you'll be home in a few weeks, right?

That's what matters."

I hesitate. I can go home. Gilchrist and I are both free, but the realization doesn't make me as happy as I would have imagined.

"What's the matter?" Mama asks. "You are coming home soon, aren't you?"

"Of course," I say, but Daniel's family doesn't know what happened to him, Elder Binyamin and Nasira's daughter is still missing, and 15 million would go a long way to help the refugees in New Lithisle.

"You don't sound very happy about it," says the deputy.

"Farren," says Mama, her voice sharp. "She's been through a lot. Don't push her."

But the deputy is right. I'm not happy. I'm confused.

Mama disconnects. Gilchrist and the deputy break camp. "Let's try to get to the girls by midafternoon," says the deputy. "We'll have to travel slower with them, of course, but I'm quite sure we can make it across the valley and up the opposite ridge by nightfall."

"The girls?" My eyes narrow. "You aren't honestly thinking about bringing them back to Old Lithisle, are you?"

"What else would I do with them?"

"They want their father."

The deputy bares her teeth, like she's an attack dog. "They're mine."

My frustration boils over. "Mira's hair is growing out. The roots are as blue as the feathers of a blue-jay."

"I know." The deputy rolls her eyes. "I told their mother to lay off the crazy colors, but she wouldn't listen."

"Sadie too?" I ask.

"Cardinal." She shrugs. "I brought dye."

"You can't take them to Old Lithisle. If someone suspected, just once, they would fail genetic testing, and be put to death as abominations."

"I'm willing to take the risk."

"I'm not" I say. "I'm going back in to find their father. He deserves custody."

Fear crosses the deputy's face. "You can't do that. I betrayed Prime Minister Zeller. I'd never be able to see them again."

"Amy," says Gilchrist. "You just told your mother you were coming home."

The deputy shoots me a smug look.

"As for you, Farren," Gilchrist goes on. "Why don't you just stay here?"

The deputy scowls. "Were you not listening? I said I can't go back into New Lithisle."

"I mean here, in the valley, with the settlers. Their father can visit, or move out himself."

"That's an awful lot of people living in the Wilds," I say. "Won't they draw too much attention?" From both Old and New Lithisle.

Gilchrist waves away my concern. "A couple of more people won't make a difference." He turns. "What do you think, Farren?"

"I'm not going to live with fish people." She turns her head and sticks her chin in the air.

"Someone's got to keep an eye on them," he says. "Now that they're loose."

The deputy taps her chin. "Their presence in the Wilds is disturbing."

In that moment, I know she's going to do it. From zookeeper to aquarist.

But I'm still lost. I hadn't been eager to return to New Lithisle, but leaving the mess to someone else to go home doesn't feel right.

Gilchrist and the deputy return to organizing their things. I walk to the wall. My reflection shimmers in the aegis, like an angel, or a ghost, the way it did months ago, but although the image looks the same, I know I'm not. Daniel would want me to help. No, he would expect me to.

There are footsteps from behind. "You aren't coming back with me, are you?" Gilchrist rests his hand on my shoulder.

Tears fill my eyes. "I can help. I should."

"I thought you might say something like that." Gilchrist reaches in his pocket and takes out a small white box. He lifts the cover. On white cotton is a sterling silver pendant with a piece of amber. Inside the resin is a tiny insect wing perfectly preserved.

Gilchrist fastens the brown organza and silk strands around my neck. The round pendant rests between my collar bones. "Your ID is inside. I was supposed to have it injected in your brain when you were a baby, but I wasn't so hot about sticking a six-inch needle in your skull." He wipes away a tear. "I should have given this to you the first time. Could have gotten you out of a fix or two."

Or into a very big one.

"Thanks," I say anyway. "For the necklace, and keeping needles out of my skull."

"You're welcome." He gives me a hug. "I'm proud of you, Pumpkin. Your mother would be too."

I turn to the wall, then back to Gilchrist. "Why do you call me Pumpkin?"

"Pumpkin pie was my favorite, so that's what I used to tell your mother. 'Allie, you're as sweet as pumpkin pie.' And she was. Once upon a time, she was."

Maybe Pumpkin isn't such a bad nickname after all.

Gilchrist glances over his shoulder. Farren has shifted her attention to us. "Best get going. Before you-know-who catches on."

"What about Mama?"

"I added a new chip to your sparkle controller," he says. "You'll be able to connect with the satellites, even on the inside."

Gilchrist gives me a quick hug. I kiss him on the cheek, then leap through the wall. Gilchrist waves, the aegis swirls, and he's gone.

The clearing inside the aegis is empty. I was hoping for a terrarider, but I should have known better. The Coyote aren't the type to leave anything behind. I take a sip from my water bottle, adjust my pack, and head down the trail.

A tall, bald man with red, mottled skin, runs from the trees.

I pull Leroy's knife from its sheath and flash the blade.

The man stops. He doesn't have fur or a tail. There are no scales, gills, or racht whiskers, nothing to identify who he is, or what he wants.

"Amy," says Daniel.

I tremble. The voice is his, but it can't be. Daniel is gone.

"Amy," he says again. "It's me."

My chest tightens. *Daniel.* Could it be? I re-sheath the knife, and take cautious steps toward the man. The nose is Daniel's, as is the broad chin, strong jawline, and high cheekbones.

I gasp. "You're here. You survived." I shake my head. "How is that possible?"

Daniel's lips part, but he says nothing.

I laugh, run to him, and wrap my arms around his waist.

Daniel stands stiff. His arms hang at his side.

I push away. "Am I hurting you?"

"No," he says, but his expression remains strained.

Dread grips me. "Are you all right?"

"I'm fine. We just need to get you out of here."

I take his hands, and bring him close. "What's wrong?"

Daniel pulls away. "The Coyote are waiting beyond the no-trespassing zone. They're here to take you."

"That's not what I'm talking about."

Daniel looks to the ground. "This probably isn't the best time."

"You're scaring me," I say.

Daniel hesitates. "I was trapped in the elevator under the rubble for ten days. By the time rescuers found me and got me to the hospital, it was too late."

No, dear God. Please. Don't let him be dying.

"Too late for what?" I whisper.

"Some of the scarring will be permanent."

"But your lungs," I say. "Are they all right? And your heart?"

"It's not that." Tears fill his eyes. "I'll never look the way I did, even if my hair grows back, and they aren't sure it will."

For a second I'm lost. He's worried about his looks when he could have died? But then relief floods me. "Why would I care about how you look?"

"Because I do."

Dear, sweet Daniel. I close the space between us and touch his cheek. His skin is thick and dry beneath my fingertips. If only I'd seen his humanity sooner, gotten the patch installed before the aegis started to fall. He and so many others had suffered needlessly.

But he is alive, and I have a second chance. "I love you, Daniel. You. Not the way you look. Your heart. Your courage. The way you've loved me." I stand on my tiptoes, bring his face to mine, and press my lips to his.

Daniel doesn't kiss me back.

"Please," I whisper.

Daniel's chest heaves.

"You're beautiful, Daniel, just the way you are."

Uncertainty clouds Daniel's face. He takes my hand, and holds it tight. I kiss him again, and this time, a shy smile lifts his lips.

"I love you, too," he whispers.

I look into his eyes, green as the summer pasture. His eyebrows are gone, but his lashes aren't even singed. They're long, dark, and curled. Beautiful, and human.

Rondi Bauer Olson is a reader and writer from Michigan's Upper Peninsula. Her debut novel for young adults, ALL THINGS NOW LIVING, was a finalist in the 2012 Genesis Contest. She and her husband, Kurt, live on a hobby farm with their four mostly-grown children, along with a menagerie of animals including, but not limited to, horses, cows, alpacas, goats, dogs, cats, rabbits, chickens, and parrots. Rondi also works as a registered nurse and owns a gift shop located within view of the beautiful Pictured Rocks National Lakeshore.